My Name is
Polly Winter

My Name is Polly Winter

VERONICA BLACK

St. Martin's Press
New York

Library of Congress Cataloging-in-Publication Data
Black, Veronica.
My name is Polly Winter / Veronica Black.
p.   cm.
ISBN 0-312-08858-2
I. Title.
PR6052.L335M9   1993
823'.914—dc20   92-40800   CIP

First published in Great Britain by Robert Hale Limited.

First U.S. Edition: February 1993
10 9 8 7 6 5 4 3 2 1

My Name is Polly Winter

One

The agent had given Jessica the address with the air of one handing over a secret to a privileged person.

'Mr and Mrs Clare are really most particular about the lodgers they accept,' he had confided. 'They are quiet people and rather reserved. But if they do like you then I'm certain you'll be very happy at The Cedars. You drive?'

Jessica nodded towards the window beyond which her Mini was parked at the kerb.

'Then I can give you a sketch map. The house is about ten minutes out of town, but there are local shops and a library. A very select neighbourhood. If, by any chance, you don't get fixed up there come back and tell me and we'll try something else.'

He sounded as if the prospect of her not being suited was remote.

'Thank you. I'm sure I'll like it,' Jessica said. 'Do I –?'

'Pay Mr Clare two months' rent in advance and then he will reimburse me,' the agent said pleasantly, rising as she rose. 'If there are any difficulties, please don't hesitate to contact me.'

Shaking hands, feeling the slight oiliness of his grasp, she resisted the temptation to wipe her hand down the side of her jeans as she went through the door. In the car she glanced through the window and saw the pointed nose and ruffled grey hair snouting in her direction like a ferret-scenting rabbit. Behind thick-lensed spectacles his eyes were sharp points of light. He had seemed almost avuncular in his cosy office but seen through two layers of glass he appeared subtly different, a Dickens' character set down by mistake in a Liverpool office.

'Rubbish,' Jessica said very quietly under her breath and started up the car. She would go and look at the room before she paid her bill and collected her things from the small hotel where she'd spent the last couple of days. If it didn't suit her then she'd continue the search, perhaps consult another agent. The small resolve made her feel unexpectedly cheerful and she gave her reflection in the driving mirror a wide smile as she negotiated the corner.

At the top of the road she slowed, pulling into the kerb, turning over the sketch map she had been given. It wasn't too far from the centre of town, she reckoned, which would be convenient for when she needed to go in to consult the archives or talk to someone from the university. This was her first important commission and she wanted it to succeed.

Blundell Road stretched beyond a cluster of shops, its pavements tree lined, its houses set back behind high walls with curving drives. Late Victorian? Probably earlier, she thought. Mid-nineteenth century had been a period of expansion for the city with immigrants pouring in and the dockyards crowded with high-masted ships. People had made quick profits and built large houses away from the commercial centres where their wives and daughters could live like ladies.

The Cedars had its name scrolled in ironwork over the main gate. Parking at the kerb Jessica stepped out of the car and stood looking through the bars at the short drive that ran between flower-bordered lawns to a handsome brick residence, its outlines softened by rust-shaded creeper, panes of coloured glass in the bay windows hinting at a vanished fashion to emulate the medieval. Definitely mid-Victorian with later additions in the shape of a carriage lantern mounted outside the front door and a deeply recessed porch with oak benches set at each side. It was a house that stood proud in its lack of subtlety and its belief in its unchallenged supremacy.

That had been an age of certainties, Jessica thought. Its atmosphere both attracted and repelled her. The women with their drooping ringlets and wide skirts at one end of the social scale and the women with their caps and ragged shawls and clay pipes at the other end – all knowing their place. She had read somewhere that when women forsook couch and corsets they had thrown away their most powerful weapons.

She pushed open the gate and went up the drive. A lower gate at the side gave on to a short, broad pathway leading to a large brick garage. Glancing at it she went up to the main door and pressed the brass bellpush at the side. Its jangling within the house made her jump; she had expected something more tuneful, more in keeping with modern electronic melodies.

Footsteps. The rattling of a chain being released. The door opened wide, a mouth with a tongue of red carpet waiting to lick her up.

'Yes?'

The woman was middle-aged with a flowered overall on and a perm that was growing out round a face that had settled into lines of habitual discontent.

'Mrs Clare? I'm –'

'I'm Mrs Tate, the cleaning lady. The agent rang and said as how a Miss Cameron was on her way.'

'Yes, I've come about the room,' Jessica said, readjusting her ideas. In this house the mistress wasn't likely to be opening the door in a flowered overall.

'I'm to show it to you,' Mrs Tate said, standing aside so that Jessica could step into the wide hall with the red carpet that flowed down a staircase that rose to a railed balcony that ran midway between floor and ceiling at the back of the hall. To left and right of the front door were closed double doors with carved panels. A big square of red covered the parquet in the rest of the hall, and light slanting through the panes of coloured glass in the arched windows at the back of the balcony made lozenges of red, blue and green in the otherwise shadowed hall.

Mrs Tate moved to close and chain the front door and then plodded up the stairs. She walked as if her feet hurt and her knees were sympathizing. From the back, her figure had a curiously square outline, like someone cut out of cardboard and slotted into a stand in the middle of a toy farm. Following, Jessica felt light and boneless, long legs rising from step to step, short curly hair outlined by the light as she ascended.

'Here we are.' Mrs Tate turned to the right and mounted two steps on to a half landing with two doors which she thrust open with an inviting air.

'Take your time,' she said with unexpected amiability. 'I'll be downstairs.'

Jessica looked in at the small and thankfully modern bathroom and went into the larger room, though 'larger' was comparative since it was of modest proportions.

'So,' she said aloud, looking round with interest. A room with white walls and an ink-blue carpet covering the floor, matching the curtains that hung at the window. A wardrobe with shelves had been built into a recess; there was a bed covered by a dark-blue quilt and a capacious dressing-table with triple mirrors, a cane armchair with flowered cushions, a small but sturdy table. Neat, clean, anonymous.

Jessica went to the window and looked down into a yard with pot plants and a washing-line strung between poles. A girl was hanging out some sheets, presumably to whiten them in the sunshine. Jessica watched her idly, deciding that the Clares must be prosperous if they could afford so much help in the house. Then her gaze wandered over the low wall that separated the yard from the rest of the garden. Here the short grass and clipped bushes and weed-free flower borders had given way to higher grass, beds of straggling rose bushes and overgrown vegetables, apple trees and pear trees blocking the horizon. Whatever the financial position of the Clares they obviously didn't employ a gardener.

The girl in the yard had turned slightly, bending to pick up the washing-basket, casting up to the window a swift, startled glance. Fourteen or fifteen, with dark hair tied back and a plain little face. A daughter probably. Jessica turned to survey the room. It had no imprint of personality, not even a picture though there were hooks in the walls. She could certainly work here.

Coming out on to the landing she looked down into the hall just as the bell jangled and Mrs Tate hurried from the back regions to unfasten the chain.

'I'm sorry, Mr Clare. I wasn't expecting you back yet.' She sounded flustered.

'I understand someone came about the room.'

A pleasant, cultured voice. Middle height with fair hair already greying and blue eyes that moved past the cleaning lady to where Jessica stood at the top of the stairs.

'I like it very much, Mr Clare.'

She came down the stairs, conscious of the unwavering blue gaze. Forty? Late thirties, probably. Regular features – too regular for current tastes.

'Miss Cameron? The house agent rang me to tell me that you were on the way so I took French leave from the office. Have you had a cup of tea?'

'No, I –'

'Mrs Tate, bring us some tea, will you?' He spoke pleasantly, with the firmness of someone who expects his instructions to be carried out promptly.

'Yes, Mr Clare.' She plodded to the back of the hall and went through a door beyond the staircase, the sort of inconspicuous door that leads to servants' quarters.

'Shall we go in here?' He opened the nearer door on the right and ushered Jessica into a small room with embroidered silk panels on the walls alternating with the wooden ones and furniture of the same pale pine. In the bay of the window a coffee table and two cane armchairs with pastel cushions were placed.

'What a pretty room!' Jessica looked round with pleasure.

'It is rather, isn't it? My wife is very fond of it.'

'Mrs Clare is –?' Jessica hesitated.

'Visiting her parents in London. I was hoping to get the matter of the room settled before her return. Sophy hates dealing with business matters. Do sit down, Miss Cameron.'

He had indicated one of the cane chairs. Jessica sat.

'Do you have any family?' she enquired.

'A son and a daughter.' He didn't elaborate further but broke off as Mrs Tate came in with the tea.

'How nice,' Jessica said as the woman went out again.

'The cups are Spode. We are rather fond of them.'

'I meant the children – having a son and daughter.'

'Children are a responsibility.' His voice was grave and the smile had faded from his face. 'Now tell me something about yourself, Miss Cameron. You're of Scottish descent?'

'My grandfather. I was born and reared in London.'

'And you've come up to Liverpool. Student? Secretary?'

'Social historian – though that sounds rather grand for what I actually do. I amass and correlate data for a company specializing in the preservation of documents appertaining to local history. You know so much of our past is disappearing under new tower blocks and motorways that in another hundred years it will be very difficult to know exactly how people used to live. What we're hoping to do is mount a semi-permanent exhibition, concentrating on specific periods in selected towns and villages.'

'And you're covering Liverpool all by yourself?' He looked amused.

'Only a preliminary survey of the nineteenth century. I shall be spending most of my time in the libraries and archives, trying to build up a dossier that can form the basis of more detailed research. Sorry.' She gave an apologetic grin. 'This is the first time I've been given an assignment to carry out alone and I want to make a good job of it.'

'For how long would you want the room?'

'Three to six months. It's an open-ended job so I can't be exact. I'll be doing some typing in the evenings if that won't disturb anyone.'

'The rooms here are fairly sound-proof, and yours is over the kitchen away from the main part of the house. Isn't most of what you want already on microfilm anyway?'

'The big important events. I'm looking for the personal that will shed new light on the way people lived,' she explained earnestly. 'Letters, diaries, photographs, that kind of thing. I propose to start by building up a file on a fairly typical middle-class family – sorry, when I get started I'm apt to run on.'

'Enthusiasm in the young is pleasant to see. Well, Miss Cameron, the weekly rent is sixty pounds – to include use of the kitchen. You may take your meals in here if you like. How would that suit you?'

'It seems extremely reasonable.'

'Compared with London rents it probably is, but we aren't renting out the room primarily to make money,' he said. 'This is a large house – too large for a small family. My wife is apt to be – nervous when she's alone in the evenings and unfortunately my job entails some travelling as well as evening meetings and conferences and the like, so it will be reassuring for her to know that someone else is around. Shall we say two weeks' in advance and weekly thereafter? Heating and lighting are included but not the telephone. There is space in the garage for you to keep your Mini car there.'

'That sounds fine.' Jessica rummaged in her shoulder bag for her cheque book.

'And the receipt.' He took out a notebook from his pocket and wrote neatly. 'I must get a rent book for you.'

'You haven't rented out the room before?' Jessica exchanged cheque for receipt.

'Once. When the children were small there was always plenty of noise and company. Sophy misses that. Now I must give you keys for front and back doors and the garage. Mrs Tate insists on keeping the chain on the front door when she's here – sensible in this violent age but somewhat overcautious in this district. Fortunately we are spared the attentions of the hooligans. Now I must get back to the office and you may move in as soon as you please.'

'I have to collect my things from the hotel.' Rising, Jessica asked somewhat awkwardly, 'When exactly will Mrs Clare be back?'

'This evening. I'm meeting her at seven. I'm sure she'll be pleased that we have such a charming lodger.'

She would have liked to ask about the children, but he was holding open the door politely. Going through she enquired,

'Is Mrs Tate the only help you have?'

'Her daughter helps out too part time. Ah, you have noticed the back garden. We left it wild for the children to play in. Young things need space to climb and kick balls about in, don't they? So, we'll see you later then. I hope you'll consider this as your home while you're here. If you enjoy watching television we have a set in the room at the front.' He nodded across the hall and went to unfasten the door chain.

'You've lived here quite a long time then?' she paused to say.

'About fifteen years. Until later then, Miss Cameron.'

His handshake was firm and dry. They parted at the main gate where his grey saloon was drawn up behind her Mini. Glancing back towards the house Jessica saw that in the bay window at the left the curtain had been pulled back slightly and a small face framed in dark hair was peering through with a worried expression. Then the curtain was dropped into place again and the watcher withdrew from sight.

Jessica got into the Mini and drove back into the town. The broad, quiet, tree-lined avenue gave way to narrower, more crowded thoroughfares with jostling crowds. There was a vitality here that was lacking in the suburb. This, she reminded herself, was the city of the Beatles, the Liver Birds, Ken Dodd. Modern, quirky, brash. It would be good to have somewhere peaceful where she could write up her notes.

At the hotel she paid for the extra night since guests were expected to settle up and vacate their rooms before midday and it was nearly four. At least she had a bolt hole if something went badly wrong that evening. As that thought slid comfortingly into

her mind she wondered why she had needed to think it. Mr Clare –
he hadn't volunteered his first name – was obviously a fairly
well-to-do professional man – he hadn't mentioned exactly what his
job was either – with a wife called Sophy who got nervous when she
was alone in the house at night, and two children who liked
climbing trees and kicking balls around in the overgrown garden.
She wished she had asked a few more pertinent questions but he,
understandably enough, had been anxious to find out what kind of
lodger she was likely to be. Their second lodger, she recalled,
which suggested either that the Clares were less affluent than they
appeared or that Sophy Clare had only recently become nervous.
In any case the room was a nice one and the rent was low.

'And I'm only here for a limited period,' she informed her
reflection, putting the last towel into her large suitcase and
snapping it shut.

Her reflection looked back at her, unanswering. It was a pleasant
reflection, Jessica considered, with features that tilted towards
mischief, curly fair hair that was too fine to be grown long, eyes
that were sometimes blue and sometimes had a greenish cast. At
twenty-four she was wearing well, she decided with another of the
grins that transformed her from the coolly elegant to the
attractively gamine. Some men were drawn to the surface
sophistication; the more discerning sought the gamine. Jessica
sometimes wondered if she would ever meet the man who would
accept both parts of her, blending them into the third person she
felt herself to be.

'I may be back just for the night,' she warned the receptionist as
she lugged her suitcase and typewriter past the desk. That would
stop them renting out the room again for that night, she reflected,
carrying her luggage to the Mini. She hadn't bought any groceries.
Better to check on the kitchen and then nip to the local shops
before they closed.

Blundell Road was still sun dappled and deserted. Jessica slowed
to a crawl and played tourist. Large houses and gardens spoke of
past affluence, but a few of them had obviously been turned into
apartments and between the bars of gates she glimpsed untidy
borders, unraked drives. No signs of children or babies. Perhaps
most people who lived here were elderly, living genteelly on
reduced income like the ladies in 'Cranford'.

Mrs Tate must have been looking out for her since she plodded

round the side of the house and opened the gate leading to the
garage as Jessica drew up.

'If you'd like to come round to the back door, Miss, I can show
you the rest of the house and help you with your things,' she said.

'That's very kind of you.' Jessica handed her the keys through
the window, waited until the garage door had been raised and
drove slowly in.

It was a three-car garage with spaces clearly marked, a table and
hanging cupboard at the back holding an array of bright tools. She
parked neatly in the smallest space and got out.

'Give me that. You lock the door and come round the side after
me.' Mrs Tate put the keys on the bonnet, lifted the heavy suitcase
with ease and plodded out. Jessica took out the remaining bits and
pieces, locked car and garage and followed round the corner along
a terrace and into the yard. The washing had been taken down and
the line quivered slightly in the breeze.

'Come in, Miss.' Mrs Tate's voice issued from a half-open door.

Jessica stepped into a long kitchen. It had been modernized, the
red quarry-tiled floor polished, white tiles grouted on to walls
papered in a pattern of fruit and leaves, the large copper boiler
clearly kept only as a reminder of days past, the stove that must
have stood in the recess replaced by a modern cooker. Washing
machine and dryer were ranged next to a large refrigerator and
freezer. Down the middle of the room stretched a long oaken table
with knife marks scoring the surface. There was a tall cupboard
against one wall and several hardback chairs. Despite the shiny
tiles and wallpaper the overall effect was curiously depressing.

'Cup of tea?' Mrs Tate nodded towards a fat brown teapot.

'No, thanks. Mr Clare said that I could use the kitchen if I
wanted to cook, but I don't want to mess up your arrangements,'
Jessica said.

'Oh, I don't cook regular for the Clares,' Mrs Tate said. 'I make
a snack for Mrs Clare around 1.30 and the odd cup of tea, but I
only stay on to cook dinner if they're having guests – and that's
once in a blue moon. To tell you the truth it gets a bit quiet round
here at night. People aren't neighbourly – not like Saucehall Street.
I was born down there and it might have been common and noisy
but people didn't lock their doors and draw their curtains in those
days. So, as far as I'm concerned, you can use the kitchen
whenever you like. Feel free. I've cleared a couple of shelves in the

cupboard and in the 'fridge for your stuff. Use the dishes here since I don't suppose you've any of your own – oh, and if you put anything you want to wash in the basket there I can do it with the rest.'

'Thanks.' Jessica spoke absently, her eyes on a row of small brass bells over her head. Each one had a number over it.

'For the old days,' Mrs Tate said, following her gaze. 'There are bell pulls in all the main rooms. Before electricity was put in they used to work on a series of wires. They were all taken out but Mr Clare left the kitchen bells. Look pretty, don't they?'

'I suppose.' Jessica frowned slightly for no particular reason.

'I'll show you the rest of the place,' Mrs Tate said, casting another wistful glance towards the teapot. 'Then I'll have to get on. Mrs Clare is due back this evening and I promised to cook something. How about you? The shops stay open until seven.'

'I'll walk down and get a few groceries,' Jessica said, moving to pick up her case.

'I'll take that. I'm used to carrying heavy things. Lord knows I had to drag the old fellow upstairs often enough when he had taken drink,' Mrs Tate said.

'The old fellow?' Jessica relinquished the suitcase.

'The late, unlamented Henry Albert Tate,' the other said. 'This way.'

The inner door led into a small room with faded wallpaper and a raffia rug, furnished only with a couple of sagging armchairs and an ancient-looking rolltop desk.

Beyond that, a short passage led past a pantry lined with shelves and then Mrs Tate pushed open the door with her shoulder and they emerged into the front hall.

'Dining-room's next to the breakfast-room.' Mrs Tate nodded towards the room where Jessica had drunk tea with Mr Clare. 'The sitting-room's across the hall and the old nursery behind. You can have a bit of a wander by yourself.'

Jessica followed her up the stairs to the half landing where Mrs Tate put down the suitcase.

'The bathroom's private to you,' she said. 'The other bedrooms are on the next level. Five bedrooms and a bathroom. Big rooms. I get them done twice a month. As much as I can manage. Did Mr Clare give you a key to the back door?'

Jessica nodded.

'I like to keep the front chain on until just before Mr Clare gets back from the office,' Mrs Tate said. 'Not that we ever have any trouble round here, but door-to-door salesmen can be a nuisance.'

'What work does Mr Clare do?' Jessica asked.

'His firm arranges conferences and dinners and stuff like that. Keeps him pretty busy. Now if you'll excuse me, I'll get to the vegetables. Mrs Clare's fussy about the sauces. Make yourself at home.'

She nodded, her face settling into the lines of discontent which were so at variance with her pleasant manner and voice.

'Thanks,' Jessica said, taking her case into the bedroom.

The tour of the premises had been somewhat superficial. She promised herself a look round later and began unpacking, hanging a poster of a Spanish dancer on one of the wall hooks, filling wardrobe and dresser with her clothes and notebooks. Her typewriter fitted neatly on the small table.

When she had finished the room looked – all wrong. She scowled at the poster. It was too savagely bright, a clarion call of vivid colour seeking to dominate the quiet neatness of everything else. Jessica started to take it down, then abruptly changed her mind. The poster was cheerful and she liked it, and she wasn't about to allow the faintly oppressive atmosphere of the house to dominate her taste.

There was no lock on the door. She chided herself for minding. This was clearly the kind of house where people didn't poke about in other people's belongings. Mrs Tate had shown a commendable lack of curiosity about her.

She went downstairs again and through to the back door where the other was peeling vegetables at the double sink.

'Getting your groceries? Don't bother about condiments and such – there's plenty here,' she said, square hands making the knife flash as it turned and twisted, paring skin from flesh.

'I won't be long.' Jessica went out into the long shadowed afternoon, making grocery lists in her head.

She'd buy sufficient for a couple of meals, then go in the car the following day and load up the Mini. Meanwhile a brisk walk would do her good.

A few cars were now parked in driveways and a boy rode by on a bike, whistling. Jessica turned into the narrower road that led to the small shopping centre. There were more people here, housewives with shopping baskets, a man walking a dog on the other side of the street. A sign she hadn't noticed before directed her to the PUBLIC LIBRARY. It might prove useful to have a good look round in the reference section for local colour.

The small supermarket was neon-lit and air-conditioned. Modern and reassuring. Why had she thought of 'reassuring'? She crossed at the first set of lights and slotted the required pound into the wire basket section. Something simple would be enough. Cheese, bread, butter, frozen peas and onions, pasta, tinned tomatoes, coffee, milk. She added a couple of pears and then put them back. There had been pears in the garden. She would ask if she might take a couple.

She picked out a couple of yoghurts and hesitated over a packet of biscuits.

'Wholemeal with raisins. Terribly healthy.'

The voice belonged to a young man who had pushed a basket in the opposite direction. A tall, young man in a shabby tweed jacket and a pair of jeans that ought to have been thrown out in the last spring-cleaning session. His face was what might be termed attractively plain, Jessica thought, answering, 'You're right, though eating healthy can be pretty boring sometimes. I'll take them.'

'Live dangerously.' He gave her the kind of smile reserved for transient strangers and pushed the wire basket past. It appeared to be loaded with tins of cat food and several large cabbages.

Jessica paid for her purchases and forked out extra for a large plastic bag. She reclaimed her pound and crossed back into the narrower street.

The afternoon was waning and there was a chill in the air. She walked faster, the low heels of her shoes making satisfying little clicking noises on the pavement. A small group of children went by, some with tartan satchels on their backs, pushing one another and laughing. Right now they were endearing. Give them ten years and they might become menacing, voices louder, shoulders broader, the need to survive replacing giggling innocence. At their heels, ignored, another child tagged. Ten or eleven years old and obviously playing some game of dressing up. Her party dress had been filched from some dusty attic, its pink flounces soiled and torn, and she was clearly unused to the high-heeled shoes she was wearing, stumbling slightly on the paving stones. Her hair was a tangled mass of black ringlets and the face she turned briefly towards Jessica was heavily painted, mouth a scarlet bee-sting, eyes hard outlined with blue.

She cast a swift glance, shocking in its unchildlike hardness, and stumbled on, the hem of her skirt trailing as she tried to catch up with the others. Then a long line of homeward bound traffic came between Jessica and the group and the child was lost to view.

Feeling oddly shaken Jessica walked on, the unpleasantness of that glance lingering in her mind. Not a nice little girl, she thought. But only people who knew little of children classified them as either all nice or all impossible. No wonder the other kids, shoving and giggling at one another, had ignored the one who vainly followed them.

The smell of cooking wafted from the kitchen. Mrs Tate was stirring something with an expression of intense concentration on her face and gave Jessica only a brief, distracted smile. Now evidently wasn't the time to start using the cooker. Jessica put the stuff away, poured hot water into a mug, added coffee, took out a couple of the wholemeal biscuits and went upstairs.

The central heating was evidently working well since her room was comfortably warm. She put coffee and biscuits on the table and went over to the bed to switch on the bedside lamp. Shadows sprang to life against the white walls. Jessica crossed to the window and looked out over the twilight-purpled tangle of garden. Above the trees, the sky was a slow-moving mass of lilac bordered clouds lit by the last gleams of the setting sun. She drew the curtains across, turned and decided she had created a haven. Even the poster seemed to fit in now. Glancing at it, glancing again, she moved quickly to put on the overhead light, to flood the room with white brilliance. Surfaces became flat and stark again and the Spanish girl held the flounces of her pink dress high above her dancing ankles, all scarlet fled from the poster.

Two

It must be an effect of the light, she thought, staring at it. Under artificial light colours did change, blur into one another. She had brought the poster back after a family trip to Spain, had seen it often since then under artificial light, had been teased by her friends because the poster was so touristy. The Spanish girl's flounced dress had been scarlet, not pink. Perhaps she was tired. Perhaps she was developing some minor eye defect that faded colours.

She drank the coffee hastily, not really tasting it, keeping her eyes averted, then glancing quickly at the poster but seeing every time the pink flounces. The biscuit tasted dry and powdery. She went to the window, pulled back the curtain, raised the sash and scattered the crumbs on the sill. The light from the room cast whiteness over the yard and left the rest of the garden in darkness. On the wind she could hear the far off hum of traffic in the city.

Closing the window, pulling the curtain across, turning swiftly to catch the Spanish dancer unaware, she saw there was no change. She would look at it in daylight, and seeing the dress scarlet again would be amused at her own foolishness.

The sound of the front door opening and then closing made her jump. Not until the sounds came did she become aware of the silence of the house. The cheerful bustle of cooking was inaudible from here. In the main hall below she could hear voices, footsteps. Mr Clare and his wife must be home. They were late – nearly half an hour late. She moved towards the door, hesitating. Ought she to go down and introduce herself or wait? Wait, probably. There were footsteps on the staircase now, softened by the carpet. A woman's voice, soft but distinct.

'Let me just change my shoes and tidy myself up, darling. Tell Mrs Tate to set another place.'

'Right.'

That was Mr Clare's voice, firm and pleasant.

When the knock came on her door she took an involuntary step backwards, then opened it, feeling slightly foolish. Nerves weren't something she had ever suffered from and it was annoying to feel so jumpy.

'Miss Cameron, I hope you'll join us for dinner on your first evening here?' Mr Clare stood in the dim light on the half landing, his greying head slightly inclined.

'Will there be sufficient? I don't think Mrs Tate expected –'

'Mrs Tate always cooks enough for an army, though I can't vouch for the quality. Sophy is very anxious to meet you.'

'I'll put on a skirt,' Jessica began.

'Heavens, we're completely informal,' he countered. 'No need to go to any trouble. Come along down and I'll give you a sherry while Sophy tidies herself up.'

'In that case, thank you.' Jessica moved to switch off the table lamp, flicked off the main light, and followed him down the stairs.

They went into the breakfast-room where she had drunk tea earlier. The curtains had been drawn and inner doors folded back to reveal a dining-room furnished in similar style with silk panels on the walls. The table was laid for a meal with what looked to her cursory glance like an array of glittering cutlery and crystal. Against the end wall were the outlines of a hatch which presumably connected with the kitchen quarters. Beneath a long window on the outside wall a carved chest echoed the furniture.

'Dry or sweet?' Mr Clare had moved to a corner cabinet.

'I know it's unsophisticated but sweet, please.' Jessica perched on the edge of a chair, wishing she had insisted on changing. Her jeans were out of place here.

'Sophistication lies in knowing what you want and asking for it.' He poured the dark amber liquid and handed it to her. 'So, are you nicely settled in?'

'Yes, very comfortably. Oh, I forgot to say that the agent suggested I pay two months' advance rent. You only took –'

'I'll see he gets his commission. What a scrupulous young lady you are!' His smile softened the faintly patronizing tone.

'I like to have things cut and dried,' Jessica said.

'If one could.' A shade of gravity had passed across his face.

There were footsteps in the hall and the door opened, a woman in a green dress came in, her hand outstretched.

'You're Jessica Cameron. Welcome to The Cedars. Though I daresay that John has already welcomed you very satisfactorily. My train was late otherwise I'd have been on time. I have a terribly old-fashioned notion that punctuality is very important – the politeness of kings and all that. Darling, I'm choking for a drink. My bones have been rattled all the way. Work on the lines, they said, though why British Rail has to start tearing up the rails every time I decide to pay a visit to my parents I simply don't know.'

She had a quick, light voice like rain pattering on a window pane. Jessica found that she was so busy listening to her that it was difficult to form a clear picture of what she looked like. Her face was mobile, expressions flitting across it one after the other, each one seeming to slightly alter her features. Her hair was an indeterminate ash blonde with thin strands of red in it that might have been natural or might have been dye growing out. She wore it in a cheek-feathering bob that looked too young for her at one moment and charming at the next.

'It's very kind of you to invite me to have dinner with you,' Jessica said, breaking into the flow as the other paused for breath.

'Oh, we couldn't expect you to eat alone on your first evening here. Is that for me, darling? You're an angel. I love gin – such a clean, sharp taste. Is Mrs Tate ready to serve? I wonder if I ought to pop into the kitchen and just check –'

'Far better sit down, Sophy,' her husband said. 'The poor woman's nervous enough about the sauces as it is. You set such a high standard.'

'I took a course in Paris years ago and I've been living on my reputation ever since,' Sophy Clare said. 'Come and sit down. John, bring the wine. It ought to have breathed for longer but it'll have to do. Jessica, may I call you Jessica? And you must call us Sophy and John – mustn't she, darling?'

'By all means,' John Clare said, his tone carefully neutral.

'Perhaps it would be better to –' Jessica started to say, but was interrupted.

'Nonsense, we couldn't possibly have someone living here with us whom we couldn't treat as a friend. John, the wine, darling? No, only a drop for me. Red wine brings on my migraine – such a nuisance being subject to migraine, Jessica. Do you ever get it?'

'No, I –'

'Then you're fortunate. Happily I don't get it as often as I used to – ah, the hatch is opening. Mrs Tate, how are you? Did everything go splendidly while I was away?'

'You were missed,' said Mrs Tate, handing soup bowls through the gap in which her head and shoulders were framed.

'Isn't that a lovely thing to hear? Was I missed, John? Was I?' There was a sudden wistfulness in the light, chattering voice.

'Very much – as you well know so stop fishing for compliments,' John Clare said with a somewhat heavy-handed playfulness.

The vegetable soup was good, thick and fragrant with a sprinkling of herbs.

'Is it good?' John Clare cast a slightly anxious look at his wife who was tasting it cautiously.

'Filling anyway. No, really not bad at all. One can't really go wrong with vegetables. Jessica, tell me about yourself. John was telling me on the way from the station that you do historical research. Will you find anything worth recording here that hasn't already been recorded and filed and microfilmed and the Lord knows what else?'

'I'm concentrating mainly on domestic history – nineteenth century,' Jessica said.

'What a pity we haven't got one of those dusty old attics filled with trunks crammed with old letters and photographs,' Sophy said.

'There is that old cupboard in the shed,' John remembered. 'We always meant to sort it out.'

'Anything that we intend to do in the far distant future gets shoved into the shed,' Sophy said. 'There's probably nothing in it at all, but feel free to rummage.' She nodded at Jessica and began to clear the soup bowls, handing them back to Mrs Tate who loomed beyond the hatch with a dish of chops and one of baked potatoes.

'I made that redcurrant sauce you like,' she said.

'That was very sweet of you.' Sophy took the dish of chops. 'These look very tasty. Oh, cabbage. Well, never mind. Cabbage can make a good accompaniment. Now let's start before it goes cold. Only one for me, darling – if I don't lose weight soon you'll have to widen the doors.'

Her green dress covered a thin figure with small breasts and thin hips. Her hands showed a fine tracery of blue veins.

'You're not into this slimming nonsense, I hope?' John said, passing plates.

'I'm afraid I'm one of those people who can eat tons and not put on an ounce,' Jessica said.

'John is the same. Infuriating for the rest of us. Is this your first visit to the North? You're a Londoner?'

'Of Scottish descent on my father's side.'

'Do you have the sight?' Sophy leaned forward eagerly.

'No, I don't think – you mean second sight? No, not that I know.'

'But you believe in it?'

'Of course she doesn't,' John said, a trifle testily. 'What you're pleased to call second sight is no more than a lively power of deduction and a large dose of imagination.'

'I'm inclined to agree with you,' Jessica said, 'though one does occasionally have the odd flash of telepathy.'

She had, she considered, balanced herself neatly on the fence. Sophy looked faintly disappointed, however. Her eyes, Jessica noticed, were slightly prominent. Perhaps she had thyroid trouble. Pale-blue eyes with sparse lashes whose tips had been painstakingly blackened.

'Telepathy can be scientifically measured, I believe,' John said.

His wife dismissed scientific measurements with a deprecating little wave of her hand.

'Too silly,' she said.

'Surely everything obeys natural laws,' Jessica said. 'It's only that we don't yet understand exactly how they work.'

'I'd go along with that,' John said.

'You're probably right,' Sophy allowed. 'One would like to have explanations.'

For an instant there was something so yearning and hungry in her face that Jessica was startled. It was gone directly as she said, 'And is your room comfortable? We could have given you the spare room but having the bathroom so close to the smaller one gives you a measure of privacy.'

'The room's fine. I hope my typing won't disturb you.'

'Oh heavens, there is nothing I shall enjoy more than hearing the comforting tap-tap of your typewriter on those evenings when John is working late,' Sophy said. 'He is one of the directors in a firm that arranges conferences and dinners and so on, which means that he has to attend a great many of them.'

'You know you are welcome to come with me to most of them,' John said.

'But I wouldn't know any of the people there, darling. And you know how I hate large, impersonal gatherings. No. I'm very much of a stay-at-home. In the evenings that is. I'm terribly busy during the day, aren't I, darling?'

'Sophy does a lot of voluntary work,' John said. 'Care for the aged, meals on wheels, children's library service – that sort of thing. Keeps her busy most of the day.'

'So it's really no wonder that when evening comes all I want to do is relax,' Sophy said brightly.

'I shall probably be out some evenings myself,' Jessica said. It was as well, she thought, to make it clear that she hadn't rented the room in order to provide companionship for Sophy Clare when her husband was out.

'You will want to make friends,' Sophy said. 'I'm afraid that we have very few. When the children were little I used to meet other mothers in the park and at the clinic, but children grow up and people move away. This is a very quiet district, mainly retired people living on reduced incomes and keeping up appearances.'

'Your children are not at home?'

Jessica was trying to reorientate the impression she had formed of the Clares' ages. If the children were grown up then they must both be older than they looked – late forties instead of the late thirties they appeared to be.

'They both work away,' John said. 'Social work. Julian is interested in juvenile delinquents while Robina prefers working with the younger children.'

'We only see them at holiday periods,' Sophy said with a sigh. 'Sometimes I wish they had stayed here to complete their training but young people like to be independent. John and I have never tried to hold on to them.'

'So we are really rather dull and conventional,' John said.

The hatch door was opened again and Mrs Tate looked through. 'Was it all right?' She sounded anxious.

'A trifle too much sugar in the sauce,' Sophy said, 'but otherwise everything was quite delicious. What treat have you for pudding? Something very light, I hope?'

'Tinned lychees and ice-cream,' Mrs Tate said. 'Or cheese and biscuits?'

Sophy had closed her rather prominent eyes with an expression of pain on her face that embarrassed Jessica though Mrs Tate didn't appear to notice it.

'The cheese, I think,' John said.

'And then you must get along home.' Sophy opened her eyes. 'No, I insist. The washing-up can keep until the morning and I'll make the coffee myself. The dinner was very good, really very good.'

'See you tomorrow then. 'Night.' Mrs Tate placed cheese and wafers on the ledge of the hatch and withdrew.

'I would be glad to give her a ride home but she insists on using her bike,' John said, fetching the cheese. 'I told her to buy Brie.'

'Anything more exotic than Brie is out of Mrs Tate's ken,' Sophy said.

Jessica took a sliver of cheese and a wafer and nibbled them, listening to the muffled sounds of departure from the next room, the closing of the back door.

'Shall I make the coffee?' Sophy was on her feet. 'Let's have it in the sitting-room? Did Mrs Tate show you the sitting-room, Jessica? We keep the television set there. Isn't there a panel game or something on tonight, darling? Go and switch it on and I'll bring the coffee.'

'Can I help?' Jessica asked politely.

'Heavens, no. It won't take me five minutes. You aren't going out, John?'

'Not this evening.'

'Then we shall be a pleasant little trio.' She went out, rising on her heels as she walked, in a manner that imparted an airy lightness to her gait.

'Shall we retire as they say?' John glanced at Jessica.

'Yes.' Rising, she followed him again across the hall where a lamp burned too dimly to banish the shadows from the far corners and into the room opposite the breakfast-room.

'Make yourself comfortable.' He nodded towards a long sofa piled with cushions and went over to a television set in the corner where he began fiddling with the knobs. Over his shoulder he said,

'Sophy likes you. I can always tell when she likes people.'

'I'm glad,' Jessica said politely.

The thought that being liked too much by one's landlady might impose certain burdens crossed her mind. Sophy Clare was obviously a lonely woman who craved companionship.

To distract her thoughts she looked around the room. High ceilinged with moulded cornices and a central rose of gilded plaster raying out from the chandelier-type light; walls papered in a faded William Morris paper with little bunches of flowers on it, a handsome black marble mantelshelf with an electric fire fitted beneath where the old fireplace had been, furniture with carved legs that must have been hell to polish and had probably been purchased in some antique sale. The bay window was heavily curtained. There were several standing lamps about the room. John had turned on a couple.

The announcer was informing the viewers of some forthcoming programmes. The television set looked decidedly out of place in this room. John turned it down slightly and took his seat on a low chair, leaning forward slightly as if he were reluctant to miss a word. Perhaps he had simply run out of conversation, Jessica thought, and leaned back, trying to look as interested as he was in the crop of films and soap operas now being flashed in brief snatches of scene across the screen.

Light, quick, tapping footsteps crossed the hall. Jessica glanced towards the half open door but nobody pushed it wider. A minute or two later there were slower footsteps and Sophy came in, pushing the door wider with the edge of the tray she was carrying.

'Let me take that.' Somewhat belatedly John hurried to help. 'Are we having a liqueur?'

'Would you like one, Jessica?' Sophy asked.

'No, thank you. Just coffee, please.'

'Only the instant stuff tonight, I'm afraid. Milk? Sugar? Help yourself. No liqueur for me either, darling. That wretched train journey made me so tired that I shall go out like a light the instant my head touches the pillow. Do you sleep well, Jessica?'

'Usually like a top,' Jessica said cheerfully.

Sophy, having handed round coffee, took her seat in an armchair placed at a little distance, facing the door. It still stood wide, the hall beyond shadowed. The scarlet of the carpet looked dull in the soft light.

'Shall I close the door?' John asked, glancing briefly from the television.

'Leave it, darling. The room feels a mite stuffy.' Her voice was quick. 'Don't you think it's a trifle close in here, Jessica? Possibly the central heating needs adjusting. The electric fire is separate, only for very cold evenings. Mrs Tate and I have a running battle about opening windows. She is convinced that fresh air is unhealthy.'

'With all the pollution around she's probably right,' Jessica said.

'Pollution.' Sophy turned the word over in her mouth as if it had a new and unfamiliar taste. Then she said with a curious fluttering movement that rippled across her face, 'It depends what one means by pollution.'

'The panel game's starting. We timed it well,' John said, leaning to turn up the sound.

Jessica drank her coffee and kept her eyes on the screen though the game was dull, the compère covertly mocking in a way that made her dislike him and despise the various contestants who, for the sake of a few minutes on screen, were willing to be debased. John seemed to be enjoying it. She heard him chuckle once or twice, answer a couple of questions under his breath. His classical profile and smoothly brushed, greying fair hair were more suited to someone listening to chamber music and eyeing the company through a quizzing glass. Eighteenth rather than nineteenth century, she reflected, and gave a slight start as a burst of very modern rock came from the television.

Sophy wasn't making the smallest pretence at any interest in the panel game. She sat bolt upright, sipping her coffee, her eyes over the rim of the cup fixed unwaveringly on the wide open door. Her face, as she lowered her cup between sips, was constantly in motion, half-formed expressions flitting across it like clouds in a blank, pale sky. There was something unnerving in her concentrated attention. Jessica resisted the impulse to turn her own head and look out into the shadowed hall.

'Good result!' John spoke heartily as the applause died and the credits began to roll. 'That woman from Durham had brains, I thought. Pity she fell down on the last question. Still she didn't go away empty handed. Ah, we have an animal documentary now. You will enjoy this, darling. You like animal documentaries.'

'It depends on the animal,' Sophy said, speaking for the first time. 'I like birds and monkeys. What about you, Jessica?'

'I think I'll give the programme a miss,' Jessica said. 'To tell you the truth I feel really tired. Would you think me very rude if I had an early night?'

'For goodness sake you don't have to ask permission,' Sophy said, a smile joining the other expressions chasing across her face. 'You come and go as you please. Do you have everything you need? Towels, hot-water bottle? We turn down the heating slightly at night – oh, the house stays very warm but a hot-water bottle can be very homey, don't you think?'

'I really don't need anything,' Jessica said, standing up. 'I want to make a start first thing tomorrow. I have a few ideas that I want to rough out. You mentioned a cupboard?'

'In the shed at the bottom of the garden,' John said, tearing his attention from the screen. 'It's stuffed full of old newspapers as far as I can remember. Actually it wasn't us who put it in the shed. It was there when we took the house, d'ye remember, Sophy? Old Mr Lawrence?'

'The previous owner?' Jessica queried.

'About ninety years old and deaf as a post,' Sophy said. 'Poor old soul went into a nursing-home and died shortly afterwards. He was a bachelor without any family. We bought the house quite cheaply, didn't we, John?'

'It'd be worth a lot more today,' John said.

'We could sell it, but we wouldn't be able to get anything comparable,' Sophy chattered, 'and the neighbourhood is very quiet. John spends so much time being sociable that he needs a place where he can unwind and relax.'

'Yes, well –' Jessica stood uncertainly, wondering if the conversation was at an end.

'Rummage around as much as you like,' John said amiably. 'You might find something that will spark off a line of research or something. Ah, we have elephants. You like elephants, Sophy.'

'They look so protective,' Sophy said, not looking at the television.

'Well, good night then.' Jessica made for the door. 'Shall I close it now?' Sophy shook her head, the fine ashy hair swinging against her cheek. She wasn't looking at Jessica at all but past her, out into the hall.

Jessica went out and crossed to the stairs. Along the balcony the stained glass of the windows glowed warmly in the soft light. The windows were arched at the top like windows in a church but the patterns of the glass were not particularly religious. Stars and tulips and long emerald leaves with narrow curves and rectangles to fill

out the spaces – typical late nineteenth-century work, cruder than
earlier stained glass. She mounted the stairs, sliding her hand up
the smooth oak of the balustrade. Mrs Tate evidently didn't stint
on the polishing.

At the half landing she turned, looking down the length of the
balcony, from which more steps would lead to the other bedrooms.
Five of them and another bathroom, Mrs Tate had told her. It was
certainly a big house for two people whose children only came
home in the holidays. Julian and Robina. She would have liked to
learn more about them but neither John nor Sophy had seemed
inclined to say very much.

She cast a brief glance down into the well of the hall, then went
into her own room, clicking on the main light, her eyes going at
once to the poster. The Spanish dancer still wore a pink flounced
dress. It was crazy, completely crazy.

She went in and closed the door, reached up and took down the
poster. It was possible that she'd hung it inadvertently against a
damp patch and the colour had run. Possible but hardly likely. The
wall behind was dry and white and unmarked save by the hook.
There was no trace of moisture on the shiny surface of the poster.
She hung it up again and sat down, drawing one of her notebooks
towards her. When anything peculiar occurred the best antidote to
anxiety was to concentrate on something very practical. Her first
task was to delve into whatever archives were available for
inspection and make a list of what had already been displayed and
recorded. That would take at least a week, she reckoned. After the
archives the local library might yield something of interest. What
she wanted to do was build up a picture of a family in
mid-nineteenth – and what was that?

Her head jerked up as she heard the quick, light, tapping steps.
Someone was walking along the polished floor that wasn't covered
by the carpet. She had heard the sounds before when she had sat
downstairs waiting for Sophy to bring the coffee. That was what
Sophy herself had been waiting to hear as she sat, her eyes fixed on
the open door.

'This is ridiculous,' Jessica muttered, getting up and opening the
door. The tapping sound stopped abruptly just as the clock down in
the hall chimed musically. Jessica stepped out on to the balcony
and frowned at the length of carpet with the wide border of
polished parquet at each side. A very slim person might have

walked along it without touching the carpet, but why would they want to? Anyway there was nobody there. She stepped to the railings and looked down, seeing the patch of light from the open door of the sitting-room. The television set had been turned down but she could hear the low murmuring of a voice as the last chime of the clock died into a throbbing vibration. Were they still sitting there? John Clare with his air of past elegance leaning forward to lose himself in the programme? Sophy seated in her chair with her rather prominent eyes fixed on the shadowed hall?

This was a fairly old house. In old buildings boards creaked and foundations settled. There were also various species of unpleasant beetles gnawing their way through wood and plaster, tapping and ticking. Central heating made odd noises too sometimes. Odd gurgles and bangs and thumps. She turned and went back into her room, closing the door firmly. Once a problem had been rationalized there was no point in worrying further about it. She read through the list she had made with concentrated attention. She would have to check with her boss whether or not her idea of gathering as much information as possible about one small section of society was better than collecting a little data on a wider scale. Letters and photographs were more likely to have been kept by the middle class than by the working classes who would have been largely illiterate at that period. She made notes for a letter in which she intended to lay out her ideas for the board to approve, and felt a sudden unexpected sleepiness which made truth of the white lie she had told down in the sitting-room.

She undressed, slipped on her robe and went into the small bathroom to shower. The water was pleasantly hot though the general warmth of the house had cooled slightly. She towelled herself lazily and went back into the bedroom. It was beginning to feel like her own domain now. Despite the stupid poster. She turned on the bedside lamp and switched off the main light, banishing it further into obscurity.

With the door closed the room seemed smaller. She went over to the window and pushed up the sash. A chilly but refreshing draught of air blew through, stirring the edges of the curtains. Somewhere below, near at hand but indistinct, a voice called, 'Polly! Polly, hurry yourself up!'

There was no answering voice and after a moment she left the window and climbed into the neatly made bed between sheets starched more crisply than nylon ever was.

Three

Struggling out of dreams that fell into tangled cobwebs even as her memory sought to capture them she returned to morning reality. Light had found its way through the gap in the curtains and was arrowing the carpet. Jessica leaned up on her elbow, looking at the room with a feeling of faint unease. It looked different from the room she remembered, which was ridiculous because it was exactly the same as it had been the previous day. Why then did she miss the texture of linen sheets? Why were her toes groping for a stone bottle still warm from the night before? It had something to do with the dreams she couldn't recall.

Getting out of bed she drew the curtains and looked with disfavour at the poster. Daylight made no difference at all. The flounced dress was still pink. When something for which no obvious explanation presents itself occurs the sensible thing is to ignore it. Telling herself that she slipped on her robe and went into the tiny bathroom. She was in the bedroom again brushing her hair when footsteps on the stairs and a tap on the door heralded Mrs Tate, carrying a tray on which coffee and toast were arranged.

'I hope it's all right, Miss, but I always clean the breakfast and dining-room on this morning so I took the liberty of bringing you up a bite of breakfast,' she said.

'That's really kind of you. Thanks very much.' Jessica took the tray and wedged it next to her typewriter.

'Saves you feeling awkward about getting under my feet,' Mrs Tate said. 'I do like to keep to my routine. If I don't make an early start I never get done.'

'Are the Clares out then?' Jessica bit into a slice of toast.

'Mr Clare went to the office and Mrs Clare does meals on wheels today,' Mrs Tate said. 'Oh, Mr Clare said as how there are some old books upstairs you might find useful and to help yourself. Second bedroom on the right. Now I must get on.'

She nodded amiably and withdrew. Jessica sat down and applied herself to the unexpected breakfast. It had been a nice gesture even if Mrs Tate's motive had been to keep her domain free for cleaning. She had also been provided with an excuse to satisfy her curiosity about the upper rooms. Thinking of this she made a small grimace because curiosity had never been one of her faults. Interest in the past, yes, but not this wish to pry into her neighbour's affairs.

She finished off the toast and coffee, completed her dressing, made the bed and carried the tray downstairs with a satisfyingly virtuous feeling and found Mrs Tate in the kitchen up to her elbows in soapsuds.

'Just leave it there, Miss. I want to get the dishes out of the way before I start on the floors,' she said. 'The dinner went down a treat, didn't it? Mrs Clare was very pleased.'

'It was delicious,' Jessica assured her, thinking as she retraced her footsteps upstairs again that Mrs Tate was definitely a throwback to an age when domestic servants took a pride in their work and regarded praise from their employers as adequate compensation for low wages and bad working conditions. Not that Mrs Tate probably suffered either. Daily ladies were worth their weight in gold these days and she obviously had the latest in cleaning devices to make the labour easier.

At the end of the balcony was a half landing matching the one outside her room with stairs twisting up from it – a mere half dozen bringing her on to a wide semi-circular hall with doors opening off it. Feeling slightly guilty Jessica opened doors, contenting herself with merely popping her head into the rooms thus revealed. There was a big, somewhat gloomy bathroom with an integral lavatory and a second lavatory next to it which had probably been adapted out of a large broom cupboard. A large bedroom next to it with double bed and a range of fitted cupboards clearly was used by the Clares; next to it a narrower room held a single bed and there were models of aeroplanes suspended on wires from the ceiling. Julian's room, Jessica decided, and looked into the next one which was similar but without the aerial models. Probably Robina's room. The next apartment was the one where the books were according to Mrs Tate. She skipped it for the moment and looked into the one nearest the stairs, the opening door revealing a spare bedroom with twin beds and modern furniture that didn't look quite happy in the high-ceilinged, wainscoted chamber. All the rooms were large with marble washbasins and gilded cornices and high, narrow fireplaces reminiscent of hip baths before the fire.

Jessica opened the door of the designated room and went in, happy in the consciousness that she was supposed to be here. It was like the other chambers with the same plaster rose on the ceiling, bits of coloured glass in the windows, slightly faded wallpaper and marble washstand. There was a wide bed against one wall and bookcases at each side of the fireplace. Here, as in the other rooms, the grate had been taken out and a small electric fire fitted. Jessica went over to the bookcases and started running her index finger along titles. Bound sets of Austen, Eliot, Brontë and Dickens which didn't look as if they had been much read, paperback copies of Agatha Christie and P.D. James, well-thumbed copies of the *Katy* and *Pollyanna* books, Grimms' *Fairytales*, some science-fiction. Nothing there to engage her professional interest. She moved to the next case, scanning the titles of various romances by Daphne du Maurier, Denise Robins, and – ah, these looked more promising.

Jessica sat cross-legged on the rug and pulled out a couple of thick volumes with battered covers. *History of Blundell Road* and *Mrs Beeton's Book of Household Management*. She opened the former first with lively curiosity, wondering what was so special about the road that someone had chosen to write about it. The author was the Reverend Edward Makin. He wrote like a Reverend too, Jessica thought, having struggled through a couple of paragraphs. The Reverend Edward Makin went into great and wearisome detail about his motives in wishing to lay before his public (irritatingly spelt with a K) that *closely observed and carefully judged history of a small portion of our Sceptred Isle that future generations may profit from the knowledge therein.*

The book had been published privately in 18— in a mock Gothic script that was guaranteed to put off any prospective reader. She closed it and picked up the other book, relaxing as she saw the clear, plain script, the charmingly anachronistic bits and pieces between the recipes. Her mother had a later edition of the book and they'd giggled together over the quantities of eggs, butter and cream required. There were loose pages in this book, sheets of lined notepaper on which fragments of shopping lists and variations on ingredients had been written in a different hand. The ink had blurred and faded in places. Jessica wasn't sure if the books would be as useful as all that but she would read through them later. She took another sweeping look along the shelves, added a thin pamphlet with a sketch map of Victorian Liverpool on the cover to her trophies and glanced up as someone looked round the door.

'Oh, I'm sorry, Miss.'

The girl she had seen hanging out the washing withdrew hastily and went past down the half-dozen steps, the wood creaking slightly to mark her descent. Jessica opened her mouth to say something but someone from below called loudly but indistinctly, 'Polly! Polly, have you –?'

Obviously Mrs Tate needed her daughter downstairs. Jessica picked up her books and took them to her room. From below came the whine of a vacuum cleaner energetically used.

What she had planned to do was drive into the city centre and start the process of elimination of subjects already covered and made available to the public, but the idea was less attractive than the impulse she felt to take a look round the immediate neighbourhood. Her best starting point for that was the library.

'Did you find what you wanted?' Mrs Tate called from the breakfast-room over the noise of the vacuum cleaner.

'Yes, thanks. I hope so anyway.' Jessica paused as the other switched off and let the whine die into a silent scream. 'I'm going to the local library. Did you want anything in the shops?'

'No, I don't think so, Miss. Thanks all the same. My daughter can pop down if I do. Have a nice morning.'

The cleaner came to life again, shuddering up dust.

Blundell Road, she reckoned, when she was outside the gate and walking, was both long and broad, curving gently at each end. She took the familiar way towards the shops, turning at the library sign into the parallel road. The library was a large Gothic-windowed building set in a piece of land too large for a normal-sized garden and too small for a park, with shrubs in pots and benches hopefully waiting for occupants under a couple of fine chestnut trees.

She went up the shallow steps into the foyer where notices advertising Keep Fit classes, a Children's Story Hour and an amateur production of *The Sound of Music* were pinned to a cork board. Beyond double glass doors were neat rows of bookshelves and a long counter with a smaller area at the side containing tables and chairs and racks of newspapers.

'Yes?' The girl stamping books behind the counter looked up.

'Do you have a local history section?' Jessica enquired.

'In the reference section past the biographies. Was there any particular book you had in mind?'

'I think I'll just browse for the moment,' Jessica said, warming to the other's helpful air. 'I may take out a couple of books but I'm new here.'

'You can't borrow books from the reference section, I'm afraid, but from anywhere else is fine. You just fill in a form at the table over there and give it to me. You can take out two books each time and keep them a month. After that the fine's five pence a day. They're a bit fussy about us collecting the fines because it helps funding.'

'Thanks.' Jessica went over to the table, took one of the forms and filled in the few details required. Against profession she wrote 'researcher', and saw the girl's eyes brighten with interest as she looked at it.

'Are you doing a thesis?' she enquired. 'I only ask because under certain circumstances we are allowed to loan out some reference books for scholastic purposes. Or you can study them here. We stay open until ten twice a week. Not that many come in.'

'I'll probably do that,' Jessica said, making for the reference section. There was hardly anything in the local history section about the immediate neighbourhood. She took out a book of survey maps and another on the history of Blundelsands and sat down at one of the tables. The former gave her some excellent points of reference; the second one gave details about the history of the nearby village during the Elizabethan era but not much after that. This had been an area where Jesuit priests had been smuggled ashore to spread the Catholic faith in a land where Papists were feared and persecuted. Blundell Road was only mentioned in a footnote as having been built between the years 1812 and 1816 as a suburb for businessmen wishing to live further out of the city. Add another ten years for the completion of the houses and that fixed the date at 1826, eleven years before Queen Victoria's accession.

'Hi there!'

Startled, she looked up at the rangy young man who had paused to greet her.

'I don't – oh, the supermarket. Hello.'

'Did you enjoy the biscuits?' He pulled out an adjoining chair and sat down.

'I hope the birds did,' Jessica said.

'Too healthy for you?' He grinned, revealing a chipped front tooth that oddly made him more and not less attractive. 'You're new around here.'

'Yes.' Jessica put her finger hintingly on the book but he wasn't so easily deterred.

'You have an odd taste in books,' he remarked, pulling one towards him.

'Local research.'

'So I see. Are you tracing your ancestors or something?'

'No, this is general research – and we ought not to be talking.'

'Nettie doesn't mind. It's generally quiet here in the mornings. Most people are at work.'

'Like me,' Jessica said snubbingly.

'You look,' he said, not troubling to lower his voice, 'as if you need a break.'

'I'm busy.'

'A coffee break. I always have one at this time. You wouldn't want me to sit all alone gazing mournfully into my coffee, would you?'

'It honestly wouldn't break my heart,' Jessica began, then broke off, grinning despite herself at the tragical mask into which he was distorting his features. 'Oh, all right, maybe a coffee wouldn't be a bad idea.'

'There's a café next to the supermarket. My name's Adam, by the way. Adam Darby.'

'Jessica Cameron. You don't have a Liverpool accent.'

'Probably because I hail from Manchester. I've only been here a couple of months myself so I haven't acquired the nasal tones. I'll put those back for you. You're from London?'

They left the library together, strides almost matching.

'How can you tell?' Jessica enquired.

'Shoes and the way you hold your head – also I sneaked a look at your card while I was at the counter. What are you researching?'

'Local history. I work for a firm that specializes in mounting exhibitions of social history from various parts of the country. I'm the advance guard so to speak.'

'Any special period?' He looked interested.

'It's my first independent assignment so I've been given a fairly free hand. I want to concentrate on a typical middle-class family from the mid-nineteenth century.'

'And you're staying in Blundell Road.'

'You did read that card thoroughly, didn't you?'

'I live at the far end. In what is laughingly called an apartment. Number twenty-two. I'm an artist, by the way.'

'Struggling?' she asked as they crossed the road to the café.

'Sometimes affluent, sometimes wondering if I can afford a Sunday newspaper. At the moment I'm fairly affluent so the coffee's on me.'

The café was fairly empty. They found a corner table and ordered a couple of coffees.

'You want scones?' The waitress looked at them hopefully.

'Not this morning. I'm still suffering from the last batch,' Adam told her. 'You can bring some currant buns, if you will. They do very good buns.'

'Just coffee for me. I ate some breakfast and I had an enormous dinner.'

'You're too skinny. Pretty but too skinny.'

'Is that an example of that northern bluntness that's supposed to be so much more desirable than London hypocrisy?' she asked.

'Ouch. I think I'll backtrack.' He looked wry as the waitress brought coffee and buns.

'You said you were an artist.' Jessica decided to forgive him. 'Am I supposed to know your name?'

'Most of the work I do is commercial. I've just finished a series of posters for a new fashion chain opening in the north-west. Hence the affluence. What's wrong? You have something against posters?'

'Only when they change colour.' She was surprised at the quick sensitivity with which he had picked up her slight start.

'Do they?' he asked.

'Not generally.' Jessica bit her lip and took an unwanted currant bun.

'Is that an example of that female mystery that is supposed to be so much more desirable than male straightforwardness?'

'*Touché.* No, I had something odd happen to a poster I brought with me, that's all.'

'It changed colour?'

'It's a poster I bought in Spain – a girl in a flounced scarlet dress. Pretty kitschy really but it's cheerful. I put it on the wall last night –

yesterday afternoon to be exact and then I went out to buy some groceries – that was when you saw me. When I got back the girl was wearing a pink dress. I thought it might be the effect of artificial light but this morning it was still the same.'

'The colours ran?'

'No. Only the dress changed colour.' She stopped abruptly, frowning.

'You've thought of something?'

'Nothing. Merely a silly little coincidence.' In her mind the little girl in the bedraggled, pink party dress trailed after the other children.

'You're being mysterious again,' he accused.

'Sorry. It's ridiculous actually but I noticed some children yesterday, crossing by the lights. One of them was dressed up in her mother's high heels and a frilly pink dress. She'd probably pulled it out of some trunk of dressing-up clothes or something. It can't possibly have anything to do with the poster.'

'Could the poster have been switched for another one before you came here?' Adam said.

'I never thought of that.' Jessica brightened at once and then shook her head. 'No, it was hanging on the wall and I took it down and rolled it up and that was just before I started out up here. There wasn't anyone around to play tricks.'

'How about after you arrived?'

'But why would anyone want to do that? They'd have to have an exactly similar poster in pink instead of scarlet.'

'You've got an apartment?'

'A room with adjoining bathroom and free use of the kitchen. The house isn't split into apartments. A couple called the Clares live there and I honestly can't see either of them running around changing posters. They're a middle-aged, respectable couple.'

'Children?'

'Grown up and living away from home. They're trainee social workers or something. No, the picture changed and there's no logical reason for it, so the best thing to do is to forget it. Just one of those things.'

'I'm wondering,' said Adam, 'why you brought it with you in the first place.'

'I brought a couple of things that I hoped might make me feel more at home. I had some idea of renting a place to myself but landlords prefer a long lease and the agent recommended The Cedars. It's a very roomy, comfortable house and the Clares have made me very welcome. This is the second time they've ever taken a lodger, so they obviously want to make a success of it. Anyway, the dress turned pink and that's all. I've decided to forget about it.'

'But you haven't,' Adam said, with a sudden keen glance.

Jessica returned the glance with a rueful one of her own and shook her head.

'When you're in a strange place by yourself,' she said, 'small, unimportant things loom larger than they should. Sorry if I bored you.'

'You haven't. You've intrigued me.' He offered her the last bun and when she shook her head again bit into it himself.

'Anyway I'll probably get the job finished within three months,' Jessica said, 'and then I hand over my findings for the rest of the team to arrange into some kind of exhibition.'

'You don't do that part yourself?'

'No, just the initial research which is the bit that interests me. Do you have exhibitions of your paintings?'

'I've had a couple – in what they call modest galleries, but I sold most of them.'

'Are you painting anything in Liverpool?' she asked.

'I've promised myself a couple of weeks doing nothing. Then the lease on my apartment is up – I took it over from a friend. So I shall see what commissions come up. Being a freelance gives one independence but no security, though so far that hasn't bothered me.'

'No frail wife and starving children?'

'Not one. You?'

'Too busy with my career.'

'But not too busy for friends, I suppose?' He cocked an eyebrow.

'Friends would be nice,' Jessica said and felt some unacknowledged weight of loneliness lift from her.

'More coffee?' Adam looked at her.

'No, thanks. I intend to get back to work. Right now I'm prowling round the district picking up local colour.'

She hoped that he wouldn't offer to accompany her, since impressions were diluted by company.

'How about coming out with me on Saturday?' he suggested. 'That's three days off which gives you time to make a good start on your project.'

'Yes, that would be nice,' Jessica said promptly.

The invitation had been couched in the easy manner and for a date far enough ahead for her not to feel pressured.

'Are you allowed followers?' he asked teasingly.

A wave of giddiness swept through and over her. His face blurred, dissolved.

'What?' Her voice was gasping.

'Isn't that what they used to call the boyfriends of servants back in Victorian times? Hey, are you all right? You're white as a sheet.'

'Fine.' She ran her tongue over her dry lips, forcing his face back into focus.

'In other words is it OK if I call for you?'

'Yes, of course.'

The dizziness was going, outlines becoming sharp and clear again.

'Seven on Saturday then. We'll paint the town red.'

'Pink will suffice.' She felt a small surge of triumph as she made the joke.

'Well, you're looking better.' Adam surveyed her. 'Sure you wouldn't like another cup of coffee?'

'No, honestly. I ought to get on. Thanks and I'll see you on Saturday.'

'I think I'll have another cup,' Adam said, half rising as she rose. 'Take care now.'

'I will. See you then.'

To her relief the pavement outside was firm under her feet, everything in focus. She wondered if the rich food the previous night had caused a delayed attack of indigestion or something. Whatever its cause the feeling had gone. She crossed the road briskly and turned into Blundell Road, slowing her step as she calculated how old the houses were, where added to, by whom occupied in the previous century. Probably by small mill and ship owners, she decided. The really wealthy would have moved further out.

At The Cedars she turned in at the gate and went round to the back door, mindful of the fact that Mrs Tate had probably put the chain on the front door.

The cleaning lady had evidently finished the breakfast and dining-rooms and was seated at the long oak table with a cup of tea

before her. In her flowered overall with her crimped and dyed hair
she looked out of place. She ought to have worn black bombazine
and drawn her hair back into a tight knob at the back of her head.

'Like a cup of tea, Miss?' Her cheerful voice, so at variance with
her careworn face, was definitely twentieth century.

'No thanks, I just had some coffee. I'm going up to look through
the books I got from upstairs.'

'Mrs Clare said as how you were doing research into old houses,'
Mrs Tate said, with an air of wanting more information.

'Something like that. I'm more interested in the people who used
to live in them. This house for example – a Mr Lawrence used to own
it, I believe.'

'Died in the nursing home.' Mrs Tate nodded. 'I never met the old
gentleman. I came to do for the Clares about – oh, must be nearly
fourteen years ago. They hadn't been here very long then.'

'The children would have been small then,' Jessica said.

'Yes, in junior school. They went to boarding-school later on.
Came home for the holidays. Lovely youngsters. Always so polite.
Well, I'd better get to the silver. Be careful of the floor in the hall. I
just polished it. I like to give it a good old-fashioned going over –
none of your spray rubbish. It takes a bit more time but it lasts the
month and looks ever so good.'

'See you later then.' Jessica went through to the hall and trod
cautiously on the shining parquet.

In her room she settled at the table, opening the two books and
deciding that while the Mrs Beeton looked more entertaining the
Reverend Edward Makin would probably provide more information about Blundell Road itself.

She had ploughed through a chapter and a half of the estimable
clergyman's early career before she realized that he had actually
been born in this house. That accounted in some measure for the
book. Like many self-absorbed people Edward Makin had believed
his life story was worth recording. It might have been, Jessica
thought, had he ever done anything worth recording, but though he
went into great detail about his early spiritual struggles – cold baths
and brisk early morning jogs had cured what he coyly referred to as
'physical temptation' – he was maddeningly vague about names and
dates. Jessica supposed that his own personality had been so
fascinating to him that he had seen others merely as bit players in his
own show. There had been a mother about whom he tossed out the

occasional sickly sweet sentiment.

Mama derived great joy from reading aloud to me when I was a small child. For her the constraints of daily life were mitigated by literature, which was always of that moral and improving character designed to strengthen the ethical fibre of feeble human nature.

Jessica grimaced at the picture of Mama thus conjured up, and went on reading. Papa made far fewer appearances in the narrative. He had gone to work in the bank every morning and to his club in the evenings – driven there, no doubt, by his wife's constant reading aloud. Probably he had been a partner or something in the bank since the salary of a mere clerk wouldn't run to the upkeep of such a large house. He had also apparently enjoyed the odd brandy or glass of port.

Well do I recall the beautiful phrases in which Mama couched her petitions for Temperance, her hands clasped together as she besought the Almighty to fill the hearts of her loved ones with that self-control so essential to the running of society in all its myriad aspects.

'No wonder you went to your club,' Jessica muttered to the invisible shade of the late Mr Makin, Senior.

She went on reading, occasionally annotating a page in her notebook, but without much enthusiasm. If one were planning to mount an exhibition about a self-satisfied prig then there was plenty of material but apart from the ubiquitous Mama and a few short paragraphs about Papa there wasn't one word about anyone else. Presumably there had been servants to clean the house and cook the meals, but Edward Makin evidently didn't regard them as worthy of inclusion in a book.

The clock downstairs chimed the hour and she stuck a bit of paper in the page she had reached and went downstairs to make herself a snack.

Four

Mrs Tate was in the kitchen, polishing a variety of silver tureens, plates and cutlery with ferocious concentration. Jessica made herself a cheese sandwich and a cup of tea and carried it through to the breakfast-room. Sitting there with the afternoon sunshine flooding through the bay window was pleasant. The doors into the dining-room were closed and the breakfast-room had an intimate and cosy air. John Clare had told her she could use the room to eat her meals in. Thinking of that Jessica decided to eat after the Clares had finished their dinner. To sit in an adjoining room would be like an intrusion on their privacy.

When she carried the dishes back into the kitchen Mrs Tate looked up from an elaborately fluted silver dish to say,

'Leave your bits and pieces. I can finish them off with the rest. Going out?'

'I think I'll take the car and stock up with a few groceries,' Jessica decided. 'I may have a stroll around the neighbourhood afterwards. I got side-tracked this morning.'

'There isn't much to see,' Mrs Tate said. 'Unless you like old churches. There's one in Fairfield Road – High Anglican. I'm Methodist myself.'

Churches meant vicars and Edward Makin had been a clergyman. Having a look round might be fruitful. Jessica thanked her and went out to the garage.

Buying the groceries she caught herself glancing round in the expectation of seeing a rangy young man with an attractively plain face. Well, there was no joy in pursuing that line of thinking. Adam Darby had finished his commission and was leaving soon. Nevertheless it was pleasant to think that she knew somebody apart from the Clares and Mrs Tate.

The latter was washing-up again when Jessica returned with

several carrier bags bulging with food. She was obviously what would have been termed a 'treasure' in the old days, efficient, plodding and devoted to her employers. Probably her own life had been less than fulfilling.

'If you're going out again,' she said, 'don't forget your key. I'm taking my daughter to the dentist so I'm leaving a bit early today.'

'I saw her this morning,' Jessica remembered. 'When I was getting the books from upstairs.'

'Yes, she went up to give the bathroom a wipe round. Mrs Clare is very fussy about the toilet,' Mrs Tate said. 'About cleaning your room, Miss –'

'Oh, Lord, I can easily do that myself,' Jessica assured her. 'I quite enjoy housework.'

'If you're sure – it would be a help, Miss. This is quite a big place to do.' It was the nearest she had come to a complaint.

'It'll be good exercise,' Jessica assured her, stacking tins in the cupboard.

'Exercise is as exercise does,' Mrs Tate said, and ran hot water vigorously on to the plates.

Jessica finished her task and went out again. A walk to the local church, a look at the registers might help her place the Makins, though she doubted if they were a typical family. Edward Makin hadn't mentioned any brothers or sisters, so as an only child he would have been unusual. On the other hand he had probably married and founded the kind of sprawling family the Victorians approved. So far she had read only about a quarter of his excruciatingly dull autobiography. The one thing the book wasn't was a history of Blundell Road. So far not a single neighbour had been mentioned.

Fairfield Road was a couple of streets away, the spire of the church rising above the roofs. Jessica spotted a side alley and cut through it, coming out almost opposite the church. Victorian Gothic, she decided, pausing to look at it. The spire looked too high for the length of the building as if it were trying to pass itself off as a cathedral. The probability that it might be closed to deter vandals crossed her mind, but when she walked through the low gate and down the drive she saw the front door was fastened open against the wall and two harassed looking ladies were carrying in bunches of flowers.

'Excuse me, but is it all right to have a look round?'

She addressed the nearer one who peered at her around a large bunch of long-stemmed gladioli and answered with a vaguely distracted air,

'You're not from the bishop?'

'No. I'm doing some research on local history.'

'The bishop's coming for the Confirmation Service on Sunday,' the woman said.

'Isn't it rather soon to be arranging the flowers?' Jessica said.

'Oh, far too soon, but they're not in full bloom yet,' the woman said, lowering her voice slightly. 'Mrs Parkinson will insist – you know how it is. Of course we shall water them and er – hope they settle.'

'Does the vicar live near here?' Jessica looked about her.

'Oh no, he lives nearer Blundelsands,' the woman said. 'The old vicarage was pulled down and a nursery school built. Much more sensible but one regrets the loss – excuse me. I must get on.'

She darted off, clutching the gladioli as a woman in tweed skirt and jacket raised a flushed face from the boot of a car parked at the side and boomed, 'Do get on, Phyllis. These geraniums weigh a ton.'

Jessica walked through the open door into the soaring coldness of the church. The interior was certainly undistinguished, the stained glass of inferior quality, the oak pews and pulpit varnished a peculiarly sickly yellowish-brown that looked as if it might stick to one's fingers. There were faded red hassocks and some rather nice pieces of copper on the altar. Vases and containers were grouped by the door and the gladioli woman was on her knees by them, pushing long stalks into a too-short container.

Jessica went to the altar rail, seeing a door at the left that clearly led into the sacristy and on the right a smaller altar with a brass plaque fixed to the wall behind it. She stepped to the latter and saw that it was a memorial list from the two world wars, the closely inscribed names bringing a sad, nostalgic feeling as she read down the two columns.

The altar below was covered with a white cloth beneath which at the front of the altar was a shorter list of names. Jessica crouched down to take a look. A list of clergymen met her gaze with dates that presumably marked their tenure. It was highly unlikely that they'd all fallen in battle. The list looked like a clutch at some kind of immortality. And the Reverend Edward Makin was there, sandwiched between a Lloyd and a Petrie. Next to his name were the dates 1851-1860. Then he had either died or resigned to be succeeded by the Reverend Arthur Petrie.

Jessica took out her notebook and made a note of the dates. Edward Makin had given the information in his tedious book that he had been born (or as he phrased it, 'entered this Vale of Tears') in the year 1827, which made him twenty-five when he was appointed as vicar. Jessica wondered cynically if it had been his exceptional qualities or his papa's position in the bank that had secured him the appointment at such an early age. And he had held it for only eight years, which meant he had either died young or resigned early. She wondered again if he had been married and stopped the gladioli woman who was approaching with a large container of geraniums.

'Excuse me, but would it be possible to have a look at the church records? Births, deaths, marriages, that kind of thing?'

'They're kept in the reference section in the local library.' The woman put the geraniums on a ledge where they clashed with the stained glass of the window above.

'Not in the sacristy?'

'Woodworm in the cupboards,' the other said succinctly. 'Our present incumbent thought it wiser to entrust them to the library, where they may be consulted on application to the assistant. Yes, coming.'

She bobbed her head in a distracted fashion and scurried into the aisle again as a booming voice yelled, 'Phyllis!'

'So it's back to the library,' Jessica murmured, taking another look at the sad list above the little altar before she turned and made her way out again.

She looked around as she emerged into the sunshine but there was no sign of any graveyard.

'It's Miss Cameron, isn't it?' The assistant, Nettie, looked pleased with herself as she greeted Jessica a few moments later. 'You came in this morning but you didn't take out a book.'

'I'm more interested in the reference section,' Jessica told her. 'I believe you have the church records here. Could I see them?'

'All of them?' Nettie looked slightly nonplussed. 'They go back to the seventeenth century.'

'The church isn't that old surely.'

'No, but there used to be another church quite near up to the beginning of last century. Then the population got bigger and the new church was built. The old one was pulled down, I think.'

'I'm interested in the years 1820 to 1860,' Jessica said.

'Oh, those are here. Five years in each volume. They're complete, I think. Some were damaged during the war and then there was woodworm so the rest were brought here to be kept safe. They're kept in a special case.'

She trotted importantly into the reference section and went to a glass-fronted cupboard against the far wall within which a series of leather-bound books, many of them extremely shabby, were ranged.

'The current one is kept by the vicar and he brings it to the church when it's needed,' Nettie said, opening the case.

'You're a churchgoer?'

'Not every week, but now and then. The services are really quite good,' the girl said defensively. 'Here we are. 1820 through to 1860. You can take them out as you need them. You'll put them back in order, won't you?'

'Yes, of course. What time do you close?'

'We're open late tonight, but I won't be here. Miss Mitchell takes over at six.'

'I'll be finished before then.'

Nettie returned to her counter, leaving Jessica with the records. The neat clerkly hand scarcely altered between one incumbent and the next. She ran her index finger down the section for 1827 and found the entry she sought.

Baptism – Edward George Makin. Born the second of April.
Eldest son of George Makin and his wife, Constance Makin
née Lloyd. Godparents – James Smythe. Cecilia Morney.

The vicar at the time had been a Lloyd. Jessica wondered if Constance had been a relative. She turned back the yellowing pages carefully, counting back nine months. In those days married couples usually started their families immediately.

Ah, here it was! The marriage between George Makin and Constance Lloyd on the fifth of April, 1826. The wedding had been solemnized by the Reverend Frederick Lloyd, father of the bride. James Smythe and Cecilia Morney had signed as witnesses. So Edward Makin's grandfather had also been a clergyman. Jessica wondered why he had chosen his grandfather's profession rather than his father's. Judging from what she had read in the book the mother's influence had been much stronger than the father's which probably accounted for it.

Now to find out if Edward Makin had married. She recalled reading somewhere that clergymen were expected to set an example to their flock by marrying and begetting large families. It probably accounted for the huge, draughty vicarages that had been built – or had Edward Makin stayed on at The Cedars? In that case were his parents dead by then? She would have to make a thorough search of the registers. In the back of her mind she heard the probable reaction of her boss. 'You were supposed to come back with a folder of ideas and examples of a particular section of society, not spend all your time delving into one very uninteresting family.'

It would be fair comment, she admitted to herself, but on the other hand she had plenty of time in which to widen her field. And living at The Cedars gave her a certain advantage. Already she was building up a so far unproven picture of the deeply religious mother, the somewhat intemperate father, the prissy son. It would be interesting to find photographs had any been taken, or letters. The nineteenth century had been a period of feverishly intense journal and letter writing. She put back the two volumes she'd taken from the cupboard and after a moment's quick mental calculation took out the 1850 to 1855 volume. During most of this time Edward had been vicar in his local church, so he had probably married during that time. Sitting down again at the table she opened the book and began running down the entries.

Death of George Makin aged fifty-nine years on June the seventh, 1851. Funeral conducted by the Reverend Frederick Lloyd.

And less than three months later old Frederick Lloyd, Edward's maternal grandfather, had also died. The funeral had been conducted by the Reverend Edward Makin. So he'd taken over his grandfather's living. Jessica ran her finger more rapidly down the pages, feeling a sense of excitement as if she were on the trail of something important. Research had that effect, often drawing one away from the main subject into fascinating highways and byways of personal experience.

She found the marriage a year later and jotted the details into her notebook. On the first day of July, 1853 the bishop had joined together the Reverend Edward Makin aged twenty-six years and

Amelia Benson, aged twenty-four. Witnesses had been Constance Makin and Philip Benson.

'I'll be going in a few minutes,' Nettie said, coming over. 'Did you find what you wanted?'

'I managed to make a good start,' Jessica told her. 'I'm staying at The Cedars, so I'm interested in the Makin family.'

'Yes, it was on your card that you filled in,' Nettie said. 'As far as I know there aren't any Makins round here now. Died out or moved away, I daresay. Shall I turn on the lights for you? It's getting very dim.'

'Also rather late,' Jessica said reluctantly. 'I think I'll come back and carry on tomorrow. Would the local café be open?'

She didn't feel like cooking anything for herself.

'Oh yes, you can get a very nice snack there,' Nettie assured her.

Jessica thanked her and put the heavy volume back behind its shielding glass.

If Edward Makin and his bride had raised a family then she had her typical nineteenth-century household. The prospect of finding letters and photographs and other souvenirs was an exciting one. She walked briskly down the road towards the café, her mind revolving happily around the prospect of future exhibitions.

'Ham salad and a pot of tea, please.' Giving her order to the assistant waitress, she found herself wondering briefly what had caused her fit of dizziness earlier in the day. Adam Darby had said something but she couldn't now recall what it was.

'The ham's off, Miss. There's some very nice smoked beef,' the waitress returned to say.

'Fine. And some bread and butter, please.'

She was filled with healthy hunger as the meal was put on the table. The café with its plastic-topped tables was pleasantly modern. It was a relief to lift her head from old books and see the everyday world going on around her smoothly.

The beef was tasty and the salad fresh. She ate and drank, watching people as they went past the windows. Housewives with shopping bags, two elderly gentlemen with their walking sticks tapping in time, a couple of schoolboys. No child in a pink party dress with make-up heavily and expertly applied to her mouth and eyes. Grey eyes, Jessica recalled, with something unchildlike and unpleasant in their depths.

She paid for the meal and walked back to the house. The earlier sunshine had waned and on the pavement behind her her shadow was long and thin. Skinny, she thought with an inward grin and turned in at the gate. The front door was unchained. She let herself into the hall where the lights had already been lit and heard, just before she closed the door, a voice calling somewhere from outside, 'Polly! Polly, you're wanted.'

Someone from next door probably. She must remember to check up and see if the Reverend Edward Makin mentioned any neighbours in his book. Not that their descendants were likely to be living next door still.

There were swift footsteps along the balcony at the back of the hall and a voice calling in a loud, nervous tone, 'Who is that? Who's there?'

'It's only me.' Jessica moved further into the light. 'I just let myself in.'

'Oh, Jessica!' There was relief in Sophy Clare's voice. 'I wondered who – but it's you. Mrs Tate left early as she had to take her daughter to the dentist. She said you found the books that John thought might be useful for you. They were here when we came and we always said that we'd get down to reading them some time, but with one thing and another – you know how it is.'

She came lightly and trippingly down the stairs, rubbing her hands together as if she were cold though the hall was pleasantly warm. Her dress was green, cut on the same gently flowing lines as the one she had worn the previous day.

'Would you like a cup of coffee? Or perhaps a sherry? I generally have one before John comes home. Will you be eating dinner with us tonight? I can put on extra fish if you'd like to join us.'

'I already had something in the café,' Jessica said, 'but another coffee would be nice.'

'Let's have it in the kitchen. I can keep an eye on the baked potatoes.' Sophy cast a sweeping look over the hall as if she hoped to catch something unaware and went through to the back, Jessica following.

The lights were on in the kitchen too and there was something cooking slowly on top of the cooker. Sophy moved in the quick nervous way that seemed habitual to her to pour coffee and add a dash of brandy to her own.

'Just to pep it up,' she said with a deprecating little laugh. Jessica wondered why she felt the need to make any excuse. Perhaps her

so-called nervousness was the result of drinking or was the drinking
the result of her nervousness?

'How is the research going?' she asked, seating herself at the long
table. 'I'm run off my feet at the moment. So much voluntary work.
You wouldn't believe how it piles up after one has been away for a
few days.'

'I'm afraid the nearest I get to doing voluntary work is buying a
poppy on Poppy Day,' Jessica admitted, joining her at the table.

'Well, heavens, you're busy with your career,' Sophy said with
another light little laugh. 'I used to be terribly busy too when the
children were younger. Now I find I've time on my hands. Of course
I could sack Mrs Tate and spend the entire day cleaning, but
housework was never my favourite occupation. Cooking is different
now. There is an art to – what was that?'

She broke off sharply, head tilted in a listening attitude.

'I didn't hear anything,' Jessica said.

'I thought – the house has odd echoes,' Sophy said. 'Many old
houses do, I find.'

'That's true.' Jessica sipped her coffee and watched, while trying
not to appear to watch, the other's fingers curling and uncurling
about the handle of her cup.

'So how are you getting on? Will you be able to find sufficient
material for an original exhibition?'

'I think so. Mind you, my boss has to give the final go-ahead,'
Jessica said. 'I usually work as part of a team. This is my first solo
assignment.'

'The nineteenth cent – excuse me a moment.' Again the listening
look before she rose and went through the adjoining rooms to the
hall again.

Jessica found herself listening too, for a creak of a board, a
syllable uttered by an unfamiliar voice. There was nothing except
the soft bubbling of whatever fish was poaching on top of the cooker
and an occasional clang from the refrigerator.

'I thought I heard John's key in the lock,' Sophy said returning.

'Is he due home at this time?' Jessica asked.

'Unless he's working late. He often works late.'

Was that why she was nervous? Or did she suspect her husband of
having an affair and use nervousness as an excuse to persuade him to
stay at home?

'It must be interesting, arranging conferences and so on,' she said politely. The other hesitated and then nodded.

'I used to be quite a social kind of person,' she said at last. 'One gets out of touch and then our closest friends moved back to Ireland and since then – well, John enjoys the challenges anyway. More coffee?'

'Thank you, no.' Jessica stood up. 'I'm going to get to grips with the life story of Edward Makin this evening.'

'Didn't a family called the Makins live here once?' Sophy said. 'There was something about it in the deeds when we bought the house. Old Mr Lawrence didn't seem to know much about it. I think his father bought the place from the Makins.'

'He was a local clergyman,' Jessica said.

'Sounds rather dull,' Sophy said.

'So far. However I'll persevere. It would be nice if I could concentrate on one particular family as an example of mid-nineteenth-century, middle-class living. This sounds like your husband now.'

Footsteps crossing the hall, the opening of the door leading to the kitchen quarters. Sophy had also risen again, her face tense, her pale blue eyes straining towards the door. What was it, Jessica wondered, that she expected to see?

'Not too late, am I? There was the usual snarl of traffic.' John Clare came in, shedding his overcoat, kissing his wife on the cheek, acknowledging Jessica's presence with an amiable nod.

'Dinner's on the way,' Sophy said gaily. 'Jessica says she ate already. I hope she wasn't just being polite.'

'I'm sure she knows that she's welcome,' John said.

'I've promised myself an evening's work,' Jessica said. 'Excuse me –' She went out, hearing Sophy's voice chattering on with an unmistakable note of relief.

'Jessica is reading up about the family who lived here before the Lawrences. She thinks it might form the nucleus of an exhibition or something. It was Makin who built this house, wasn't it?'

Jessica went into the hall and stood for a moment, not precisely listening but testing the air. There was a faint stirring as if someone passing had left some trace of themselves upon the atmosphere. John Clare? She shook her head at her own foolishness and went on upstairs. Surely Sophy Clare's nervousness wasn't infectious.

On the half landing she paused to look along the balcony with its stained glass windows dimmed by the gathering dark. This was a pleasant old house, the modern improvements blending in surprisingly well, the slight shabbiness of some of the rooms suggesting that the Clares, though comfortably off, were not wealthy.

Switching on the light in her room she glanced hopefully towards the poster but it still showed a pink flounced dress.

'Forget it,' she urged herself aloud and sat down at the table.

Knowing something about the author of the book on Blundell Road didn't render the book itself any more interesting. The Reverend Edward Makin had actually included the full text of the first sermon he had ever preached – on the subject of the Second Coming which, judging from the clergyman's beliefs on the subject, was going to be terribly uncomfortable for everybody save a select few – himself and his mother included. His wife hadn't been mentioned though she was halfway through the volume and he was now installed as vicar in the local church. His grandfather, apparently another of the elect, had 'gone to his everlasting rest'. Jessica grimaced and closed the book, deciding that an hour of the Reverend Edward Makin was about fifty-eight minutes too long.

Mrs Beeton looked more entertaining. She leafed through it conscientiously, paying particular attention to the inserted bits of paper with their odd household hints and half-completed shopping lists. The Makins, if the lists dated from them, had eaten an inordinate amount of beef and dozens of oysters. But the latter had been cheap in Victorian times.

She paused to read through a selection of dinner menus. Choice of three soups, two fish dishes, a savoury, the main course with its attendant vegetables, two desserts, cheese and biscuits to fill up the gaps. Surely they hadn't eaten like this every day! There were wine lists too, but she guessed that George Makin had imbibed most of those unless his son had been a hypocrite as well as a bore.

There was no sound from below. Presumably the Clares had finished their meal and were now seated in the sitting-room, John Clare watching anything and everything that was being shown on television while Sophy sat, looking through the open door into the dimly lit hall.

Jessica flipped over the pages of the book, telling herself that the habits of the Clares were of no interest to her. She was merely renting a room here at a very reasonable price. It was a nice room but with window and door closed it was becoming stuffy.

She went to the window and lifted the sash. The curtains hadn't been drawn and the tangle of garden beyond the yard seemed to stretch farther than she remembered it doing during the daylight.

There was a tiny sound behind her at the closed door. So tiny that she couldn't make up her mind whether it was a scrape or a sigh. It was sufficiently loud to make her start violently and swing round.

'Yes?' She spoke loudly.

Nothing. Neither scrape nor stir. Jessica strode to the door and opened it wide. The half landing, the carved banister at the top of the stairs, a restricted view of the balcony. She moved further out and looked along it narrowly. Nothing moved.

She went to the rail and looked over into the well of the hall. Light made a rectangle outside the open door of the sitting-room and she could hear the murmur of an announcer's voice from the television which had evidently been turned low.

From the room behind her came the soft sighing sound again. Jessica turned sharply and retraced the few steps she had taken. A half sheet of paper was fluttering down from the table, disturbed she realized by the draught from the open window and door.

She went in, bent down and picked it up, the quick beats of her heart slowing with relief. It was one of the loose pieces of paper from between the pages of the Mrs Beeton book. Not a shopping list or a menu, she thought, glancing at it idly. Some child had been practising writing on it, in faded ink, the pothooks wavering.

My na ... name is ... my name is P ... My name is Polly Winter.

Polly's Tale

My name is Polly Winter, though I can't remember when anyone called me by both names together. Usually I get just 'Polly', and sometimes, when cook's in a temper, 'Girl'. Nobody ever said to me 'Good morning, Miss Winter. Isn't it a lovely day?'

Sometimes when Cook's soaking her feet, I set out the second best cups in the kitchen and sit at the table entertaining a friend like Mistress does. I make the tea weak like they have it in the drawing-room, with the cream from the top of the milk in a little silver jug and sugar lumps in the bowl.

'Do try a slice of lemon, my dear. So refreshing in this heat,' I say, and my friend smiles and inclines her head.

If I'm lucky cook dozes off with her feet in the basin and my friend and I have a genteel chat, little fingers crooked as we sip our tea and nibble a biscuit.

The trouble is that it's hard for me to see my friend clearly. I never had one, you see. Not really. Not a real friend. Only people who've been good to me from time to time.

'You are a fortunate girl,' Master says to me. 'A most fortunate girl, Polly. I trust you give constant thanks for your narrow escape from the burning pit?'

'Oh, yes, sir,' say I, folding my hands together and lowering my lashes. That is the proper humble attitude to be adopted by one rescued from the burning pit.

Not that anyone knows about that except him and me. It's our secret. We have a secret, the Master and I. Mistress doesn't know of it and Cook doesn't know. It is our secret, to be held close and never spoken about.

'My wife would be deeply distressed to learn that such misery even exists,' Master says. 'She is a most innocent and gentle lady. I wish her to remain in that happy state of childlike innocence.'

That's a bit of a laugh, this childlike innocence he goes on about. As if he didn't have the evidence of his own eyes and ears to know that not all children are innocent, only the fortunate ones with their hair neatly braided and lace on their drawers – and I'm not so sure about them sometimes.

But not Miss Julia. She never had a bad thought in her little head in her life. Like a little doll she is with her starched petticoats and her big blue eyes. Master Robert is a baby still, in his little lace caps and bibs. Oh, they are lucky ones and one can't deny it.

How can I make you see this family? There's the Master, of course, with his black frockcoat and high cravat and smooth fair hair and the gold watch chain across his middle. He has a habit of consulting it, drawing it out and looking at it with a little smile as if he knew he could turn back time if he cared to do it. Master likes the day to be parcelled out in periods of work, quietness and study.

Not for the staff, of course. Cook can read and write already and there isn't really any need for me to learn.

No need for me to look pretty either. Beauty is a snare and a delusion. So says Master, looking at me in the grave, kindly manner he has. Goes down a treat in church does that manner. Oh, you should just see the old cow – sorry, ladies simpering at him as he mounts into the pulpit. The Mistress'd be dead and worms chewing at her if some of them had their dreams come true.

'We're to have a governess for Miss Julia,' Cook says to me. 'What do you think of that now?'

She looks at me in a triumphant kind of way over the pastry she's slapping about on the table. Sometimes she puts crystals of sugar in the dough that make it go crisp and brown, but this dough is for a beef pie so there's no sugar in it, only a scatter of dry mustard to give it a tang.

'A real governess?' I say. 'I didn't know.'

The truth is that I've not been too well recently. Cook says it's my age. She says the same about Mistress too though Mistress is years older than I am. When she isn't well she stays in bed, wearing the fluffy little jacket that makes her look young. When I'm feeling poorly I take longer to fill the coal scuttle and sometimes my head gets in a bit of a muddle and I can't quite remember if it's one day or another day.

'Of course she's a real governess,' Cook says now. 'Miss Julia's five, isn't she? Time she started lessons.'

'I thought Mistress would be teaching her,' I say, and Cook snorts.

'Mistress has the baby, hasn't she? No time.'

So there's to be a governess. She will teach Miss Julia how to read and make her letters, and how to embroider a sampler that can be framed and put on the wall for visitors to admire. She will give her lessons on the piano too. Mistress used to play but then the baby came and now she hardly ever touches the keys.

'Looks like it's going to be a nice day,' says Cook. 'You'd better get those sheets hung out.'

The sheets are cold and damp and white as rich folks' shrouds. When the sun has dried them they'll need to be ironed with the hot smoothing iron and then folded into exact creases and piled up in the big airing cupboard. We have a woman comes every two weeks to do the washing in the big copper and on those days Cook puts her feet up or goes into town to meet her friend. I don't have any friend to meet, and even if I had I'd still have to help with the washing, the steam rising and turning my face bright red.

So out I go into the yard and struggle with the sheets, wishing I was bigger and had muscles in my arms. I'm doing that when I see a movement at the window of the landing room and look up, startled like, to see someone looking down at me.

That must be the new governess. I hadn't expected her to arrive so quickly, before Cook's even got the pastry in the oven. I stand with my arms reaching up to the line and look at her. She looks too young to be a governess, which is a silly thing to say, because she's the first real governess I ever saw. Big Tildy used to dress up as a governess in a black dress with a long, sharp cane in her hand.

'Now, sir, who's been a naughty boy? Bend over, sir, and let your governess discipline you.'

How we used to grin, smothering our giggles, as we took turns to peep through the crack in the door and watch.

But this is a real governess, with her hair cut short as if she's had a fever.

She's pretty, I think, though it's impolite to stare at someone for a long time. Now she's looking away from me over the garden. They have a man in three times a week to look after it. The man has horny hands and a flat boxer's nose and he looks as if he could be mean.

'Keep away from temptation,' Master advises. 'Fix your eyes upon the Lord.' If the Lord is thinking of sending me to the fiery pit I'm not sure I want to fix my eyes on Him. It's less worrisome to fix them on Master as he stands tall in the pulpit, with all the old cows simpering at him.

'That governess person is here already,' I tell Cook, going back into the kitchen.

'Tell me something new,' she invites. 'She's gone to pick up her things from the station. You'd better light the fire in the drawing-room. It'll be chilly later.'

The drawing-room is at the other side of the hall. Master and Mistress sit there after dinner in the evenings, he reading, she sewing with one ear listening to the sounds from upstairs where the children sleep. Sometimes the baby cries and then she rustles up the stairs to soothe him. Miss Julia never cries. She was born not crying and nobody's given her cause to change since.

I go into the drawing-room to see to the fire. First I go to the big bay window and look through it. The hackney cab is outside and the new governess is getting into it. I wonder if her coming will make any difference to us.

The fire catches easily and I straighten up and put my two hands hard against the small of my back. Sometimes my back aches something cruel, but Master says that honest labour is better than a life of sinful luxury. Master talks a lot of bloody nonsense sometimes, but being a clergyman I daresay he feels he has to. It would be easier if they kept more staff but Master says that money doesn't grow on trees. So there's only Cook and me, and the laundry woman every two weeks and at spring-cleaning time a couple of girls from the Home because Cook and I simply cannot get everything done by ourselves – not even if Mistress does a bit which she never does.

I don't say anything. Sometimes, when Cook's busy and I open my mouth at the wrong time I get a clip over the ear for saucing her.

'She seems a nice enough young lady,' Cook says now. 'Spoke to me very civil. Provided she doesn't become demanding –'

Governesses, in Cook's experience, often become very demanding, wanting cups of tea at odd hours, and talking a lot about the virtues of their former charges. She believes in 'nipping such things in the bud'. Legion are the things that Cook has nipped in the bud. 'The fishmonger was going to fob me off with skate, but I soon nipped that in the bud.' 'She looked as if she was going to charge extra but I nipped that in the bud.'

The governess had her dinner with the Master and Mistress. I don't wait at table because the Master thinks that clergymen ought to serve themselves, though he doesn't think they ought to cook for themselves too. Anyway I haven't been trained up to wait at table. There's some as might say that I haven't been trained up to do anything that would interest a clergyman but them as say that don't know much about the clergy.

'Among my best clients, dear,' Madam used to say. 'They start off by wanting to save your soul and they end up by coming regular on Tuesdays.'

After dinner the Mistress comes into the kitchen because she likes to make the coffee herself. She takes no notice of Cook and me, but Mistress is like that. She doesn't mean to be unkind. It is her way, Cook says. I leave her to it and come across the hall to see if they need any coal on the fire. The door is half open and I pause, seeing the firelight leaping on the ceiling and not liking to interrupt. I can hear the murmuring of the Master's voice. He has a lovely voice, very calm and stern. It was his voice I heard first before Madam called me in, saying, 'I think you will find Polly suitable for your requirements, sir.'

'She's no more than a child!' Master said.

'And of very good family. She speaks most prettily,' Madam said. 'Of course, if you wanted someone older –'

Master says he determined then that I was a brand to be snatched from the burning.

I go back into the kitchen and start on the washing-up. Cook does the good china herself, dipping each piece in the soapy water and lifting it out dripping. I get to do the ordinary china and the silver. They have some nice pieces of silver, Cook says.

'Go up and check that the room is all right for the governess,' Cook says. She's to sleep in the small room off the half landing. It used to be Cook's room but when I came it was decided that we'd share a room, so now we both sleep on the upper landing with Cook snoring away in the big bed and me in the truckle bed under the window. Next door to it is the spare room, though nobody ever comes to stay. The Master's mother died in that room and sometimes I fancy I can hear her shuffling about. On the other side of that room is the sewing-room and then the children's room and the big bedroom where Master and Mistress sleep.

I go up the stairs and into the little room. There is flowered paper on the walls and a knotted rug on the floor, and the bed is too wide for the room and sags in the middle where Cook used to lie. The governess has returned and started to unpack. Her carpet bag is open in the middle of the floor and there is a hairbrush and a comb on the dresser. I look round to see if anything is required and then I notice that the picture of the Lord pointing a sinner towards the fiery pit has been taken down and another put in its place. A lady with long black hair is dancing, the flounces of her skirt whipping above her ankles. The dress is bright red. It reminds me of something but I stare at it for several minutes before I remember. My dress was a bit like the dancer's, but pink and not red. Nobody except me and the Master ever saw that dress out of this household. I think he burned it, but I'm not certain. It was a lovely dress, cut low over the shoulders and I used to pad out the bodice until Madam said her clients were the gentlemen who didn't like breasts. I wear a plain linen bodice and a dark skirt now, and there's nobody to tell me that I looked grand in the pink one. I wish I could tell the governess that I didn't always look such a dull rat of a girl, but I don't suppose that I'll get to speak to her at all.

'You took your time,' says Cook when I get down again.

He went to see Madam, Master says, to find a brand to snatch from the burning. The others were too old, I daresay. Anyway I got snatched up and put here and I have to be very grateful, though nobody asked me what I thought of it all.

'Have you no parents, Polly?' Master asked.

I thought that was a funny kind of question. I mean everybody has parents, don't they? Except Adam and Eve, and they came ready made so to speak. I couldn't remember mine very clearly. My mother wore a plaid shawl with a ragged fringe and coughed a lot, and people called her Mrs Winter. There was a man too. Perhaps he was my father. He wasn't there all the time. He came when my mother died. I remember having a new black dress and being pleased about that and then seeing my mother's shawl folded up and not round her shoulders and wanting suddenly to cry and then the man who might have been my father taking my hand and hurrying with me down a narrow street. And after that there was Madam and the girls and sleeping in the day and staying awake at night, and the pink dress with flounces and the girls painting my face until I looked ever so pretty.

Mistress comes into the hall with the coffee she's made on a tray. She'll go into the drawing-room and Master will make a big fuss, telling her she ought not to tire herself out. He never says that to Cook and me.

I'd better get the hot-water bottles in the beds. The bottles are made of stone and have to be filled with the boiling water and corked up tight and wrapped in a small blanket and carried upstairs one at a time. One for Master and one for Mistress, and one for Cook and now there'll be an extra one for the governess. The children get their beds warmed before they go to bed and I don't have a hot bottle at all, on account of my feet are used to being cold and anyway I've got sins to cancel out.

At least I've got comfortable shoes now. the ones with high heels were never very comfortable even though they were made specially for me. These have low heels that make little tapping noises when I walk down the balcony at the back of the hall. The floor there is polished and I have to walk carefully, carrying the heavy stone bottles and wishing my back didn't ache so cruel. Coming back is easier. I can do a bit of a dance under those coloured windows, though Master says that dancing can lead to trouble.

When I've put in all the bottles I peep in at the children. They're both sound asleep, but Miss Julia has stuck her thumb in her mouth which will spoil the look of it, so I creep in and take it out. Then I go downstairs again and out to check the gates are closed. That's my last job of the day. After that Cook and I will have a cup of tea and a slice of toast and dripping and go up to bed.

I go out into the garden to check the gates. It's dark and chilly out here and the gas lamp makes funny hissing noises as I pass underneath. Down at Madam's the girls will be getting themselves ready for the clients and getting a toss of gin to make their eyes sparkle and loosen their muscles. If you don't loosen your muscles it can hurt cruel.

'Polly! Polly, hurry yourself up!' calls Cook.

I hurry myself up and get back indoors. The wind has made one of my back teeth ache. The local barber pulls teeth but he charges threepence, and I don't get any pay. Master says I'd spend it on worldly vanities. He's probably right. I wonder if an aching tooth counts as worldly vanity.

So I get myself off to bed, hearing the creaking of the house and the rising and falling of Cook's snoring. My feet are cold but my tooth aches worse. Master says that before we compose ourselves to sleep we must examine our consciences. I always mean to do that but I always fall asleep before I get very far.

Getting up in the morning is always hard. I get up first and get the fire going and the water boiling while Cook struggles into her corsets. Then there's the breakfast to be started and hot water to take upstairs and the table in the dining-room to lay. I seem to be on the run until prayers start, when Master thanks the Lord for the beginning of a new day to be devoted to His Glory. Well, it might be the start of the day for Master but I've been on my feet for hours already. So has Cook, and Mistress too, because though she doesn't do housework she does look after the children.

'Other women have nursemaids for their children,' Mistress complains.

'Other women are not clergymen's wives,' says Master. 'We must set a good example, my dear.'

I suppose that the governess will look after Miss Julia now. She hasn't started yet. I go up into the sewing-room to get a length of thread that Cook needs to tie up the suet pudding, and there she is, sitting on the floor if you please and looking at the books in the two bookcases at each side of the fireplace. She looks up when I go in with a kind of startled look on her face.

'Oh, I'm sorry, Miss,' I say, and quickly retreat because she looks busy.

Today is going to be shed day. I call it that in my mind and my mind shivers away from it. Shed day doesn't come very often but I know when it's due. Master has a certain look at the back of his eyes – a kind of hunger but not for solid food. It's more a craving, I suppose, for things like sugared grapes and nips of brandy and plum cake when it isn't yet Christmas. All the things that are bad for your insides but that make your mouth water.

'It is necessary,' says Master when he has summoned me into the garden. Mistress is resting on her bed and Cook has put her feet up and it isn't laundry day and the gardener has gone home. There's just Master and me, going into the shed.

'If we never sin,' says Master, 'what use to seek for forgiveness?'

So we get in a good bit of sinning in that dusty darkness, and it isn't a bit like it was in Madam's where the beds were soft and I had a flounced pink dress.

'Wickedness,' says Master. 'You tempted me and I being weak and human fell. Dirt and filth. Harlot of Babylon.'

He uses other words too. You'd not credit that a clergyman could know such words. If one of Madam's clients had used them he'd have been out on his ear, I can tell you. Madam was very particular about language.

'Cover your vile body,' Master says, and turns away, shuddering.

I hate shed days. No, that's not quite true. On shed days I feel a queer kind of excitement. I don't know why that is, because every time I go in the shed I feel sick enough to vomit. There are so many different feelings inside me and none of them match. I wish I could talk to someone. I wish I could talk to that governess. Someone ought to know. But who would believe me? Who would listen to Polly Winter?

Five

'Census forms?' Nettie leaned on the counter and looked doubtful. 'We don't keep any here. What year were you wanting?'

'1860 would have been nice,' Jessica told her, 'but there was no census in that year, so it'd be 1861. What about parish registers? Apart from births, marriages and deaths, I mean. Confirmation lists, anything like that.'

Nettie shook her head. 'There's only what I showed you,' she said. 'What exactly were you looking for?'

'I'm trying to find out about someone called Polly Winter.'

'Do you know anything about her?'

'Nothing,' Jessica admitted, 'but I've a feeling she may have been a servant during the time that the Reverend Edward Makin was vicar here, so I –' She paused, seeing the other's start.

'Makin?' said Nettie. 'Now that's funny your saying that. I was reading about him not long ago.'

'Reading what?' Jessica asked.

'In a book about famous English mysteries – that was the name of the book, as a matter of fact. You know the sort of thing, Spring Heel Jack, and the Ripper and things that never got solved. They had a chapter for each one. I remember that particular one because it all took place nearby. Shall I get you the book? I don't think it's out.'

'If you would.' Jessica waited while the other went to the shelves, returning with a fairly thick volume in her hand.

'Here it is. Published 1946. I don't think the author ever wrote anything else.'

'I'll take it.' Jessica restrained her impatience while the book was stamped.

'I hope you find what you're looking for,' Nettie said cheerfully.

Jessica wondered what she was looking for exactly. What drew her to the period when Edward Makin lived at The Cedars and why was she so sure that the child who had written her name on a spare bit of paper had lived there at the same time? There was nothing to connect the two save a gut feeling inside her, the same feeling that had led her the previous year to recognize an Adam fireplace in a job lot of old furniture and fittings.

She resisted the temptation to open the book until she was back in the house. The Clares were out as usual, John Clare at his office, Sophy helping with some charity or other. Mrs Tate was sorting groceries.

'Did you take your daughter to the dentist?' Jessica asked on her way through the kitchen.

'She needed an extraction, fortunately right at the back but it was quite nasty,' Mrs Tate said. 'She stayed home today, put her feet up.'

Jessica went through to the hall and upstairs. Her small room looked cheerful with the autumn sunshine beaming through the window. She sat down and opened the book, rifling through the pages until she came to the chapter headed 'The Makin Mystery'.

The style was flat and factual and there were no illustrations. The cover of the book was green with a black question mark printed large. The quality of the paper was mediocre and the binding was beginning to fray. When it had been published the war had only just finished and materials were in short supply, she reasoned. Perhaps it had had only a limited print run. She wondered what had led the author to choose that particular subject. In the aftermath of conflict with the world picking itself up after chaos, had he turned to older, more comfortable mysteries that had lost the sting of immediacy and become intellectual puzzles divorced from the realities of the postwar era?

There was no biographical information on the back flap, nothing to give her any information. Not that it mattered, she thought, settling herself deeper in the armchair. What was important were the contents.

The Cedars is a handsome, early Victorian house in a residential part of Liverpool, with a large garden at the back and the customary lawn and short curving drive bordered by shrubbery at the front. There are no cedar trees nearby from whence it might have derived its name but there may have been one at the time the house was built. Its original owner was a certain George Makin, a native of Liverpool with interests in a local bank and shares in a small cotton mill in the Wirral. His increasing prosperity and his marriage in 1826 to a Miss Constance Lloyd, daughter of a clergyman, probably decided him upon the course of establishing himself and his bride in a pleasant district out of the hurly-burly of the city. George Makin, from the little that can be deduced from what is known about him, was a thrusting, energetic person who, as his prosperity increased, spent more and more of his time out of the house, immersed in his various business enterprises and also socializing in the gentlemen's clubs of the day. His wife, Constance, seldom went out socially but devoted herself to the only child of the marriage, a boy named Edward. Possibly Constance consoled herself for her husband's neglect by clinging more tightly to her son even to the extent of undertaking his education herself. She was a deeply religious woman of an evangelical cast of mind who no doubt imprinted her own high moral standards upon the child.

Edward Makin, born in 1827, a year after his parents' marriage, was finally sent to school – one imagines over his mother's protests. He was entered as a pupil at a minor public school in 1842 when he was fifteen. Probably his father wished him to be prepared for the university entrance examinations and it is also possible that the elder Makin felt his son lacked companions of his own age.

Edward Makin had an uneventful school career and seems to have made no close friends. His vacations were spent at home and his mother rather than his father seems to have been the parent who attended speech days and prize givings. The fact that by this time George Makin was nicknamed 'Soak' Makin may account for his absences and for a growing rift between his wife and himself.

Edward does not appear to have distinguished himself particularly at school since he did not enter Cambridge until 1847 when he was twenty, having spent the previous year making the customary Grand Tour of Europe, not with companions of his own age but with his mother.

He obtained a Degree in Classics in 1850 and was ordained as a curate the following year, without immediately taking up a curacy as the illness and death of his father necessitated his presence at home. The elder Makin died of a liver complaint which probably was caused by his excessive drinking.

In the following year he was appointed as vicar of St Michael's Church in Fairfield Road, succeeding his maternal grandfather, Frederick Lloyd whose death had left the living vacant. Instead of taking up residence at the vicarage, however, he continued to live with his widowed mother at The Cedars.

In 1853 he married a Miss Amelia Benson, the daughter of a former business associate of his father. Edward was now twenty-six, his bride some four years younger. The newly-wedded couple continued to make their home with Mrs Makin the elder, and one can only guess at the ensuing tensions. However Amelia was spoken of as a very gentle, amiable young woman and it's possible that she didn't chafe against the continuing rule of her mother-in-law.

Two children were born of the marriage, Julia in 1854 and Robert four years later. Mrs Makin the elder died in 1857 before the birth of her grandson. The cause of her death was given as cancer. Edward Makin preached the funeral sermon over his mother in a manner described as 'profoundly affecting and literate'.

Shortly after this he began work on a memoir which was later published privately. In this memoir he gives few personal details about his wife or children but concentrates upon the devotion between his late mother and himself hinting strongly at the distress caused by the intemperance of his father. He also touches very obliquely upon what he refers to as his 'rescue missions in the houses of soiled doves', a common nineteenth-century euphemism for brothels. The practice of frequenting such places in the hope of persuading the prostitutes to mend their ways was later a habit of Mr Gladstone and other reform politicians but often provided slanderous ammunition for their political rivals.

In 1859 Edward Makin was thirty-two years old, a respected clergyman, described in a newspaper item relating to the visit of a bishop as 'darkly handsome and with an eloquent tongue'. Indeed it is surprising that he was not quickly promoted and given a more prominent and demanding ministry. Possibly his somewhat holier-than-thou attitude was not attractive. His home life, from all accounts, appears to have been a tranquil one. His wife, Amelia, was reputed to be a devoted wife and mother, to the extent of caring for her two babies herself instead of engaging a nursemaid. Indeed, at a time when domestic labour was both cheap and plentiful, and bearing in mind the size of the house, the Makins employed only a cook-housekeeper called Eliza Tatum, and given the title of 'Mrs' according to custom though she had never been married. There was also a housemaid living-in known as 'Polly' and in her early teens. Her surname apparently was not considered important enough to preserve. When extra help was required, girls were employed as temporary workers from the local orphanage. A gardener named Higgs came three times a week to tend the plants and do any odd jobs the women couldn't manage. Apart from an occasional visiting clergyman the Makins seldom entertained guests and they were on polite but distant terms with their neighbours.

In 1859 a governess was engaged, apparently at the request of Mrs Makin, to instruct five-year-old Julia.

It is possible that Amelia was in ill health that year and found the care of a lively little girl becoming too much for her. Whatever the reason a Miss Dorothy Larue was engaged and duly took her place in the household. Though her surname suggests a French connection nothing is known of Miss Larue beyond the fact that she was in her twenties and came highly recommended, though by whom is not known. She apparently quickly gained the confidence of her small pupil and was regarded by her employers as a most respectable young woman.

In the early autumn of that year Miss Larue took Julia for a walk which was customary in the mid-afternoon when the weather was fine. She had then been employed at The Cedars for about six weeks and the neighbours were used to seeing her set out, holding Julia by the hand. Their walks usually took them past the church in Fairfield Road to a patch of common ground where Julia was permitted to bowl her hoop. That was the last time anything was ever seen of either of them.

At four o'clock, the usual hour for tea, Eliza Tatum prepared a tray as she always did when she rose from her afternoon rest. The servant girl Polly was not in the kitchen and after waiting a few minutes Eliza carried the tray through to Amelia Makin who had just risen from her own nap and was playing with the baby, Robert. Eliza then returned to the kitchen to drink her own tea where she was joined by Polly who had been picking fruit in the orchard at the far end of the garden. About half an hour later Edward Makin returned from the church vestry where he had been clearing a cupboard and sat down with his wife, ringing for fresh tea which Polly took in.

At five o'clock Amelia expressed concern at the late return of Miss Larue and Julia and Edward Makin ordered Polly to walk over and see if they were on their way home. The servant girl went but returned after an hour saying there was no sign of them. By this time it was growing dark and had begun to rain and Amelia Makin was becoming deeply distressed. Edward Makin persuaded her to take a dose of laudanum, the universal remedy of the Victorian era, and to lie down while he went out himself, calling in at the households of several of his parishioners in the vain expectation that Miss Larue and her charge might have called there to shelter from the rain. He returned to the house at eight o'clock and having drunk a cup of tea informed Eliza and Polly that he intended reporting the matter to the police. By this time it was raining heavily and very dark which hampered any search. The hoop belonging to Julia was found however at the far end of the common. No other traces of either Dorothy Larue or Julia Makin ever came to light. Both were registered as missing persons and the case 'held on file'. Amelia Makin suffered what was clearly a nervous breakdown after several weeks of suspense. Edward Makin continued his ministry but in the following spring he resigned and took his wife abroad, presumably in the hope of effecting a cure. The child, Robert, accompanied them. Presumably the sad memories that surrounded The Cedars had proved too much for Amelia's nerves since the sale of the house was arranged through an agent while they were still abroad. Edward Makin died the following summer, of a typhoid attack contracted while they were staying in Venice.

His widow remained abroad, surviving her husband by fifteen years. Their son, Robert, was then eighteen and had just been commissioned as an officer in the Guards. He went with his regiment to India and was killed during a tiger shoot six years later, leaving neither wife nor children.

The disappearance of the governess and the child remained unsolved. It seems that Dorothy Larue abducted Julia but no definite leads as to the route they took ever came to light. Detectives who examined the governess's belongings found only a modest selection of garments but nothing that would throw light on her past career.

The case itself poses several interesting questions. Why did Edward Makin not check out the references provided by the governess, if indeed such references were provided? It seems highly unlikely that a clergyman would engage a governess without first checking into her background. Why did he delay for several hours before informing the police of the disappearance of his cherished only daughter and her governess? And how did he miss the hoop which was found later at the far end of the common? These questions were not apparently asked at the time, possibly because the police were reluctant to cause further pain to an obviously distraught and highly-respected couple.

The Cedars was sold to a retired clergyman called Mr Laurence and later inherited by his son whom I interviewed but who displayed little interest in the past history of the house. No members of the Makin or Benson families apparently left descendants.

And that was the end of the chapter. Jessica sent a small scowl after the absent author as she closed the book. He seemed to have recorded the main facts but he hadn't indulged in any speculations as to what might have happened. He hadn't mentioned what had happened about the two indoor servants, Eliza Tatum and Polly for example. Presumably they belonged to the lower classes and were not considered very important. Had Eliza stayed on as cook after the house was sold? And where had Polly gone? Polly Winter, Jessica thought, who had taken a pencil and written her name, established her identity and pushed the slip of paper in between the pages of a cookery book. No, nobody had bothered much about Polly, nor thought to ask why she hadn't heard the cook calling her to help make the tea when, by her own admission, she had only been in the orchard picking pears.

Jessica seized a piece of paper and started jotting down questions as they crowded into her head.

Who was Dorothy Larue? Where did she come from, what were her references, if any, and had Edward Makin checked them out? If not, then why not? If the governess had abducted the child why did she leave her clothes behind and why were there no letters, diaries, personal mementoes among her things? Why had the hoop been left on the common and why hadn't Edward Makin seen it?

Had Polly really been in the orchard when the cook called her to help make the afternoon tea? Come to that, why hadn't Polly seen the child's hoop since she'd gone out before Edward Makin to see if the governess and Julia were on their way back?

She put the paper with its questions on it into the file she was starting to build and stood up. It was nearing lunch-time and the sun was shining. She'd walk along to the café and eat a snack there. She told herself that it was because she felt like another walk, didn't feel like cooking, but the rangy frame and pleasant features of Adam Darby had come into her mind. If he was around it would be fun to bounce ideas off him. They were due to go out together, she recalled, and felt a stirring of anticipation. It would be good to have a date, to spend an evening in the real world instead of feeling herself drawn back to the past, a past in which she had no part but which seemed to be intruding into the present.

Sophy Clare was just coming in, having apparently walked through from the kitchen. She looked tired and a little strained as she paused to greet Jessica.

'How is the project going?'

'Slowly. I'm becoming interested in the Makins.' Jessica shot a glance, but the older woman showed no reaction.

'The family who lived in this house about a hundred odd years ago?' she said. 'Didn't one of them write a book?'

'A memoir, yes. It was among the books upstairs.'

'I don't get much leisure for reading,' Sophy Clare said in an excusing tone. 'My welfare work, you know.'

'Like your children.'

Now there was a reaction. Sophy started and said, 'What? What did you say?'

'Your son and daughter are social workers, aren't they?' Jessica said.

'Oh, yes. Both of them,' Sophy said, brightening. 'Of course they have to work very hard. My voluntary work is simply – a means of filling the time, you know. Just that.'

'Yes, well, I have to get on anyway,' Jessica said, feeling unaccountably awkward. The other's bright, brittle smile and voice jarred on her for no reason she could understand.

She went out through the front door, having to undo the chain, aware of the other watching her. She had the impression that Sophy wanted her to stay, but she wanted time alone, a space to think.

In the small restaurant she ordered eggs on toast and coffee and sat, her eyes turning constantly towards the window, towards the lunch-time crowd.

'Waiting for someone?' the waitress enquired in a friendly tone.

'No. No, I'm not waiting,' Jessica said.

Yet the sensation of waiting stayed with her. For Adam? No, though she hoped he would come by. For whom then? For a child with a painted face in a pink dress? But the child, briefly seen once, had nothing to do with anything. Except the poster perhaps, fading from scarlet to pink? The quick, light footsteps along the gallery, the scratching, low at the bedroom door, the piece of paper that fluttered out in a windless room? Jessica scowled, pushing her half-eaten lunch aside, pouring more coffee, resting her chin on her hands.

'Waiting for me, I hope?'

Adam's voice made her jump violently. Jessica stared at him as he pulled out a chair and sat down, the smile on his face turning to concern.

'Sorry if I gave you a shock. You're white as a sheet,' he said.

'I've a lot on my mind – nothing connected with you. Adam, did you know there was a mystery about The Cedars?' she asked abruptly.

'No. What mystery? Tea and toast, please.'

Having given his order he turned his attention to Jessica.

'Edward Makin inherited the house when his mother died,' Jessica said. 'He was vicar of the local church, married with two small children. There was a cook and a servant girl living in at the house and then a governess was engaged, a young woman called Dorothy Larue. After six weeks she took Julia, the five-year-old daughter, for a walk one afternoon and they both vanished. They were never seen again.'

'Where did you find out all this?' Adam enquired.

'From a book in the library. I've been doing some research into the Makins. After it happened he and his wife and baby son went abroad and the house was sold. They both died abroad and the son, Robert, was killed out in India.'

'And the case was never solved?'

'It was put on file and eventually forgotten. Back in 1859 detection wasn't as easy as it is now. I mean there were no fingerprinting techniques, and people didn't need passports to travel, though I don't think the governess did abduct the little girl.'

'Why not?'

'She left all her clothes behind and there was nothing in her things to prove exactly who she was or where she'd worked before.'

'She might have done that herself to blur the trail,' he pointed out.

'There were other puzzling features,' Jessica hurried on. 'The servant, Polly, said she was in the orchard gathering pears during the afternoon but when the cook called her to help make the afternoon tea the girl didn't come. And Edward Makin waited until quite late on in the evening before he reported the matter to the police. By then it was raining hard and all the police found was Julia's hoop on the far side of the common, and that's odd too, because first Polly and then Edward Makin had both gone that way to look for them.'

'What I'm wondering,' Adam said, 'is why this is bothering you so much. There's something more than interested research in all this, isn't there?'

'I think,' said Jessica, 'that there's something very odd about the house. It has a peculiar effect on people. I keep – hearing things.'

'What things?'

'Someone calling for Polly – and I heard that when I first got there, before I knew anything about the Makins or read the book. I heard footsteps a couple of times before anyone came and a slip of paper fell out of a copy of Mrs Beeton that I was looking through. Someone had printed on it in a very childish hand – *My name is Polly Winter*.'

'The servant girl?' To her relief he wasn't laughing.

'Her surname isn't given anywhere in the book. I think she was practising writing, maybe trying to establish some sense of her own identity. Adam, do you think it possible that the dead can linger, try to set something right?'

'It isn't a theory I've ever thought much about,' he said.

'If we accept the idea in theory,' Jessica said slowly, 'then it's possible this servant, Polly Winter, knew what had happened and wanted to set it right.'

'But why wait more than a hundred years?'

'We don't know that she did,' Jessica argued. 'Perhaps the conditions weren't right before. Perhaps she tried and nobody took any notice. I'm here to research into that period so I'm more tuned in.'

'Or the situation in the house resembles the one she knew so she can function in it – what's the matter?' He looked at her sharply.

'The Clares,' Jessica said in a low voice.

'What about them?'

'They're both very pleasant, very welcoming,' Jessica said, 'but Sophy, the wife, is afraid of something. She watches the door all the time as if she listens for something. Her husband said she gets nervous alone in the house in the evening. I suspect she has a drink problem.'

'That's hardly likely to be caused by something that happened over a hundred years ago.'

'I suppose not. They're obviously happily married with two children – grown-up children, actually, Julian and Robina. They're away, training as social workers. What's wrong?'

·'Julia and Robina,' Adam said. 'Julia and Robert.'

'It has to be a coincidence,' Jessica said.

'I'm sure it is, but the initials – they almost reproduce the situation when the Makins lived there.'

'Well, my name's Jessica Cameron and not Dorothy Larue,' she said, 'and there isn't anyone called Polly working in the hou – but the daily woman is called Mrs Tate and the cook-housekeeper in the time of the Makins was called Mrs Tatum. I only just realized that. Adam, what's going on?'

'Some odd coincidences,' Adam said. 'They might mean something or they might not, but you've intrigued me. Where are you going from here?'

'Home to get my notes written up,' Jessica said. 'Adam, thanks for not suggesting that I've got an over-active imagination.'

'Is it still on for Saturday night?' He touched her hand as she rose.

'I'm looking forward to it. Thanks for listening to me,' Jessica said, going to pay the waitress with a definite feeling of optimism. She'd talked to someone and he hadn't laughed, hadn't derided.

She walked back more briskly, feeling the sharp snap of autumn in the air. A girl ahead of her was turning in at the front gate of The Cedars just as Mrs Tate opened the door, her voice scolding forth.

'You shouldn't have come over with your tooth still so sore,' she said loudly. 'Oh, Miss Cameron, did you have anything to eat? I can fix you something on a tray if you want.'

'Thanks but I had a snack,' Jessica said, catching up the girl. 'This is your daughter. We me –'

She had been going to say 'met before', but the face crowned with spiky blonde hair under a floppy beret, one cheek still slightly distended after her dental treatment, wasn't the girl she'd seen hanging out washing, looking through one of the lower windows as Jessica got into her car. This wasn't the girl who'd come into the room where she'd been looking over the books in the bookcase.

'Pleased to meet you,' said Mrs Tate's daughter. 'I don't think we've bumped into each other before, have we?'

'No,' said Jessica. 'No, I don't believe we have.'

Six

When she woke up the next morning Jessica reached at once for the notes she had made the previous day. She had hoped that after a night's sleep her subconscious might have presented her with possible solutions but as she read through what she had written nothing new came into her mind.

Known Scenario ...

   September 1859 (note – check exact date?). Early afternoon, Dorothy Larue takes Julia for a walk to bowl her hoop on the common; Amelia Makin lying down, presumably with baby, Robert; Mrs Tatum lying down;

Edward Makin over at church; Polly gathering pears in garden (though presumably she wasn't doing that for the whole afternoon).

At four o'clock Mrs Tatum rises and prepares tea, calling Polly who doesn't respond. (Why?) Amelia Makin has risen and is playing with Robert. Polly comes in from garden, presumably with the fruit she has picked.

4.30 – Edward Makin returns from the church and Polly takes in fresh tea.

Five o'clock – Edward Makin tells Polly to go and look for Miss Larue and Julia.

Six o'clock – Polly returns, saying she hasn't seen them. Question. If the governess was in the habit of taking Julia to bowl her hoop on the common, why didn't Polly find the hoop?

Shortly after six – Edward Makin persuades his wife to calm her nerves with a dose of laudanum, and himself goes out to look, calling in at various (unspecified) houses along the way. It is now growing dark and raining, which may account for his failure to see the hoop.

Eight o'clock Edward Makin returns, drinks a cup of tea, goes out to inform the police.

The people involved:

1. Edward Makin, 32, clergyman. Well respected, noted for eloquence of his sermons. Greatly influenced by his mother (at this time deceased), rather self-satisfied judging from his memoirs. Seems to have been one of those clergymen who tried to persuade prostitutes to reform their lives. Why did he wait so long before informing the police? He spent the afternoon sorting out a cupboard in the vestry of the church. Did anyone check this statement?

2. Amelia Makin, 30, (the author of *Mysteries* got this wrong), Edward's wife. A loving mother since she looks after the two children herself. Her wish to employ a governess for Julia suggests that she herself doesn't feel competent to teach the child and there being laudanum already in the house may point to her being of a nervous disposition.

3. Mrs Tatum, cook-housekeeper. Age not known but probably middle-aged. Has secure position in the house and, apparently, the right to put her feet up in the afternoon.

Nothing else known of her.

4. Polly (Winter?) in early teens, general servant. Nothing else known about her.

5. Dorothy Larue, in twenties, governess. Had been employed for six weeks. No clues to her previous career found among her things by the police. Was Larue her real name? Were her references, if any, checked out by Edward Makin?

6. Julia Makin, 5. Evidently liked the governess and went off happily enough to bowl her hoop on the common.

Jessica read through the notes again, interrupted herself to take a shower and dress, and went back into the bedroom, running a comb through her short hair, pulling back the curtains, switching off the light, half consciously postponing the moment when she would read over the rest of the notes. So far what she had written was a theoretical incursion into the past, with nothing personal appertaining to her own situation. A puzzle for a rainy day. But her pen had run on late into the day, and she had begun to feel that she too was entering the story.

She sat down, took up the thin sheaf of papers and continued to reread.

The situation today –

The Cedars is now owned by John and Sophy Clare, a married couple in their forties, with two children (twenties) training or working as social workers. Names are Julian and Robina (note similarity to Julia and Robert).

John Clare – works for firm arranging conferences et cetera, frequently out in the evenings. Television addict. Question. Why does he refer to Julian and Robina as if they were still children?

Sophy Clare – trim, elegant, immerses herself in voluntary work, obviously eager for company and nervous in the house. Possibly has a drinking problem?

Mrs Tate – daily-help but seems to function more as live-out housekeeper. A widow. One daughter. Works hard, chatty. Note similarity of name to Mrs Tatum.

Personal Experience –

When I arrived I saw a young girl hanging washing in the garden. I saw same girl looking through the sitting-room window after me as I went to my car. The same girl entered the upstairs room where I was looking through the books. I assumed wrongly she was Mrs Tate's daughter. When I was in the sitting-room I heard footsteps across the hall a few minutes before Sophy Clare came in with the coffee. Later I heard footsteps along the gallery and a brief sound like scratching low down on my bedroom door. I have seen a child dressed up in a pink party dress with heavy make-up on her face and my Spanish poster has faded from red to pink.

Jessica took up her pen and wrote underneath.

I have heard someone calling for Polly out in the garden. The first night I slept here I dreamed (fancied) that as I dozed off the sheets were linen not cool nylon. Is it possible that Dorothy Larue slept in this room, that somehow or other I entered into her experience?

From downstairs came the clatter of crockery. Mrs Tate had arrived and started on her daily tasks. Jessica folded the papers and slipped them prudently into her roomy shoulder-bag.

In the kitchen Mrs Tate greeted her cheerfully.

'There's coffee made,' she said invitingly. 'How about a bit of toast? No? Well, you young girls are all the same. I tell my Linda that she'll never get roses in her cheeks if she doesn't eat right.'

Linda, not Polly or Dorothy or Amelia. Jessica accepted the coffee, allowed herself to be coaxed into eating a piece of toast, sat at the table, noting as she had noted before that it didn't blend with the modern gadgets. It was too large, its top scored by marks where meat, bread and vegetables had been sliced for a much longer time than the Clares had lived here.

' – and I said there's no point in me doing just a few things in the washing machine. Better to have a full load.'

Mrs Tate was chatting away in domestic fashion.

'You hang them on the line sometimes?' Jessica said.

'To finish them off if the sun's really hot. Haven't done that for weeks. Not much warmth in a September sun. Well, I'd better get on. The Clares go out early on Fridays. Mr Clare has business meetings, and Mrs Clare goes off to the Children's Home all day.'

'She does a lot of welfare work,' Jessica said.

'And isn't appreciated,' Mrs Tate said darkly. 'Of course that's nearly always the way, isn't it? I'm lucky in that respect. The Clares are very good to work for, though Mrs Clare is fussy about the food.'

'And Mr Clare doesn't like it when you leave the chain up on the front door.'

'Better be safe than sorry, that's what I say,' Mrs Tate said. 'When I'm cleaning upstairs I shoot the bolt on the back door too. I must remember not to do that now that you're here. Now I must get on. I want to get home early so that I can get Linda a hot drink. Her face is still a bit swollen.'

'Oil of cloves on the gum will deaden the pain,' Jessica said.

'Really? I never heard of that.'

Neither, thought Jessica, did I until this moment.

A faint chill shivered through her and was gone. She rose, speaking with firm cheerfulness.

'Mr Clare said that I could look through the shed in the garden. There's an old cupboard there that might hold some newspapers or something that will help my work. Do you think it would be all right if I took a couple of pears?'

'Help yourself,' Mrs Tate said. 'Nobody bothers much about the garden. Doesn't seem to affect the crop though. I do quite a lot of bottling.'

It was the first time that Jessica had actually walked into the back garden. It was a large plot, surrounded by a wall with a back gate that had a broken padlock. At the other side of the gate was a stretch of rough ground with the beginnings of a housing estate beyond it. The garden itself was a tangle of rose bushes, the petals large and limp with the fading of summer, several bushes of azaleas that needed pruning, an unexpectedly neat vegetable plot, an old greenhouse with most of its panes cracked and nothing inside but an old wheelbarrow and a collection of cracked and broken flower pots. There were numerous trees, the fruit hanging heavy on the branches and the spaces between them high with bramble and nettles.

The shed was a stone hut with a corrugated iron roof. It had the look of an air-raid shelter left over from the 1940s but it was clearly older than that, its stone sunk deep on its foundations. She pushed the door open and looked into the dim and cluttered space within. A couple of rusting scooters, a burst rugby ball, piles of tattered newspapers met her gaze. The possibility there might be mice here crossed her mind, but the interior was dry and there were no signs of any holes or gnawed edges. There was a small window, its tiny panes completely obscured by dirt.

She stepped inside, seeing the cupboard against the back wall at once. It wasn't a wide piece of furniture but its top almost reached the corrugated iron of the roof. She stepped up to it and tugged open the door. Piles of old newspapers, letters, bills, half-used exercise books and faded photograph albums were stacked neatly in its interior. It might prove to be a treasure trove, she thought with a stirring of excitement. Old Mr Laurence had been something of a hoarder it seemed. She hoped that he had hoarded something worth seeing.

She reached up and took a stack from the top, staggering slightly from the weight of it as she stepped back. Her first impulse had been to look through them inside the shed but the light wasn't good and there wasn't anywhere to sit.

She went back to the house, passing Mrs Tate who was up to her elbows in soapsuds, carrying the pile up the stairs and along the gallery to the upper floor. There would be more space in the spare room to spread the papers out. It took four more trips to the shed before the cupboard was empty. She wedged the outside door shut with her foot and carried up the last pile.

The newspapers weren't in any particular order and the letters were a hodge-podge of what looked mainly like bills and old shopping lists. Jessica took a deep breath and started sorting, putting the newspapers according to year, setting the photographs in a separate pile.

The temptation to start reading before she had imposed some kind of order on the mess was strong. She resisted it, promising herself that she would start with the photographs. The glimpses of them she had had told her they were old, sepia-tinted prints, probably late Victorian.

Her guess had been right. A gentleman in frock coat stood next to a seated lady at whose knee stood a sailor-suited little boy. Her hope they might be the Makins was dashed when she turned the photograph over and saw 'Laurence 1870' printed on the back. Mr Laurence whose son had become a recluse was the man who had bought The Cedars from the Makins after they had gone abroad. The next photograph showed the same trio with both parents seated and the child standing between them. All three looked grave and preoccupied and there was a faint fuzziness about the child which suggested he had moved slightly at the last moment. She picked up the next, seeing the same three, no this time there were four people. A woman in cap and apron stood at one side, her hands clasped at her waist, her plump face bearing a look of alarm as if the camera had startled her even though she was clearly posed for a photograph.

Jessica turned over the photograph and saw with a quickening of interest that the same hand had inked on the back, 'Mr and Mrs Laurence with their son, and housekeeper Mrs Tatum'.

The same housekeeper who had worked for the Makins had stayed on to work for the new owners. She turned the photograph over again, holding it nearer to the light, looking more closely at the plump face, the greying hair drawn back under a lace-edged cap. Mid-sixties, she guessed, though it was hard to tell since in the previous century women had aged more swiftly. However the age would fit in with her own private image of Mrs Tatum as a woman in her forties when she had worked for the Makins. There was nothing unusual in the plump face.

She went quickly through the remaining photographs but there was no other likeness of anyone connected with the case. There was a view of the house, taken from the front, another taken from the back with a part view of the garden which looked neater and better tended than it looked now.

She turned to the newspapers, most of them yellowing at the edges. The earliest was dated for the spring of 1915 and was full of news about the war – the First World War, Jessica realized. Very interesting, no doubt, but too late for her purposes. She piled the newspapers up in one corner and started on the letters and bills. Some of these were torn or smudged. She started to sort out letters from bills. Prices had certainly risen since a joint of beef had cost two shillings and sixpence.

It was past one. She sat back on her heels, wiping her print-stained hands together, feeling the slight pull in her neck muscles. Polly had suffered from back ache despite her wiry appearance. All those hods of coal and jugs of hot water had tired her out sometimes.

'I'm guessing again,' Jessica said firmly to herself. She rose hastily, picked up the photographs and went to the tiny bathroom to wash her hands and brush the dust off her jeans.

The house was very still. Unusually still.

Of course the Clares were out all day, she reminded herself, but it was surprising that Mrs Tate hadn't called upstairs to ask if she wanted a cup of tea or coffee. On the other hand she was under no obligation to treat a lodger as if she were a member of the family.

In the kitchen the dishes had been washed and the table scrubbed, and a start had evidently been made on the floor, the tiles around the table being damp and slippery. The window had been opened and a fresh breeze blew strongly. Jessica made herself a sandwich and a cup of coffee, taking them into the small breakfast-room. Through the window that overlooked the front drive she could see a pair of magpies amiably sharing worms. Mrs Tate had mentioned going home early to look after her daughter. She had obviously gone.

Taking the empty plate and cup back into the kitchen, Jessica washed them up and then, on impulse, tried the back door. It was unlocked and a faint exclamation of annoyance escaped her. Mrs Tate had been careful enough about locking up doors when she herself was alone in the house but she hadn't bothered to lock up when she left. If she had left.

Jessica went back into the front hall and raised her voice.

'Mrs Tate! Mrs Tate, are you still here?'

The cavern of the house caught her voice, echoed it briefly, and then absorbed it. There was no answering call.

Jessica stood irresolute for a few moments and then went briskly up the stairs into her own room. She needed to spend some time at the main library in the university where she could make notes on the political and social climate of the 1850s. Once she had the general picture then she could set her typical family within it. The growing consciousness that the Makins were hardly a typical family was something she'd think about later. She collected what she needed and went downstairs again, conscientiously locking the back door behind her before she got her car out of the garage and drove into the tranquil, tree-lined road.

The ordered bustle of the library absorbed her attention. At this time of year, before the main student body returned, it was always easy to attract the help of one of the assistants and find a vacant space where she could start to build up her dossier on whatever period was going to be the subject of the exhibition. Before she had worked with a colleague. This was the first time she had worked alone. She reminded herself firmly that she mustn't allow the mystery of what had happened a hundred years before in The Cedars to divert her from her main task, and settled to a long afternoon of research.

In the mid-nineteenth century, England had been rich and outwardly prosperous, with a vast empire and a plump middle-aged queen who adored her balding prince consort. In America the States had stood on the brink of civil war; in Europe the Hapsburgs had reigned, in Russia the tsar. Ladies had worn wide crinolines and tight corsets and had frequent recourse to the smelling salts. Others, less fortunate, had been pressed into domestic service, toiled in factories and mills and often died young after years of constant childbearing.

She stopped at last, straightening up from a collection of fashion plates of the period she had been studying, motioning to the assistant who had begun hovering.

'I've finished with these. Thank you.'

'Will you be wanting to look at anything else, only we're closing soon.' The assistant looked as if she had a date and wanted to rush off to it.

'I've finished. You've been very helpful.'

Stuffing her notes back into her bag Jessica felt a sense of regret. Several hours' concentrated attention had cleared her mind. She felt an actual reluctance to return to the big house with its tangled garden and echoing rooms.

By now the Clares would almost certainly be home. She cheered herself up with that thought as she left the university campus and got into her car.

A stream of traffic was leaving the city. Jessica joined it. The harsh neon lights were yellowing the pavements. In the evening the streets had a smoky aspect.

She was pleased, as she pulled into the driveway at the side of the house, to see light beaming through a gap in the curtains at the sitting-room window. Either one or both of the Clares was home and she wouldn't have to enter a dark house alone. As that thought struck her she felt a little shiver of shame. She had never been nervous in her life and it annoyed her that she seemed to be developing fears and fancies now.

'Is that you, John?'

Sophy Clare put her head out of the back door as Jessica approached along the terrace.

'I'm afraid it's only me,' Jessica said, raising her voice slightly as she crossed the yard.

'Oh, Jessica, how nice!' Sophy held the door wider. 'I only just got back from the orphanage and I thought John might have been here. He has several big conferences to arrange this month so he's grossly overstretched. Will you have some dinner with me? I shall leave something cold for John though he usually snatches a quick bite in town – would you like a glass of sherry?'

'Yes. Yes, that would be very nice,' Jessica said.

'I'm afraid it will be a scratch meal tonight,' Sophy apologized. 'Mrs Tate usually prepares the vegetables before she goes home on Fridays but I'm afraid she didn't today. I'm poaching some sole in a butter sauce and we have asparagus.'

'It sounds lovely,' Jessica said, accepting the sherry and sitting at the table.

'I've always liked cooking,' Sophy said, stirring busily. 'Food is predictable, isn't it? I mean when one boils potatoes they don't turn into sprouts halfway through the cooking time.'

'I'm not so sure,' Jessica said. 'I mean when I put something on to cook it never comes out looking exactly like the picture in the recipe book.'

'That's just lack of practice,' Sophy said, laughing. Her laugh had a slightly blurred quality. Jessica suspected she'd already had more than one sherry.

'I suppose so.'

'Shall we go into the sitting-room. This meal cooks itself,' Sophy said in a bright, hostess voice.

'Yes, of course.' Rising, Jessica noticed that the other stepped quickly to the back door and slid home the bolt.

In the sitting-room the television had been turned on with the sound down. The room had a cosy quality with the artificial flames of the electric fire streaming upward and the lamps and central chandelier dimmed to a level of comfort that illuminated without glare.

'Leave the door!' Sophy's tone was suddenly sharp.

'Sorry.' Jessica moved aside, sat down.

'I don't want to miss the timer on the cooker,' Sophy said, and jumped as a ringing telephone out in the hall interrupted her.

'Excuse me, that must be John.' She put down the almost empty glass she had been nursing and hurried out.

Voices sounded indistinctly – Sophy's and someone obviously shouting over a bad line.

'John had to go to Birmingham so he won't be home until

tomorrow,' Sophy said returning. 'Well, that leaves just the two of us to eat the fish. You're not going out this evening, are you?'

Jessica shook her head.

'It's too silly to be nervous at my age,' Sophy said with the same brittle little laugh, 'but I suspect it may be the result of the menopause or something. It's only in the last couple of years that I've suffered from nerves.'

'This is a big house,' Jessica said. Perhaps now was the time to tell the other that she too had heard voices and footsteps.

The doorbell rang.

'Who on earth can that be?' Sophy looked at her and then stood up. 'Well, let's see who it is.'

She hadn't requested it but Jessica also rose and went behind her into the hall.

'I'm sorry to bother you, Mrs Clare, but I wondered if Mum was still here.' The nasal voice belonged to Linda and was heard the instant Sophy opened the door a crack. 'I didn't want to disturb you by phoning and so I thought I'd take the bus and go back with – she is here, isn't she?'

'Your mother left at – before lunchtime,' Jessica heard herself say. 'I haven't seen her since this morning.'

Suddenly, crazily, she wanted to add, 'Someone had better look on the common and see if they can find the hoop.'

Seven

'You'd better come in, Linda.' Sophy pushed the door close, undid the chain, opened the door wider. 'Come into the sitting-room. Now what is all this about?'

'Mum didn't come back today,' Linda said flatly. 'I thought she'd stayed on here but when it got dark I started worrying a bit.'

'You should have telephoned,' Sophy said.

'I don't like phones,' Linda said. 'Anyway I'd been stuck in all day and my face felt better, so I decided to get the bus in. What time did Mum leave?'

'I went out early this morning,' Sophy said. 'I only got back a short time ago.'

'I saw your mother this morning when I came down,' Jessica said in response to their enquiring looks. 'I went out to get those old newspapers out of the shed after that – Mr Clare told me it'd be all right. I took them up to the spare room to sort them out. It took all morning and when I came down into the kitchen to get myself a sandwich Mrs Tate had gone. I spent the whole afternoon down at the university library.'

'Could your mother have gone somewhere else?' Sophy asked.

'Not without letting me know. You don't think she's had an accident?'

'Let me get the directory and I'll check with the local hospitals,' Sophy said. She sounded brisk and practical.

'Come and sit down,' Jessica suggested, but the girl shook her head.

'I'm too fidgety, Miss. Mum never just vanishes without telling me. There's only her and me since Dad died and she was worried about me anyway because my face was hurting. She wouldn't just disappear.'

Sophy, at the telephone said, 'Jessica, could you check on the fish? Give Linda a cup of tea or something.'

In the kitchen Jessica made tea, coaxed Linda into drinking it, checked the fish. Sophy came in, shaking her head.

'Nobody has been brought into any of the hospitals who might be your mother. Does she have any friend she might go and see?'

'We keep ourselves to ourselves,' the girl said with a kind of pathetic dignity.

'Perhaps we ought to tell the police?' Jessica said.

'She hasn't been missing long enough,' Sophy said. 'I mean, don't they tell people to wait twenty-four hours unless there's a young child involved?'

'It wouldn't hurt to report it,' Jessica said. 'Especially since Linda's so sure that her mother wouldn't have gone anywhere.'

'Then I'll go with her,' Sophy said. 'Let me divide the dinner and put mine in the hostess warmer. No, you eat, Jessica, and I'll take Linda to the police station and then run her home. Honestly, dear, I wouldn't worry too much. There's bound to be a good explanation.'

Jessica had the almost overwhelming compulsion to offer to

accompany them, which was ridiculous. Far more sensible to eat her dinner. She saw them out, put the chain on the front door, carried her dinner into the small breakfast-room and sat down to eat.

The front hall was brightly lit and silent. Of course it was silent. She was alone in the house. She got up and firmly closed the door. She wasn't going to sit with her eyes fixed on an open door. The fish tasted good, faintly spiced. She concentrated on each mouthful, aware of silence.

There was a small radio on the dresser. She reached over and switched it on. Music – an old record of the Stones blared out. She turned it down slightly and set herself to listen as if she had never heard pop music before.

She would make coffee. That meant going to the kitchen again. She had left the light turned on there. It was fortunate, she thought wryly, that her rent covered electricity charges.

When she opened the door the hall was still empty. Jessica stood for a moment, looking up the staircase towards the gallery. Then she spoke aloud and crossly. 'Jessica Cameron, you're acting like a fool! The house is empty! Go and make yourself a cup of coffee and start acting like a rational being.'

She walked to the door and opened it, passed the darkened pantry, walked through the little room where Mrs Tatum must once have sat, into the brightly-lit kitchen. She put on the kettle, made coffee, resisting the temptation to slurp a tablespoonful of sherry into it from the bottle still on the side. Was that how Sophy had begun? The quick, consoling nip because the house was too quiet with the children gone and John Clare working late?

She drank the coffee sitting at the kitchen-table. From here the radio in the breakfast room was only a faint, far off throbbing. When the bell tinkled sharply she looked up, saw one of the row of bells still quivering on the wall. The wires had long since been cut, Mrs Tate had told her. The bells couldn't ring. The bell *was* ringing, its tinny echo dying into the silence again.

The tiny hairs along her forearms were standing up. A faint dampness had sprung about her hairline. Her legs felt heavy, anchored to the tiled floor. When the front doorbell sounded she let out a gasp, movement returning to her. Perhaps when the doorbell rang some mechanical fault activated the indoor bells.

The front doorbell sounded again. Jessica stood up, walked steadily to the front, raising her voice.

'Yes? Who's there?'

'I forgot my key,' came Sophy's voice.

Jessica put up her hand to unfasten the chain and saw there was no need. The short chain hung loose at the side. She had secured it when Sophy and Linda had gone out. She knew, beyond any shadow of doubt, that she had secured it.

'The police weren't very helpful,' Sophy said, coming in. Jessica stepped back, hearing the other talking, trying not to think of herself eating her dinner in the breakfast-room while someone crept across the hall, undid the chain, let themselves out into the darkness.

'If I don't eat I shall faint,' Sophy said, going past her. 'Well, I cannot imagine where Mrs Tate has got to. She hasn't had an accident and the police thought quite sensibly that she may have gone off to see a friend. I know that Linda swears she hasn't any but who knows? Mrs Tate may have a colourful private life she doesn't let her daughter know about.'

'Do you think that's likely?' Jessica found voice to say.

'Frankly I think it's highly unlikely,' Sophy said, laughing. 'Anyway, I told Linda that she must telephone if her mother came back tonight and in the morning, if there still isn't any news, she must go back to the police. Now I must eat – no, don't go. Have some coffee with me.'

'Thanks.' Jessica poured herself another cup and trailed behind Sophy into the breakfast-room where the radio was still playing.

'That sounds nice and cheerful,' Sophy said, putting her tray on the low table. 'John will be terribly late, so it's nice to have company. Did you find anything interesting in the shed?'

'Newspapers that don't relate to the period I'm researching, some old photographs – those bells are disconnected, aren't they?'

'Ages ago, when we first moved in. We kept them there as a souvenir of more prosperous times. Why do you ask?' Her voice had sharpened suddenly, the good humour fading from her face.

'I was just thinking how pleasant it would be to have a whole staff of servants ready to answer one's summons,' Jessica said.

Now wasn't the moment to talk about the bell that had rung, the chain that had undone itself. Sophy Clare's equilibrium wasn't steady at the best of times, but the changed tone of her voice had told Jessica what she wanted to know. The older woman had also heard the disconnected bells ring out for servants long since dead.

'Not so wonderful for the servants,' Sophy said, her face relaxing.

'I suppose not.' Jessica drank her coffee, feeling her inner chill ebbing.

'Have you met anyone apart from us yet?' Sophy was asking.

'A man called Adam Darby. He's an advertising artist.'

'Oh, that's good.' Sophy sounded pleased. 'I hope you'll feel free to bring your friends here. What this house needs is more life, more young people.'

'He's just a friend,' Jessica said. 'As a matter of fact I'm going out with him tomorrow night, so I hope –' she hesitated.

'Oh, John will be home tomorrow evening, I'm sure,' Sophy said. 'Well, I think I'd better play safe and wash up in case Mrs Tate doesn't turn up in the morning. I do hope Linda telephones. She isn't the brightest of girls but her mother is a treasure. No, I don't need any help. I shall clear away and then do some knitting, I think. The house is so much more friendly than when I'm here by myself.'

'If it's all right with you I'll have an early night,' Jessica said.

'Heavens, I shall be fine,' Sophy assured her. 'John fusses a great deal about my "nerves", as he puts it, but he always did worry. No, I shall be fine.'

Jessica went upstairs. She wouldn't think about Mrs Tate or the bell that had rung when it shouldn't have rung or the chain on the door that ought not to have been unfastened. She wouldn't think about any of them. She made a face at herself in the mirror as she shifted the chair until its back was wedged securely under the door handle, but she left it there.

Much later, she woke briefly, as a door opened and closed in the hall below. That was John Clare, she thought sleepily, arriving home from work. No doubt Sophy would tell him about Mrs Tate. She snuggled down into the blankets and slept again.

In the morning the chair still wedged under the door handle looked foolish. She pulled it loose and set it in place and dressed quickly, surprised when she looked at her watch to see that it was past nine o'clock. Despite the early night and the fears that had preceded it she had slept dreamlessly.

When she walked into the kitchen she was greeted immediately by Sophy who, standing at the cooker, indicated the police officer seated at the table with a cup of coffee before him.

'Jessica, this is Sergeant Penton. He's here to make a few enquiries. Sit down. I'm just making coffee.'

'Mrs Tate hasn't turned up?'

Jessica sat down at the table, the anxieties of the moment folding her round.

'It seems not,' Sophy said.

'You're –?' Sergeant Penton gave her a look that managed to be both enquiring and avuncular.

'Jessica Cameron. I'm lodging here for about three months.'

'Ah, yes, Mrs Clare told me. Doing a research project or something?'

'Historical research for a museum project. I've only been here a few days.'

'Then you knew Mrs Tate?'

'I met her, yes. She's very nice.'

'And you saw her yesterday?'

'Yesterday morning, yes. She was washing the dishes and clearing the kitchen.'

'Did she say anything in particular?' he asked.

'Only that she wanted to get finished quickly because she wanted to leave early. Her daughter had had a tooth out and wasn't feeling too good. I was bringing in piles of old newspapers from the garden shed so I passed her several times. Then I went upstairs and spent the morning sorting them and piling them. I came down at – around 12.30 and she'd already left. I made myself a snack and then I went down to the university library and didn't get back until later.'

'She must have left the house,' Sophy interposed. 'Her coat and scarf are gone from the hall cupboard where she always put them.'

'You didn't hear her leave?' He looked at Jessica.

'Not a sound. Of course I was concentrating and not listening for anything. Oh, she had left the back door unlocked – I felt a bit irritated about that because I was by myself in the house.'

'Was the door actually unlocked?' Sophy looked surprised.

'I locked it myself when I went out,' Jessica told her.

'Mrs Tate always locked up after herself,' Sophy said. 'She was very security conscious. She was forever putting up the chain on the front door.'

'Perhaps she was called away suddenly?' Jessica said doubtfully.

'You say her coat and scarf were gone?' Sergeant Penton looked at Sophy. Sophy nodded.

'Then if she had time to put those on she had time to lock the back door,' he said. 'I take it you've had a good look round the house? She couldn't have had a fall?'

'I went all over the place last night, after my husband came home,' Sophy said. 'If you want to take a look round –?'

'That won't be necessary. How did she come and go? Bike? Bus?'

'She catches the bus from the end of the road,' Sophy said. 'Usually if she's working here late, John, my husband, gives her a lift into town.'

'Her daughter gave us a full description and a snapshot,' the sergeant said. 'You recall the colour of her coat?'

'Dark – navy, I think, and a flowered headsquare – red flowers, I think.'

'That fits with what her daughter says. Well, I'd better get back to the station and put out an all-points call. Someone may have noticed her on the bus.'

'I'll see you out,' Sophy said. 'Will you want to talk to my husband? He was working until quite late last evening and he had to go out again this morning.'

'I doubt if that'll be necessary. You'll inform us if she turns up?'

'Yes, of course.'

They went out through the back door. Jessica poured herself a cup of coffee. Perhaps she ought to have mentioned that the chain on the front door had been undone but she had no proof, not even a real, inner certainty, that she had fastened it when Sophy and Linda went out.

'Well, that seems to be all anyone can do for the moment,' Sophy said, returning. 'I certainly hope she turns up.'

'Yes. It must be worrying for Linda,' Jessica said.

The sharp ring of the telephone shrilled from the hall.

'Let's hope that's Mrs Tate,' Sophy said, hurrying out.

Jessica finished her coffee, debated on whether or not to make some toast, decided against it. Sophy came back in, her voice high and brittle as she said, 'Such a nuisance! John has a luncheon to attend and my presence is required. It may go on for quite a long time. I must drag out my glad rags.'

'I want to sort through the newspapers,' Jessica said. 'I'll put them back later.'

'Oh, there's no need to do that,' Sophy said. 'We've been

meaning to clear all the rubbish out of the shed for ages. Put what you don't need in a couple of bin liners and John will carry them down for the refuse collection. I'll see you later. Oh, if he'd told me sooner I could have gone to the beauty parlour.'

'Have a nice luncheon,' Jessica said.

She washed up the cups, wiped over the table. Perhaps she'd give herself a bit of a beauty session, wash her hair, stick on a face mask she'd put into her case at the last minute and make herself glamorous for the evening date.

'I'm off. See you later.'

Perhaps Sophy had decided to spend the morning in the beauty parlour anyway, since she certainly wasn't dressed for a formal luncheon. Indeed she looked strained and tense. Probably she was one of those women who find business lunches an ordeal.

When she had gone Jessica locked and bolted the back door and flew to the hall to check the door chain was in place. If anyone wanted to enter The Cedars they would have to ring the bell.

Sophy had told the sergeant that she and her husband had looked all over the house. It would do no harm to have another look round, Jessica told herself, trying not to feel like a nervous spinster looking under the bed last thing at night. This was broad daylight on a Saturday morning. When she looked through the front window in the sitting-room she could see a couple of children on bikes ride past the front gate. The sitting-room itself had that vaguely abandoned air when the cushions haven't been plumped up. She plumped them up and went across the hall to look in at the breakfast-room and dining-room.

She hadn't yet been into the room behind the sitting-room. The door was closed and she half expected to find it locked but it opened easily and she stepped into a bare room with nothing but a carpet on the floor and ground length french windows with heavy drapes. When she pulled back the drapes she saw the windows were firmly bolted. They opened on to the terrace where in the summer it would be pleasant to sit out. Below the terrace stretched the tangled garden.

No Mrs Tate downstairs for sure. Beginning to feel foolish Jessica went up the stairs and opened the doors on the upper landing. Everything was neat, bare of ornaments. She crossed the floor in the Clares' bedroom and opened the wardrobe door to be met by a long row of garments hung innocently on padded hangers.

Nothing there and she was being overly inquisitive! Mrs Tate had left the house in a bit of a hurry, neglecting to call goodbye or lock the back door. She wasn't here.

She went into the spare room where the piles of newspapers waited, sat cross-legged on the floor and began reading her way through them, skimming through dried and yellowing pages that told her a great deal about the progress of the First World War but nothing about the period she was researching.

If she went on reading, filling her mind with useless information, she could hold at bay the necessity to think more deeply about what was going on.

'Nothing is going on!' She slammed down the paper she was reading, raising her head, addressing the empty room. Only the faint echo of her own voice, the almost imperceptible shivering of the air answered her.

Adam Darby was calling for her. They would spend the evening at a club and he would probably kiss her goodnight at the end of it. Perhaps he would want to sleep with her. No, he was more subtle than that, she reckoned. He would establish a friendship before trying to turn the relationship into anything more.

She went down to the kitchen, found two large black bin liners, took them upstairs and stuffed the newspapers into them. Dragging them downstairs, unlocking the back door, she deposited the bulging bags in the yard, relocked the door, washed her hands, made salad, buttered bread, brewed tea, felt practical and in command of each small task.

When the telephone rang she hurried to answer it.

'Jessica? Sophy Clare here. Has there been any word of Mrs Tate?' Her landlady sounded as if she were slightly breathless.

'No, nothing at all,' Jessica said.

'We'll be later than I thought,' Sophy said. 'We've been invited out for dinner – old friends. When you go out will you be sure to lock up?'

'Yes, I promise. Have a nice time.'

'You too. Oh, and Jessica –'

'Yes?'

'The young man you're meeting – do please feel free to invite him in for coffee, especially if we haven't returned when you get back. The house can be quite lonely when one is alone in it.' Her voice tinkled with laughter.

'That's very kind of you,' Jessica said.

'And if we're not back leave the bolt off the back door. Just lock it. 'Bye.' She rang off, leaving a trace of imminent hysteria in the air.

Jessica put the receiver down slowly and went into the kitchen to finish her lunch. She would invite Adam back for coffee only if they got on well during the evening. The notion of asking him back simply because she might be entering an empty house made her feel ridiculous.

The front doorbell chimed. Jessica rose again, went through to the front door, beginning to feel like a harassed housewife with no time to call her own.

'Yes?' She opened the door on the chain, saw the uniform and felt an anticipatory thrill of relief as she loosed the chain and opened the door more widely.

'Would Mrs Clare be in, Miss Cameron?' he asked.

'I'm afraid not. She's out for lunch and dinner with her husband,' Jessica said. 'Would you like to come in?'

'Just for a few minutes.' He stepped inside, looking round with a lively interest that struck her as more than professional. 'They knew how to build houses in the last century. You can't get workmanship like that nowadays.'

'Are you interested in old buildings, Sergeant Penton?'

'I like things that are solid and sturdy and don't fall down in the first gale. Mrs Clare's out today, you say? Sensible of you to keep the chain on the door. There's a right lot of rogues running about these days, making out they've come to read the gas meter and I don't know what else.'

'Would you like a cup of tea?' Jessica offered.

'No, thanks, Miss. I'm awash with tea already. My wife isn't happy unless I get two or three cups of it under my belt after lunch. I just popped in to let you know that we've made some progress on the Mrs Tate affair.'

'She's turned up?' Jessica led the way into the sitting-room and turned to face him.

'Not yet, but there have been, as we say, developments. She was seen on the bus yesterday morning. At least a woman answering her general description was noticed. A couple of separate witnesses came forward.'

'You've posted her missing then?'

'In most cases we do wait twenty-four hours,' he explained, 'but Linda Tate was so insistent that her mother wouldn't just go off without saying anything, that we thought it as well to issue a general description. Two passengers on the bus came forward independently. They didn't know her personally but at that time of day there aren't many people on the bus.'

Jessica heaved a small sigh of relief and sat down on the edge of an armchair.

'So she did leave and go into town,' she said.

'It certainly looks like it. However she got off a stop before her usual one and went into a supermarket. We've made enquiries there but so far nobody seems to have seen her.'

'Does her daughter know?'

'Oh yes, we went round at once to tell her. I'm a bit sorry for the kid. She's only sixteen and there aren't any other relatives. Mind you, Wilson Street is one of those back to back areas where everybody knows everybody else's business, but the Tates do seem to have kept themselves to themselves ever since Mr Tate died. He was a drunk, seemingly.'

'I'll tell Mrs Clare. She'll want to do what she can to help,' Jessica assured him.

'She seems like a nice lady,' said Sergeant Penton. 'Well, I'd better get on. She'll probably turn up. Might have met an old boyfriend or something. I don't suppose she tells her daughter everything. Remember to fasten the chain again.'

When he had gone the house was sunlit and silent again.

Eight

Towards evening the wind rose, bringing in its wake a spatter of rain. Jessica had been strongly tempted to walk over to the local library where the amiable Nettie would be but in the end she had stuck to her original resolve, taking a long, leisurely bath, applying a totally unnecessary face pack, washing her hair, manicuring finger and toe-nails, slipping on a narrow skirted woollen dress in a shade of yellow that made her skin creamy. Snapping a wide belt with copper medallions on it round her waist she was pleased with her reflection in the mirror. She looked smart and modern, a young woman preparing to go out on a date, not someone haunted by a past event that seemed curiously to be linked to the present in a way she sensed rather than reasoned out.

She made herself a salad sandwich and drank a glass of milk, unsure if the evening would include food or not, unwilling to risk a grumbling stomach.

When she came out into the main hall darkness had crept into its corners. She switched on the main light and went into the sitting-room. The television stared at her blankly, waiting to be activated. Was that why John Clare watched with such intensity? Because it provided sound and movement in a house that was too large and too quiet?

Sophy Clare had said they were going out for a business lunch and then out to dinner with friends. It was the first time she had mentioned their having friends. On the other hand there was no reason why she should have felt obliged to lay out all the details of her life for a lodger.

When the front doorbell rang she hurried to open the door, loosing the chain as Adam Darby called from outside the door,

'Jessica, it's me, Adam.'

'How did you know I was the one who'd answer the door?' she demanded.

'I saw you in the window a minute ago. Where is everybody?'

'The Clares are out until late tonight.'

'You've been on your own all day? Why didn't you come round to my place and let me know?'

'Because I've been busy,' Jessica said. 'I don't have to have someone holding my hand the moment I find myself alone in a house, you know.'

'Tough gal, eh?' He gave her the cheerful grin that was already becoming pleasingly familiar.

'Not really. Something's happened as a matter of fact.'

'Yes?' Walking with her into the sitting-room he looked an enquiry.

'Mrs Tate – the daily woman left here yesterday morning and never got home.' She paused as Adam whistled softly through his teeth.

'You see the connection?'

'With the disappearance of the governess and the little girl? It's a natural connection to make on the spur of the moment, I suppose – OK, I just made it, but coincidence surely? What happened?'

'Apparently Mrs Tate left here yesterday morning – I was in at the time but I was upstairs and didn't hear her leave. She left the back door unlocked which is very unusual because she's extremely security conscious. Anyway last evening her daughter, Linda, came round to say her mother hadn't come home and she was worried. So Mrs Clare went with her to the police.'

'Wasn't that a bit premature?'

'Linda says they don't mix with the neighbours and there isn't anywhere her mother would have gone without letting her know,' Jessica explained. 'Round lunchtime the policeman came over and said Mrs Tate had been seen on the local bus that goes into town. She got off outside a supermarket, went inside and that is as far as she's been traced.'

'Where are the Clares?'

'Mr Clare went out first thing this morning to a meeting. Mrs Clare went out later to join him for a business lunch and phoned me up during the day to say they were going on to have dinner with friends.'

'Leaving you by yourself?' He frowned.

'Sophy – Mrs Clare knows I had a date tonight and there's no reason why they should feel obliged to sit at home with me just because the daily woman has done a flit.'

'Do the Clares know about the Makin mystery? The governess vanishing, I mean?'

'They haven't mentioned it. Probably not.'

'Well, for the time being let's regard it as an odd coincidence.' His tone was rallying. 'I've my car outside but you might need a coat.'

'I've a stole.' Taking it up, draping it over her shoulders, she was pleased by the flash of admiration in his eyes.

'Let me check the lock on the back door.' Hurrying through she was pleased when he followed. There was something protective in his attitude that warmed her more than the stole.

'I'd better leave the bolt off the back door and just leave it key-locked in case the Clares can't get in if they arrive home early after all. What do you think of the house?'

'Solidly built, seems bigger than it really is.'

'It isn't completely furnished.'

'That probably explains it then. Even so it does seem curiously empty, as if real life never really went on here. No personal bits and pieces around.'

'I suppose it was more cluttered up when the children were small –' She broke off as they went back into the hall.

Children, even when they were grown up, left clutter behind them – cricket bats, books, photographs. There were the two rusting bikes in the shed and the burst football, but in the house itself there was nothing to suggest that two children had ever lived there. No photographs, no souvenirs of their teenage years. Nothing.

'Something you forgot?' Adam was looking at her.

'I think I'll draw the sitting-room curtains closed and leave the light on there and in the hall,' Jessica said. 'Then I can leave the chain in place on the front door and we'll go out by the back.'

'Fine.' He was still looking at her.

'Adam, the Clares don't have any photographs around of their children,' she said tensely.

'Perhaps you simply haven't seen them.'

'Well, they don't have any on show. Obviously I've not rooted through their drawers. No, what I mean is there's nothing around to suggest that they ever lived here.'

'How long have the Clares been living here?'

'Fifteen years, Mr Clare said. He and Sophy look to be in their forties – it's hard to tell. Julian and Robina work as social workers – or maybe they're still training. The Clares hardly ever mention them. When I first arrived Mr Clare mentioned the garden was nice for the children to play in and I got the impression that they were still young, until he mentioned they had left home. I don't know – it's as if something doesn't fit.'

'Is there nothing of the children here?'

'A couple of old bikes and a burst football in the garden shed.'

'Well, there you are then! Not every parent clings on to the first baby shoe.'

'And it's silly to invent mysteries where there aren't any? You're right. Shall we go?'

She unlocked the kitchen door, let Adam pass through, switched off the light, fumbled the key in the lock at the other side, her eyes adjusting to the gloom.

'Everything secure?' Adam asked.

'Everything secure. We can walk round the side of the house. Watch out for the step up to the terrace.'

'Perhaps I'd better hold your hand,' Adam said slyly, possessing himself of it.

Yielding, she was conscious of warmth, of stability at variance with his casual manner.

'Which window is yours?' They had gained the terrace and he paused, shifting his grip on her hand.

'It overlooks the yard. Why?'

'I may serenade you with guitar,' he said.

'Don't threaten.' Jessica laughed, and they walked on down the side to the road where a car was parked.

'Have you eaten anything?' he asked as they got in.

'Only a bit of salad.'

Fastening her seat belt she glanced towards the house, seeing the faint glow of light behind the thick curtains at the sitting-room windows.

'Then you can manage a cheese omelette and a glass of white wine before we go on to the club.'

'What? Oh, yes, lovely.' She pulled her eyes away from the dark silhouette of the building as he started the engine.

'I suggest that we have a relaxing meal, tell each other our childhood adventures and then listen to some music,' Adam said.

'And stop worrying about what might be going on at The Cedars? Sorry, I suspect that I'm getting to be a bore.'

'Actually, I'm as intrigued as you are,' he said. 'However I do feel that if we drop the subject for a couple of hours we might come back to it with a fresh perspective. Agreed?'

'Agreed.' She felt something like a weight slide away.

An hour later, sipping the last of her wine, the omelette neatly filling any spaces inside her, she smiled across the table at her companion.

'That was good, just what I needed. Tell me more about your painting. You aren't going to stay in advertising?'

'Advertising pays me what I need to survive during the periods when I spend time doing my own thing,' he said. 'And it's not an easy field to get into. But you're right, of course. I do want to specialize in portraiture eventually.'

'Picasso style?'

'No, more representational.' He frowned slightly, linking his fingers together. 'I've a yen for the old style – Holbein, Van Dyck – portraits that people will look at in a hundred years time and say, "I know what kind of person he or she was". You know what I mean?'

'To catch the inner self as well as the outer lineaments?'

'Something like that. Sounds pretentious, doesn't it? What about you?'

'I like what I do,' Jessica said simply. 'Finding out about bits of the past, fitting them into a coherent pattern. It's interesting and then when the current exhibition's complete it's satisfying to watch people walking round, marvelling at the bits and pieces they didn't know about. Living history.'

'Shall we come back to the present and make tracks for the club? You have that remembering look on your face.'

'Remembering?' Jessica looked at him sharply. 'What makes you say that?'

'I don't know. The words just came out.'

'Do you believe in reincarnation?' Jessica asked abruptly.

'Naturally. Mind you, when I was Holbein I did rather better than I'm doing now. I got several royal commissions.'

'Be serious! Do you think it's feasible that we come back over and over, meeting the same situations until we get it right?'

'There's also the theory of race memory. And if we all come back then what are ghosts, so-called?'

'Memory traces on the air? People who want to get something right and believe they can do it better by staying on the other side? I don't know.'

'Let's have some coffee. We can listen to the music later.' He signalled the waitress.

'I'm sorry. We agreed not to talk about it,' Jessica said.

'No, I feel like talking about it,' Adam said. 'It's an unusual situation and it won't hurt to kick around a few theories. Not that I know much about it. Presumably if a situation from a previous life needs to be resolved the same group of people have to be reborn together all in a bunch.'

'Or come together at some particular time in order to – to activate things?'

'Right,' said Adam, leaning back as the waitress brought coffee. 'Now back in eighteen – when was it?'

'1859.'

'Back then Edward Makin and his wife –'

'Amelia.'

'Amelia – they lived at The Cedars with their two children, Julia and Robert. They employed a cook-housekeeper called Mrs Tatum and a servant called Polly. Then they engaged a governess, Dorothy Larue, to look after Julia. One autumn day governess and pupil went for a walk and disappeared. Shortly after that the Makins went abroad with their son and sold the house. They all eventually died abroad. That was then.'

'And now we have John and Sophy Clare,' Jessica said, 'with two children called Julian and Robina and a daily woman called Mrs Tate who also disappears. I know the parallels aren't exact but the pattern is almost the same. You don't agree?'

'I think that we're stretching coincidence very thin. I take it that the house didn't look familiar to you when you arrived? You didn't recognize anybody?'

Jessica shook her head.

'It's only that now and then – it's like I feel a kind of echo,' she said uncertainly.

'And you have been hearing things.'

'Also seeing them,' Jessica admitted. 'I didn't realize it at the time, as I thought the person I was seeing was Linda. Linda Tate, I mean. When I first arrived there was a young girl hanging out washing on the line in the yard. I saw her from my bedroom, and when I was going to my car – I wanted to collect my luggage from the hotel – she was looking out through the sitting-room window. Mrs Tate had mentioned that her daughter helped out sometimes and I just assumed –'

'But surely someone from 1859 would be dressed differently?'

'You mean in a crinoline and bonnet? A lady might, but a servant girl would wear an ankle-length skirt and a top, wouldn't she? Plenty of people wear that kind of thing nowadays. I honestly didn't take particular notice of what she was wearing. And then I was looking through the books up in the spare room and she came in – she said something like "I'm sorry, Miss" and went out at once. I hardly looked up at her for more than a couple of seconds and I didn't think anything more about it until I met Linda.'

'Who doesn't look like the girl you saw?'

'Not a bit.'

'And you haven't seen the first girl since?'

Jessica shook her head. 'Not a sign of her.'

'And you think it was Polly – why? It could have been anyone.'

'I suppose so, but I found that slip of paper in between the pages of the Mrs Beeton cookbook – "My name is Polly Winter". Anyway I have a feeling –'

'Which you can't prove.'

'No,' Jessica said reluctantly. 'No, I can't prove it at all.'

'Let's assume for the moment that the girl you saw was Polly,' Adam said. 'If she's wandering around as a ghost then she obviously hasn't been reborn.'

'Probably not.'

'So what about the others?' he asked. 'Is John Clare anything like Edward Makin? From what you know of Edward Makin, that is?'

'Not a bit,' she admitted. 'From everything I've been able to find out, the Reverend Edward Makin was rather a prim, pompous man with a mother complex. Mr Clare is a businessman – he arranges conferences, dinners, things like that. He's never mentioned his mother and he seems very pleasant, very easy going.'

'And Mrs Clare?'

'She's the nervous type,' Jessica said slowly. 'She's rather apt to fly to the sherry bottle at the least excuse. She definitely doesn't like being alone in the house. Amelia Makin evidently took laudanum sometimes but that needn't mean much because laudanum was used quite freely in Victorian times. It's a derivative of opium and people used to give drops to teething babies.'

'And you haven't found any photographs of the Makins?'

'Only of the Laurences who took the house after the Makins left, but there was one of Mrs Tatum as part of the Laurence family so she evidently stayed on to work for them.'

'Did she look like Mrs Tate?'

'Hard to say. In old photographs the focus wasn't always very sharp and servants pinned their hair back and didn't define their features with make-up.'

'And it wasn't Mrs Tatum who disappeared anyway.'

'When we start analysing it then it doesn't seem very likely, does it?' Jessica said.

'Unless everybody changes places the next time round,' Adam said.

'And perhaps it is all coincidence. Let's forget about it for a while. Didn't you say something about listening to music?'

'Moody blues at the Rainbow Club. Let's go.' He sounded faintly relieved as if the subject had begun to gnaw at him.

'Moody blues sounds good,' Jessica said. She pushed the Makins into the back of her mind again and rose.

'Shall we walk and pick up the car later?' Adam asked when they were outside. The rain was holding off and there was an almost country freshness in the air.

Jessica nodded, taking his arm, cuddling her stole about her as they walked along the street. People hurrying to the late-open supermarket, couples strolling arm in arm like themselves, new tower blocks rising above the old Victorian buildings that straddled the skyline.

'What is the Rainbow Club?' Jessica enquired. 'I heard of the Cavern.'

'Where the Beatles started. Funny how the sixties is looked back on now as a kind of golden age. The Rainbow's a fairly new club, a bit up-market but with an atmosphere that's a rather happy mixture of funky and traditional. I've only been there a couple of times. Here we are.'

The outside looked unprepossessing, the Victorian façade with its mock-Gothic embellishments giving it the aspect of a gentlemen's club or a small public library. Within, the theme changed, as they signed their names and descended into a series of basement rooms which looked as if Emily Post had got together with Annie Hall to produce an interior which mixed up faded William Morris wallpaper and spiky chandeliers with thick glass blocks supported on slender columns of steel. On a dais a group of musicians played softly and the rooms opened into a small dance floor where a few couples were swaying.

'May I get you a drink?' A hostess in what looked like a silver leotard with a cascade of feathers on her head had approached them.

'Just tomato juice,' Jessica said firmly. 'You go ahead and I'll drive us back.'

'A whisky and soda then. Thanks.' Adam guided her to a sofa that was more comfortable than it looked.

'What do you think?' Adam glanced at her.

'It has a certain charm,' Jessica admitted. 'The truth is that I haven't much to compare it with.'

'You mean you don't spend all your time in London rushing around night-clubs?'

'Not often,' Jessica said with a grin, letting her stole slip off her shoulders. It was pleasantly warm here with a faintly musky scent on the air. She wondered if anyone was smoking hash.

'And I took you for a sophisticate.'

'No, you didn't, so stop teasing. This all looks rather exclusive. I'm flattered that you brought me here.'

'Only the best for the best.' He raised the glass the space-age hostess had just given him in a smiling tribute.

'Flattery,' Jessica told him, 'will get you almost anywh –'

'What is it?' Adam looked at her.

'A draught coming from somewhere.' She put down her own drink on the slab of glass before them and pulled up her stole.

The little hairs at the back of her neck were quivering. The tomato juice was thick in her throat.

'I think they have extractor fans to waft away any smoke. You're probably near one. Want to change places?'

'I beg your pardon?'

'I said,' he repeated patiently, 'do you want to change places? Jessica, what's the matter?'

'Nothing. Tiredness just caught up with me, I guess. Let's listen to the music. Nice to have live music for a change.'

The child stood at a little distance, her eyes fixed on Jessica with a look that was a curious mixture of defiance and pleading. Defiant about what? Pleading for what? The pink dress was slipping off her thin bare shoulders. Jessica could see the childish collar bones, sharply angular like the wings of a young bird. The brown hair was elaborately curled, long ringlets hanging in bunches at each side of a small, heart-shaped face, with eyes outlined in black and a pouting mouth painted a deep blood-red.

This was a real child. This was a solid form with clear outlines, the flat bust rising and falling as if the child were breathing hard, the sparrow-twig ankles revealed between the frilled hem of the dress and the high-heeled shoes. She held out the sides of her dress with small, thin hands as if she were about to execute a curtsy. She shifted slightly from one foot to the other as if she were still unaccustomed to high heels.

Adam was saying something. She could hear his words as a series of separate phrases, each phrase distinct but meaningless.

'I'm sorry.' She turned her head, focusing on his face.

'I was asking you if you wanted to dance,' Adam said.

'Oh, not yet. I like sitting here, just listening to the music,' Jessica said with desperate brightness.

'What were you staring at?' He was too perceptive to be deceived, she realized.

'Nothing, I –' As if her head were attached to some string she turned it away from him, expecting empty space, seeing instead the fast breathing figure still standing there, holding out the flounced skirts of the pink dress.

'The child,' she said, in a voice that scarcely reached a whisper. 'The child in the pink dress is here.'

'Where?'

To her immense relief he sounded interested, not dismissive.

'A couple of yards off. Adam, I'm so cold.'

'What is she doing?'

'Nothing. Just standing there. Looking at me.'

'Ask her what she wants,' he suggested.

'I can't.'

A kind of horror was creeping over her. The child was out of place, out of time. Her presence was – wrong. It denied the logical progression of the years. It mocked normality.

In her mind Jessica spoke firmly and fiercely, 'You don't belong here. Go away.'

And the child went, twitching into nothingness, leaving only a little shivering on the air.

Polly's Tale

Now why did she do that? Why did she send me away? Maybe she thought I'd nab her masher. Fat chance with that one. He don't look as if he fancied young meat. Nice looking but not a toff. Looks like he enjoys his fun straight. Come to the wrong place, hasn't he? I mean straight is cheap and Madam has to make her profits.

She's new is Dot. Come up from London. Speaks ever so nicely

and says her papa was French. Well, that's not likely to be true. I
mean if her dad was a Frenchie she'd be over in Paris, wouldn't
she? But she does know some French and she's ever so polite. It's
all 'Would you mind if –?' and 'I do beg your pardon –' Ladylike.
Funny but when she said she was new to all this and only started
because she couldn't get on with her stepmother I believed her.
She sure as hell wasn't brought up to it like me. There's still a kind
of cleanness in her face. I reckon she don't do specialities yet.

'What I would really like to do is be a governess,' she tells me
when I take her up a cup of tea in the morning. 'A real governess.
But when Papa took a second wife he began spending his money on
her and my own education was sadly neglected. However I am sure
that I could contrive to look after a small child.'

I didn't like to ask her if she felt like that why she didn't just go
and do it instead of coming to Madam's, but the money here ain't
bad. A lot of the girls here get caught that way. They tell
themselves they're doing it temporary, but they don't often get out.
I wish I could get out sometimes, grow up all respectable. Fat
chance of that too. But Dot might do it yet. She's new to it and her
face is still clean. I wonder why she told me to go away just now.
She ain't usually so sharp.

Nine

Jessica drew a long shivering breath.

'She's gone.' The two words came out shakily.

'Look, it isn't possible that you – don't jump down my throat –
imagine her?' Adam said.

'Not unless I'm going crazy and starting to hallucinate,' Jessica
said tensely, 'and I don't feel as if I'm going crazy, but that might
be a sign that I am, I suppose.'

'You don't strike me as a crazy lady,' Adam said. He spoke
judiciously, not smiling, and she felt a small surge of relief.

'Then Polly – I'm sure that it is Polly – is appearing to me from
time to time. Adam, how are ghosts supposed to behave? I mean,

don't they usually appear where they were when they were alive? Especially if they're no more than a kind of memory trace on the atmosphere?'

'I'm no expert,' he said. 'Until now I'd have sworn that I didn't believe in ghosts anyway, but I'm inclined to agree with you. They are usually tied to particular fields of activity. I mean Anne Boleyn stays around the Tower of London; she doesn't float round the local Cash and Carry.'

'Then Polly must have been here at some time,' Jessica said. 'What did this place used to be? Can you find out?'

'I can ask,' Adam said. 'Maybe the manager will know. He may have seen the original plans when he took over.'

He was beckoning the waitress who came over, smiling beneath her feathers.

'Could we see the manager if he's around?' he asked.

'Is there some complaint, sir?' The space-age woman suddenly looked apprehensive.

'None at all. My friend and I were merely interested in the building. We can see it's pretty old and we wondered if it had a history.'

'I can tell you that myself,' the waitress said, her expression relaxing.

'Oh?' Jessica looked at her with sharpened interest.

'I used to like history at school,' the other said. 'Even thought of teaching it at one time but teaching it is all dates and acts of Parliament, not the interesting bits about people.'

'Sit down and have a drink with us,' Adam interposed.

'Thanks very much. Shall I bring three?'

'By all means.' As she moved off Adam glanced at Jessica. 'You don't mind? She is probably expected to sit with the customers.'

'Would you like me to make myself scarce?' Jessica teased.

'She's not my type.' He broke off as the other returned.

'Same as before and a shandy for me. There's no nonsense about ordering champagne and getting coloured water here,' the waitress said, setting down the tray and pulling up a backless cube masquerading as a chair. 'My name's Astrid.'

'I bet it isn't,' Adam said.

'Actually it's Sharon. Nerdish, isn't it? Anyway, what were you wanting to know about the Rainbow?'

'Something about the history of the building. My friend – oh, sorry, this is Jessica Cameron and I'm Adam Darby, by the way –'

'I've seen you here once or twice before.'

'It's a nice place – good music.'

'And not too loud. Mr Cheyney – he's the manager – he's very keen on what he calls ambience. Soothing music that's never too loud to drown the talking. Anyway, Mr Cheyney was telling me about the place only the other day. He knows I'm keen on old things. You'd never guess what it used to be.'

'A brothel?' said Jessica.

Astrid/Sharon stared at her. 'Gosh, are you psychic?' she demanded.

'No, but I thought it might be,' Jessica said.

'Well, as a matter of fact it was,' the other said. 'You wouldn't think it, but the Victorian age wasn't everything it was cracked up to be. I mean the respectable gentlemen got up to all sorts you wouldn't credit. And this place used to be one of those places. It was closed down by the police in 1890-something. I think it was empty for a bit then, and then during the First World War it was a club for servicemen – a real club, no funny business. After that it was a restaurant for a bit but then it was a club again during the next war, and then it was a night-club but the owner sold out and last year it was remodelled as the Rainbow. Of course it's been redecorated lots of times but it's still the same building. Are you reporters or something?'

A faint apprehension had crept into her eyes.

'Nothing like that. Just interested,' Adam said. 'Anyway, thanks a lot. You've been a marvellous help.'

'I'd better go and see to my other tables. Glad to have helped.' She rose, the apprehension gone, and went off, head feathers swaying.

'What made you say it used to be a brothel?' Adam asked.

'The way Polly – the child was dressed,' Jessica said. She was no longer cold and her mood was approaching normal again. 'Little girls in the Victorian age didn't wear lipstick or paint their eyes. Not ordinary little girls that is. Neither did respectable women. But child prostitutes would. They would be dressed as miniature women – miniature prostitutes, that is. There was a lot of that kind of perversion in the nineteenth century, all hidden under layers of respectability when piano legs were covered up and ladies never showed their ankles.'

'Then it can't have been Polly you saw hanging out the washing. Or are we getting confused? If Polly was the maidservant she can't have been a child hooker.'

'The child in the pink dress is a year or two younger than the girl I saw in the house.'

'Was it the same person?'

Jessica closed her eyes for a moment, summoning images. 'I don't know,' she said at last. 'It might have been – something about the eyes, but unless I saw them side by side I really couldn't swear to it.'

'Which you wouldn't be able to do if they're the same person.'

'We're talking as if they're real,' she objected. 'Look, don't ghosts repeat the same actions over and over again like a record with the needle stuck?'

'I think some of them do.'

'OK then.' She frowned slightly, marshalling her thoughts. 'Let's just suppose for the sake of argument that for some reason we don't understand, certain actions, certain events leave a strong imprint on the atmosphere and can be seen or heard under certain conditions years and years later. Eventually they would fade, wouldn't they?'

'Which is why one never sees a stone-age ghost. Go on.'

'Only that if that's so the same person could leave traces of themselves at different ages in different places.'

'Did you say the girl spoke to you when she came into the spare room?'

'Where I was looking through the books? She said, "Excuse me, Miss –" or words to that effect, but that doesn't mean she was conscious of me. She might have been in the habit of going in and then excusing herself.'

'What if this figure does have a certain residue of consciousness?' Adam asked. 'What then?'

'Then she's trying to tell me something? Why me?'

'Because you're the only one who can see her?'

'Thanks for not saying "Imagine she sees her",' Jessica said wryly. 'Maybe she's around because a situation similar to the one she knew is developing.'

'But if Polly was a child hooker how did she get to be a servant girl at The Cedars?' Adam asked.

'Because Edward Makin rescued her,' Jessica said on a note of triumph.

'I thought you said he was a pompous clergyman with a feeble wife.'

'He went round sometimes, trying to persuade soiled doves, as he called them, to change their way of life. He actually mentions it in a roundabout kind of way in his deadly dull memoirs. He could have found Polly here and given her a job in his household. I don't suppose he told his wife where she came from.'

'It does seem to hang together. So where do we go from here?'

'Nowhere,' Jessica said firmly. 'What happened a hundred years ago has absolutely nothing to do with me today. I'm getting to be a bore on the subject. Would you like to ask me to dance?'

'I thought you'd never ask.' He rose, holding out his hand to her.

He danced well, holding her firmly but not too close, not intruding on her space. The music was slow and rhythmic, nobody was hustling.

'It's a lot more restful than disco dancing,' she commented as they moved to the patterns of sound. 'I didn't know there was anyone of my generation who knew how to actually hold their partners and move at the same time.'

'Traditional is coming back in.' He swung her gently into a reverse turn.

'Thank you, kind sir.' She sketched a curtsy as the music flourished to a close.

'More?'

'What time is it?'

'Just gone ten. You didn't give a time when you'd be back or anything?'

'No, but I wondered if the Clares were home.' She bit her lip, aware that the music hadn't entirely banished her anxieties. 'Look, I'm sorry if this sounds completely neurotic but if they're not home and I went back now I could have a look round just to make sure –'

'That you're not entertaining any visitors unaware? It's better if two of us check.'

'As a companion for a pleasant evening out I must be a pain in the neck, and I'm sorry,' Jessica began.

'You're nobody's pain in the neck and you've nothing to be sorry about,' Adam said. 'Come on. You can drive if it makes you feel better, but I'm cold-stone sober.'

'Then you can drive,' Jessica said. 'Not that I'm expecting to find anyone apart from the Clares at home. I locked up like Fort Knox.'

They walked out into the neon-lit street and took the short

distance to the car-park at a steady pace. Jessica had wondered if he would stop and kiss her, establish something more than friendship between them before they got into the car, but he made no move to touch her.

Only when they were in the car did he cast her a faintly mischievous glance, saying, 'I'm trying to make up my mind if you want me to try anything on with you or not.'

'I got the impression that you weren't –' She hesitated.

'Weren't interested? I'm interested. It's only that I get the distinct impression that your mind might be somewhere else if I go rushing into anything. Why don't we put it on hold until this business is cleared up? And don't try to convince me or yourself that you're just going to walk away from it all, pretend it doesn't exist.'

'All right.' Jessica shrugged and smiled. 'Yes, I am still curious. I don't know exactly where I go from here but I suppose if this sequence of events means anything at all then sooner or later I'll see Polly again.'

'The next time you do you might try talking to her, ask her what she wants,' he suggested, putting the car into gear.

'No thanks. She might answer.'

'So?'

'So then I'd know for sure she wasn't just a memory trace. I'd know she was conscious of me personally and that – it'd scare me to death, Adam.'

'I think you're selling yourself short,' Adam said casually, slightly accelerating into the road, 'but I appreciate your point.'

'If the Clares are back do you still want me to come in with you?' He glanced at her.

'Why not? In fact Mrs Clare made it plain that I was welcome to invite you in. Then you can meet them.'

'Fine. If they're not there we'll have a good look round. What, by the way, are you expecting to find?'

'Nothing. It's just for my own peace of mind.' Jessica made an impatient gesture. 'Stupid to feel this way! I've never been nervy in my life and now I'm jumping at shadows.'

'I think I'd be feeling the same way,' Adam said.

'I doubt it but it's nice of you to say so.' She sent him a grateful glance, liking the firm profile that would look craggy in later life. There was something about Adam Darby that could only be described as niceness. The word sounded dull but Adam wasn't dull. She found herself hoping that he'd stay around even though his own advertising commission was over.

They had left the town and were driving through the suburbs which became leafier as the roads widened. She felt herself tensing as they neared The Cedars and made an effort to relax, deliberately uncurling her fists, scolding herself for giving way to the odd, insistent feeling that something threatened but hadn't yet revealed itself.

'The sitting-room light's still on.' Adam nodded towards it as he drew up.

'I don't suppose the Clares would have turned it off. I'll try the front door first.'

She went up the drive and fitted her key into the lock. The front door opened an inch and was restrained by the chain.

'They're either asleep already or not home yet,' she said, closing the door again as Adam joined her.

'Do you want to go round the back?'

'I really wasn't thinking of shinning up the drainpipe.' She felt a tiny surge of light-heartedness as she answered. Adam was with her and she wasn't going alone into a large, empty house.

She led the way round to the terrace, her eyes growing accustomed to the darkness as her feet negotiated the step. The kitchen door opened to her key and she switched on the light, unable to hold back a small sigh of relief as she saw the empty room with the long table dominating the central space.

'Did you expect Polly to be sitting here?' Adam asked.

'Don't read my mind. No, of course I didn't. It was only –'

'Only what?' He took her by the shoulders, turning her gently to face him.

'Only that I was pleased to find everything here the way I left it.' Not for the world could she tell him that, as she had switched on the light, she had had in her mind's eye a brief, flashing picture of Mrs Tate, seated at the head of the table, looking at her.

'Let's have a quick look round the other rooms first,' Adam suggested. Before he let her go he bent his head and kissed her quickly and firmly on the lips. The kiss was a promise, not a fulfilment but her spirits rose as she went through into the shabby little servants' room and past the butler's pantry into the hall.

'Mrs Clare, are you home? Sophy?' She raised her voice in

question, heard its faint echo in the recesses of the gallery.

'Doesn't look as if anyone's come back yet.' Adam walked across to the sitting-room and looked in. 'No, nothing. Just the light on as you left it.'

'I'm beginning to feel silly,' Jessica confessed, opening the door of the unfurnished room behind and briefly turning on the light as she looked in.

'Don't be. Coming in alone late at night might unnerve anyone.' He went over into the small breakfast-room with the dining-room beyond.

'Nothing?' Jessica followed him.

'Not a soul. This is all rather swish, isn't it?' He was looking at the panels of silk on the walls.

'The Clares have been furnishing the house bit by bit,' she explained.

'How long have they lived here?'

'Fifteen years.'

'They took their time then,' he observed. 'You said it wasn't completely furnished.'

'I've an idea the money ran out. Perhaps John Clare works on commission or something.'

'Shall we take a look upstairs?'

'I'm certain there's nobody else here but – yes, please.'

Following him up the stairs and along the gallery to the short flight of steps that twisted to the wide upper landing she mentally crossed her fingers against the possibility of the Clares coming back to find their lodger and her boyfriend looking through the bedrooms. Inviting him in for a cup of coffee was one thing, but this ...

'All a bit impersonal, isn't it?' Adam commented, looking round the main bedroom. 'You're sure they've been here fifteen years?'

'John Clare told me and Mrs Tate mentioned she'd worked here for fourteen years. You're right though. It does look as if – as if they only stayed here. I know what you mean but I can't express it exactly.'

'As if their real lives were lived elsewhere?'

'Yes, just like that!' Jessica nodded. 'Everything neat and tidy, no mess, no photographs of their children on display. Of course they might have albums full in their drawers but we can hardly go looking through their private possessions.'

'I suppose this Julian and Robina do exist?' Adam said. 'There's no chance they're doing a Virginia Woolf, talking about invented children because they never actually ever had any?'

'I never thought of that – no, Mrs Tate mentioned them.'

'What did she say?'

'Only that they were nice, polite children. Apparently they went off to boarding-school and I got the impression that after that she didn't see much of them if anything at all. No, they obviously exist. This is the spare room along here. I was looking at the books in the bookcases when Polly came in and said "Excuse me, Miss" and went out again. I assumed she was Mrs Tate's daughter and didn't give it another thought until I actually met Linda.'

'There's nowhere for anyone to hide,' Adam said, and gave her a straight look. 'That's what you're really afraid about, isn't it? Not ghosts that nobody else can see but something else. Who?'

'When I was in the house by myself,' Jessica said, not sure whether to be glad or sorry at his quick perceptions, 'the chain was on the front door. Mrs Clare had gone out that way with Linda to report Mrs Tate's disappearance to the police and I put up the chain after them. I went into the breakfast-room to eat my share of the dinner Mrs Clare had just made, and I closed the door into the hall and switched on the radio, because the house was too quiet and – oh, I don't know. I closed the door anyway and listened to the music. When I came out into the hall again the chain was off the door.'

'And you're sure that you put it up? Yes, of course you are. Did you hear anything while you were eating your meal, apart from the radio?'

'I don't recall hearing anything. I was listening to an old track of the Rolling Stones,' Jessica said. 'If someone had actually opened and then closed the front door I think I'd have heard that. It's a fairly heavy door.'

'Then someone took the chain off very quietly, probably realized the door might make a noise when it was opened and closed and went out – the back way? Was the back door locked?'

'Locked but not bolted. I checked it myself. And I didn't make a mistake about the chain. I definitely secured it after Mrs Clare and Linda went out.'

'And you didn't mention it to Mrs Clare when she came back?' Jessica shook her head.

'She'd given Linda a ride home and she was anxious about Mrs Tate. I told myself that I'd forgotten to chain the door myself.'

'But you didn't believe it.'

'Not for one second,' Jessica said.

'And ghosts wouldn't need to unlatch chains or open doors to get from one place to another – or at least one assumes so. Then someone left the house while you thought you were here by yourself.'

'Who?' Jessica shivered slightly.

'Mrs Tate? Could she still have been here?'

'I never thought of that.' Jessica considered for a moment, then shook her head. 'Why on earth should she hide in the house for hours? Anyway she was seen on the local bus at midday that day. Sergeant Penton told me so. Honestly, Mrs Tate is the least mysterious person you could hope to meet. She's a solid Liverpool woman, down to earth, works hard, obviously adores her daughter –'

'And doesn't mix with her neighbours? You said she hadn't any friends.'

'She hinted her late husband was a drunk,' Jessica said. 'Maybe she preferred to keep herself to herself? Anyway it wasn't Mrs Tate who took the chain off the front door.'

She jumped violently as the front doorbell chimed.

'Who on earth's that?' Instinctively she had clutched at Adam.

'Why don't we go down and see?' Adam suggested.

'Yes, of course.' She went swiftly ahead of him down the stairs. From outside Sophy Clare's voice sounded loudly.

'Jessica, are you in yet?'

'Just coming!' She hurried to unclasp the chain and admit Mrs Clare with her husband behind her.

'We tried the back door but it seems to be bolted,' Sophy said, stepping inside.

'I bolted it as we came in without thinking. Sorry. Oh, this is Adam Darby. You said it would be all right if I invited –'

'Yes, of course. I'm so glad you did.' Sophy's hand was outstretched. 'How are you, Mr Darby? John and I are so pleased that Jessica has made a friend. It would be dreadfully dull for her otherwise with an old married couple. Did you have a pleasant evening?'

'Very pleasant, thank you. Did you –?'

'Oh, today's been a positive whirl,' Sophy said. 'What with the business lunch and then meeting old friends – has there been any news?'

'The sergeant came to say that she'd been seen on the local bus about midday yesterday,' Jessica said.

'On the –? Ah, then she'll probably turn up and explain everything in due course,' Sophy said brightly, tripping past them to the staircase. 'Enjoy your coffee and make sure you lock up last thing. I am absolutely exhausted. Are you coming, John?'

'Nice meeting you,' John Clare said politely and followed his wife up the stairs.

Ten

Jessica woke to the dawn chorus and lay for a few minutes savouring the pleasant feeling of knowing she had slept well and didn't need to get up yet. The return of the Clares had inhibited whatever might have happened between Adam and herself, almost as if they were disapproving parents she thought with an inward grin. In the kitchen she had made coffee and they had sat at the long table, talking in low voices though it would have been impossible for anyone to overhear unless their ear was pressed to the door.

'They seem like nice people,' Adam said. 'She's a bit over bright but she's probably that sort of woman.'

'And the house has nothing to do with it?' Jessica looked at him.

'Well, they've lived here fifteen years,' he pointed out. 'If anything had been going on for a long time they'd have moved surely.'

'She's nervous in the house when she's alone here,' Jessica argued. 'She as good as admitted that was why they take lodgers.'

'Meaning that you're not the first one?'

'The house agent mentioned the Clares were fussy about the lodgers they took, so I assumed there have been others. One, actually.'

'It might be interesting to find out if Mrs Clare was always very nervous or if this is a recent thing.'

'Or if anyone else saw or heard anything peculiar.'

'I'll have a word with the agent and see if I can find out anything. Who is he?'

Jessica told him, adding doubtfully, 'He might not reveal that kind of information.'

'I'll think of some excuse. I'm rather good at persuading people.'

'And modest with it?' Jessica gave him an amused glance.

'I suspect that's the cue for my departure,' Adam said. 'The lady is starting to see through my charm. Or do you want me to stay?'

Jessica hesitated. She wanted him to stay but she felt instinctively that their first night together ought to be an occasion of mutual delight, not an antidote to her own nervousness. His support during the evening had been a help but she needed time to probe her own feelings, to find out if what was happening around her was affecting her to the point when it would be wiser to leave.

'May I postpone but not cancel?' she said at last.

'I don't think I've ever been rejected so prettily.' Adam reached across the table and took her hand. 'And when we do get together it'll be somewhere very modern and very unshadowy. Agreed?'

'Agreed.' She let her hand rest in his for a moment, aware of strength and a delicately expressed affection that would need space to grow in an atmosphere free from strain and the burden of nebulous fears.

'Lock up after me,' he said, beginning to rise. 'Look, if anything that really frightens you happens, ring me up and I'll be down the road in two minutes flat. Here it is.'

He was scribbling the number on the back of the pad which hung with its attendant pencil by the fridge, tearing off the page, giving it to her.

'Thanks. I don't suppose that I'll need to use it but –'

'You don't have to wait until you're scared to ring me.' He pulled her gently towards him, tracing the curve of her cheek with his finger. 'It's Sunday tomorrow so I'll have to wait until Monday to go and see the agent. Are we going to spend part of the day together? Get in the car and drive out to the Wirral or somewhere for a breath of fresh air?'

'Sounds good.'

'Then if I don't see you before I'll pick you up at three. And don't worry too much. I don't think you're imagining anything and I do feel that there's something odd going on. 'Night, Jessica.'

His mouth was warm and she wanted him to stay, but the prospect of making love a few doors away from the Clares, pleasant though they were, made her stick to her original decision.

She had locked and bolted the door after him, stood for a moment in the brightly lit kitchen listening to the soft hissing of the 'fridge, feeling the house settling around her. The row of bells on the wall hung motionless. She switched off the light and walked firmly through to the hall, turning lights on and off, checked the chain was on the front door, climbed the stairs and went into her own room without even remembering that was the one place she and Adam hadn't checked earlier.

And she had slept dreamlessly as a log, waking now in the greyish light before dawn woke the rest of the world, cuddling down in the warm bed, half inclined to believe that she had been making connections between things that had no connection. What was it she had read somewhere? It is not the personality of the murderer that is important but that of the victim. The victim seeks the killer, not the other way round. She couldn't remember where she'd read it, and it was ceasing to matter because she was sliding back into sleep.

In this quarter of the town, Sunday morning retained the drowsy quality that selective childhood memory insisted it had. She showered and dressed and met Sophy Clare coming up as she started down the stairs. The older woman looked her age in the stark morning light, lines etched at mouth and eyes, a faint darkness at the roots of her hastily combed hair revealing her fairness wasn't due to unaided Nature. She had on a housecoat of the green that seemed to be her favourite shade but this morning it emphasized pallor rather than grace.

'I always take a tray up for John and myself on Sunday mornings.' She indicated the tray she was carrying. 'I'm afraid we're rather lazy by the end of the week. Do you have everything you need? If you've run out of anything then just rummage.'

'Thank you. Enjoy your lazy morning.'

Jessica went on into the kitchen. The blinds had been raised and the sun was streaming in. There was the comfortable scent of coffee and some burnt crumbs of toast around the rim of the refuse bin. Beyond the window a bell was distantly chiming. Calling the

worshippers to church, Jessica thought, putting on the still warm
kettle and getting down a cup and saucer. She couldn't remember
the last time she'd gone into a place of worship for any reason other
than research. In Victorian times churchgoing was obligatory. Not
only public worship either, she reminded herself. There would
have been morning as well as evening prayers, particularly in a
family where Papa was also a clergyman. She could picture Edward
Makin reading aloud in his sonorous voice while his wife sat – or
would she have knelt? – with the baby on her lap and little Julia at
her skirts. Mrs Tatum and Polly would have been somewhere in the
background, she supposed, probably having been up for hours,
carrying jugs of hot water, preparing the enormous nineteenth-
century breakfast that people considered necessary before they
began the day.

Where had the governess taken her place? By the wife or further
back, not quite among the two servants? Kneeling with her black
skirts spread around her and her hair demurely netted. Dorothy
Larue. Where had she come from? The absence of any
identification on the clothing she had left behind suggested she had
wanted to remain anonymous, to blur her past.

Jessica made her coffee and sat down with it at the table, stirring
it round and round thoughtfully. Dorothy Larue had vanished. If
she had gone of her own accord she would surely have taken her
belongings with her unless – it was possible they were too heavy for
her to carry, too awkward for her to get out of the house
unnoticed. She might not have wanted to be traced, so had
removed all identifying marks. But if she disliked the situation she
could have given in her notice. But she had taken the child with
her. Why? What was going on at The Cedars that made it desirable
for the child to be removed?

Jessica drank the coffee, her mind teasing at the problem. Look
at it in a different way.

Dorothy Larue didn't want her background to be known. She
had removed any indications of her past before coming – no, that
wouldn't do. Edward Makin was hardly likely to engage a
completely unknown woman as governess for his daughter.

Suppose that Dorothy Larue hadn't gone away of her own
accord. Suppose she had been lured away, had an accident, been
murdered – and the identification removed later? That pointed the
finger straight at Edward Makin. Without one shred of proof,

Jessica reminded herself. Because he wrote dull memoirs and appeared to have a mother complex was no reason to suspect him of murder.

Edward Makin was in the habit of 'rescuing' unfortunate girls who had somehow or other entered the twilight world that lay like a cancer beneath the smooth skin of Victorian respectability. Didn't prostitutes of that era – of any era – often take fanciful, foreign-sounding names? Couldn't Dolly Larue have become Dorothy? But why keep the surname at all? Why would a young woman, leaving a shady past behind her, entering into a new life retain her surname? Was she trying desperately to hang on to some part of her own personality? To keep a tiny portion of herself independent in a life where she had become merely 'the governess'. That made a curious kind of sense.

Edward Makin, Jessica reflected, seemed to make a habit of employing servants with suspect backgrounds. Polly Winter, taken out of her frilled pink dress and high-heeled shoes, her face scrubbed clean, set to do the housework in a large house that needed more domestic help than the Makins employed. Dorothy Larue, taken from the same brothel – surely not! No, she would have been taken from another one, a different town perhaps, agreeing to be 'rescued' but insisting upon retaining the surname she had bestowed upon herself.

Don't think of the killer. Consider the victim. Except there was no evidence that there had ever been any killing at all.

Jessica poured herself more coffee and sat down again, her brow furrowed. Wasn't it the victim who, superstition said, returned to demand justice? She herself had seen Polly. Why Polly? It was the governess and Julia who had gone.

Jessica pushed the half-drunk second cup of coffee aside and rose, moving her shoulders impatiently as if she were pushing off a burden. If anyone could have read her thoughts at that moment, she decided ruefully, they'd have good reason to look at her askance. She was actually feeling irritated because Dorothy Larue hadn't put in an appearance!

On a fine Sunday morning the sensible thing would be to take a leisurely stroll round the neighbourhood, but she wanted to get out of the immediate district, to drive somewhere and – she couldn't think exactly what she wanted to do but she unbolted the door and went out to the garage anyway.

The road was even sleepier than it was on a weekday. In the front driveway of a house near the traffic lights a man was washing his car, helped by a small boy who seemed to be getting most of the soapy water on himself rather than the chassis. A woman came round the side of another house and whistled to a small dog who bounded towards her. Life was blessedly dull.

She drove aimlessly into town, seeing it almost empty of crowds now, the pavements sunlit, the barred windows of jewellers' shops keeping temptation away, the neon lamps thin giants of concrete with long steel heads. The new part of town lacked warmth, needed the patina of age to give it character.

She had rolled down the side window and the breeze on her face had a freshness that was momentarily free of petrol fumes and the breathing of long-distance tankers.

She drew up at a pedestrian crossing to allow an elderly man to cross, bulky newspaper under his arm. He had a tight, lined, Liverpool face, turned briefly towards her as he acknowledged the courtesy.

'Excuse me.' She stuck her head out of the window, not knowing what she was going to say until she heard herself ask, 'Do you know Wilson Street?'

'Wilson Street?' He came towards the car. 'Yes, you're not too far from it actually. Go to the next set of lights, turn left, second right. It's one of them old back to back streets. Nothing to see there.'

He turned and went off, clutching his Sunday morning reading.

Of course there was nothing to see. Jessica started up the car again. Wilson Street was where the Tates lived – Mrs Tate and Linda. She didn't know the number but there was bound to be somebody who could tell her where they lived. Her feeling of purposelessness had vanished. She admitted to herself that she had had it in her mind to go to Wilson Street all along. Presumably Mrs Tate didn't come in to work on Sundays. Hopefully she was now at home, retailing the explanation of her disappearance to her daughter. But surely she would have telephoned and Sophy Clare hadn't mentioned – well, at least she could have a reassuring word with Linda. It couldn't be very pleasant for the girl to be stuck at home not knowing where her mother was.

Wilson Street was inordinately long and narrow, its houses festooned with television aerials, front doors painted in aggressively bright colours, the doorsteps scrubbed. Every door was closed. Slowing to a crawl Jessica abandoned her romantic vision of gossiping neighbours eager to help. Those days had probably disappeared during the fifties, she reflected, stopping as she spotted a small newsagent's.

'The Tates?' The newsagent took her money and handed over the tabloid she'd picked at random. 'That'll be number forty-seven, the other end of the street. Linda usually comes in about this time to pick up their paper but I haven't seen her yet. Are you a friend?' He gave her a sudden, sharp look of suspicion.

'I've a message for her from her mother's employer.'

'Went off somewhere a couple of days ago, didn't she? Not bad news, I hope?'

He sounded hopeful, his voice lip-licking.

'No,' Jessica said. 'I can take the paper round for Linda, if you like. I'll pay for it with mine.'

'It goes on the book. They pay every month, regular. Not like some I could name. Keep themselves to themselves. People do these days. All this new welfare business knocks private charity on the head if you ask me.'

'Yes, I'm sure. Thanks.' Jessica nodded amiably and went back to the car.

Number forty-seven had an empty house with boarded-up windows at one side of it and a narrow entry at the other side. Jessica parked the car and got out, looking at the red painted door with its shiny knocker, the side window across which flowered curtains were still drawn. It was likely that Linda had slept in, possibly after a disturbed night during which she had worried about her mother. Well, now that she was here she might as well knock.

The knocker clanged against the door plate. She waited for footsteps from within but none came. Perhaps Linda slept at the back. She went down the narrow alley and turned left into a yard with only a low brick wall to divide it from the adjoining one. The view from the windows when the curtains were drawn back would be very dull, she realized, since beyond the yard what looked like an old warehouse reared up, its windows boarded and anonymous. It was no wonder the Tates worked so willingly at The Cedars.

She went to the back door, looked in vain for a bell or knocker, then used her knuckles, rapping sharply. The door swung open under the pressure of her fist and she looked into a small kitchen,

with some dishes in the sink waiting to be washed and a frying pan
with some bacon in it on an unlit cooker.

'Linda! Linda Tate!' She raised her voice but not too stridently.
If Linda still slept she might not appreciate being yelled into
wakefulness – but she wouldn't surely have gone to bed and left the
door unlocked? These days people locked their doors. Trust
between neighbours had gone, if indeed it had ever existed.

'Linda? Are you here?'

Jessica stepped into the kitchen, its dimness sliced by the
sunlight coming through the open door, filtering through the cotton
blinds. The little house hummed with silence. Linda had
apparently slipped out.

There was a door leading into the front part of the house. Jessica
opened it and looked into a narrow hall with stairs leading up
steeply opposite the front door and another door, open this time,
on the right. Everything was narrow and neat. Mrs Tate favoured
flowery patterns and she obviously cleaned her own house as
thoroughly as the one in which she earned her living.

Jessica went into the dim front room, crossed to the window and
pulled back the curtains. Behind her the room presented a neat,
pristine aspect, the original fireplace containing a gas fire, clock
and candlesticks above, narrow shelves containing fancy china at
each side. There were two fireside chairs placed neatly at each side
of the gas fire with a coffee table between, a sofa filled one wall, its
cushions plumped up. Over the mantelshelf was a print of swans in
flight.

'Linda!'

Jessica went back into the passage and called up the stairs. If
Linda wasn't awake by now then … She went swiftly up the steep
stairs on to the slip of a landing. Tiny bathroom and a bedroom
were over the kitchen; there was a larger bedroom over the front
room. All the doors were open. The bathroom was clean but a
jumble of clothing half filled a laundry basket and the medicine
chest was crammed with tubes and jars of make-up. The back
bedroom was clearly Linda's, its carpet fitted, the curtains
patterned with leaves and matching the duvet cover on the single
bed. There were a couple of rag dolls on the dressing-table and
some school books piled on a shelf. A poster of Kylie Minogue and
Jason Donovan was sellotaped to one wall.

She stepped into the larger room, wondering what strange quirk had led Mrs Tate to cling to the room where she must have slept with her drunken husband. The carpet here was faded and the curtains thick. She pulled them back slightly as she had done downstairs and turned to look at the room with its flowery paper, faded like the carpet, its unmade double bed. The bed in the back room had been made up. She had a sad little picture in her mind of Linda coming to sleep in her mother's bed, creeping closer to childhood again. But where the devil was Linda now?

Wherever Linda was she wouldn't be too pleased to come home and find a comparative stranger up in the bedroom. Jessica's lips quirked wryly as she admitted that for someone who was entirely law abiding she did seem to be getting into the habit of snooping.

She took a step towards the door, a board creaking loudly under her foot, and froze as the wardrobe door opposite swung slowly ajar.

'A faulty catch.' She said the words aloud, testing the floorboard again by stamping her foot down harder.

The wardrobe door swung wider. Within hung a neat row of garments. Two dark skirts with flower-patterned blouses, a couple of striped overalls, a plastic mackintosh, two cotton dresses and a woollen dress with a matching jacket, a dark blue coat with a flowered red scarf tucked round the top of the hanger.

Surely Mrs Tate didn't have two dark blue coats and two identical scarves. Jessica reached in and took out the coat. Well worn with the hem recently mended in a slightly different shade of cotton, a couple of blondish hairs on the collar. Yes, it was certainly Mrs Tate's coat. And the scarf, a little crumpled, its red blossoms spraying over a grey-blue background, was surely hers too. Which meant that she had returned.

Jessica felt a great surge of relief. Whatever the reasons for her absence, no doubt they would be explained soon enough. On impulse she plunged her hand into first one and then the other pocket. Both were empty save for the folded rectangle of bus ticket with the corner clipped off. So Mrs Tate had taken the bus and vanished for a couple of days, come home again and hung up her coat. And gone out with Linda, leaving the back door open. Wearing her Sunday coat? It was feasible, Jessica decided, hanging the coat and scarf back.

She closed the door of the wardrobe and walked briskly down the stairs. She would write a quick line and leave it with the newspaper. In the front room she looked round for a pen and paper. the Tates evidently didn't write letters, since none seemed visible either in the front room or the kitchen. Well, she would leave the newspaper anyway. She put it down on the kitchen table and looked round again. Obviously they had had breakfast since there were dishes in the sink and – Jessica stepped to the cooker and looked at the frying pan with the three strips of raw bacon laid in it. Raw bacon? Then they hadn't eaten breakfast or one of them hadn't eaten breakfast. Jessica went over to the cooker and lifted up the frying pan. The strips of bacon were rock hard, curling at the edges, their fat congealed. She wondered if bacon would become so hard in the two or three hours since they would have started making breakfast.

In the sink were two cups stained with the dregs of coffee, two saucers and a plate with crumbs on. Two people had drunk coffee or one person had drunk two cups of coffee at different times. There had been cake or biscuit on the plate. No knives or forks or plate set ready for the bacon.

Jessica put down the pan again and frowned. So Linda had started making herself something to eat – and her mother had returned before she had switched on the cooker. Perhaps they'd had a cup of coffee together and then Mrs Tate had hung up her coat and scarf and put on her Sunday coat and gone out – without locking the back door, without calling in at the newsagent's to pick up the paper, without wrapping up the uncooked bacon?

Mrs Tate was a careful housekeeper. The state of this house proved that. Had she changed her coat then she would certainly have hung up the coat and scarf, and put the bacon away, and locked the back door. For a woman who was as security conscious as Mrs Tate she had become extremely careless about locking up after herself.

There was a telephone in the hall. Jessica looked at it and then shook her head. If she rang up The Cedars to enquire if Mrs Tate had called in whoever took the call would wonder what on earth she was doing here.

She went out through the back door, closed it behind her, and stood for a moment in the yard, looking across at the warehouse with its boarded windows. The Tates weren't overlooked by any neighbours. Wondering why the thought should have occurred to her she turned and went up the alley again. Her car was still parked at the kerb, being inspected now by a lanky youth who straightened up as he saw her, saying with no trace of guilty intention, 'You keep that in good nick.'

'I try to.' Jessica nodded at him. 'Are you interested in cars?'

'Not really. Bikes are my scene. Thought I'd hang around in case anyone took your wheels. There's some round here would pinch the gold out of their granny's teeth.'

'Thanks, that was nice of you.'

'Oh, we're not all juvenile delinquents,' the boy said with a grin. 'New round here, aren't you?'

'I came round to see Mrs Tate,' Jessica said.

'Linda's old lady?' The boy looked at her. 'She's done a bunk. Hadn't you heard?'

'Yes, but I assumed – you know Linda then?'

'Not to say know. She's a bit of a wimp actually. I mean I don't hang out with her or nothing like that. Her mum's a bit of a snob, works in one of the big houses out Crosby way. Anyway she never came home on Friday. I know that because Linda asked me if I'd seen her and then yesterday I saw the policeman here.'

'Mrs Tate had caught the bus into town,' Jessica said. 'Have you seen Linda since?'

'Nah!' He shook his head vigorously. 'Tell the truth but I didn't know what to say. I mean Linda's not a girlfriend or anything, and when there's police around – well, I'm law abiding, but there's no sense in pushing yourself under the coppers' noses, so to speak. Anyway I figured someone else was looking out for Linda.'

'And you haven't seen her or her mother since?'

He shook his head. 'Are you from the police?' There was a sudden, native suspicion in his face.

'No, I'm a kind of historian,' Jessica said.

'And you know Linda?'

'I'm lodging where her mother works.'

'I thought you talked a bit posh for a lady copper,' the boy said.

'I don't suppose you'd know,' Jessica said on an impulse, 'if Mrs Tate or Linda used to leave the back door unlocked when they went out?'

'Round these parts? You must be joking!' He gave a smothered laugh. 'Mrs Tate was ever so particular about locking up. Linda told me. Acted as if we was all a bunch of thieves and hooligans, which a lot of us are, mind.'

'Look, if you do see Linda or her mother would you give me a ring?' She dug into her bag and remembered she had no pencil. 'D'ye have something to write with? I'll give you the number of The Cedars. Ask for Miss Cameron.'

'What's the number then?' He fished a biro out of the pocket of his anorak and a cigarette packet.

Jessica gave it to him, adding, 'It's Jessica Cameron, by the way.'

'Darren Parks. Pleased to meet you,' he said belatedly.

'Happy to meet you too. There don't seem to be many people around.'

'A lot of the houses round here are empty and nobody can sell them,' he said. 'Whole street needs blowing up if you ask me. It's been here for about a hundred years already – used to be called Victoria Street till the Labour lot got in.'

'Well, thanks for keeping an eye on the car anyway.' Jessica took out her keys and opened the car door.

'I really wasn't thinking of nicking it,' Darren said with a trace of anxiety. 'Tell the truth I'd have gone on past but I saw that little kid hanging round and I thought I'd better keep an eye open.'

'Kid?' Jessica wasn't sure why she asked.

'Not from round here. Leastways I never saw her before. Ever so silly she looked, all dolled up in a frilly pink dress trailing round her ankles. Anyway when I got here she'd skulked off somewhere or other, so I stayed around just in case. You can't trust anyone these days.'

Eleven

She was too shaken to return immediately to The Cedars, so drove round aimlessly for a while, paying particular attention to road signs, trying to calm the wild beating of her heart. Someone else had seen the child in the pink dress. Polly wasn't a figment of her private imagination; she had some kind of objective reality. She had turned up in Wilson Street and Wilson Street had once been Victoria Street, so it wasn't beyond the bounds of possibility that

Polly had been born there, if one accepted the theory that ghosts could only appear in the places they had known in life. From her birth-place she had gone, by what means Jessica couldn't fathom, to the brothel where the Rainbow Club now was.

She was in the centre of town near a restaurant. Jessica parked the car and went in, ordering a glass of wine and a pizza. Her surroundings were as cheerfully, impersonally modern as plastic, and she concentrated over her meal on the newspaper she had bought. The doings of Parliament, the state of the bank rate, the latest marriage of a much-married pop star, seemed oddly remote as if these events were all taking place in some other universe.

On Sundays libraries and estate agents were closed. She wanted to do something very practical, something that would help her to learn more about the event at The Cedars that had happened more than a century before and seemed still to cast a long shadow into the present day.

She paid for her meal and went out to collect her car. It was still sunny, the kind of day on which a picnic was the best way to spend one's time. She would tell Adam what had happened, of course. And perhaps when she reached home there would be word from Mrs Tate or Linda.

She garaged the car, went round to the kitchen and opened the door without having to use her key. Sophy Clare was wiping dishes, washgloves on her hands.

'Washing-up is not my favourite occupation,' she said wryly, stripping off the gloves. 'However one cannot just leave them to pile up.'

'Mrs Tate hasn't contacted you then?' Jessica closed the door behind her.

'Not a word. I'm beginning to think that she did have a secret life after all.'

'Nor Linda?'

'No, but then Linda dislikes using the telephone. I've been wondering if we might not drive over and make sure she's all right. She hasn't any other family and I do feel –'

'She isn't home,' Jessica said. 'Actually I drove over to see if there was any news – I hope you don't mind. It really wasn't any of my business, but I happened to be in the neighbourhood.'

Sophy didn't ask how she had known the address. Instead she clicked her tongue slightly, saying, 'I daresay it must be nerve-racking for the poor girl, having to sit and wait. I hope the police will let us know if anything turns up. I shall have to advertise for a new daily woman in a week or two if nothing happens.'

Jessica hesitated, noting the older woman's casual air. She didn't appear to be unduly disturbed about Mrs Tate. Then she noticed the fingers twisting and rolling the washgloves, smoothing them out between her own hands. Above the twisting fingers her face was calm and pleasant, with no more than a vague regret shadowing her expression.

'Mrs Clare – Sophy, is there anything particular about this house that makes you nervous?' she asked abruptly.

'Oh no, dear.' The answer came too swiftly. 'Just that the house is rather large now that the children have grown up and left, and John has to be out rather a lot.'

'Then you haven't heard footsteps or the bells ring?'

Sophy's face whitened beneath the make-up she had liberally applied. She made a final twisting motion with the gloves and said, 'Oh God, you have heard it too.'

'Something,' Jessica said cautiously, coming back to sit down at the table.

'Quick, light footsteps like a child when the doors are locked and there's no child in the house?'

'And one of the bells rang, the ones that are disconnected.'

'John says the floorboards creak as they expand and contract.' Sophy threw the gloves on to the draining board and sat down herself. 'The wires from the old bells are still there, only cut, so mice might nibble them and set off the ringing. But I've never seen a trace of any mice here. John says I imagine things.'

'How long has the – how long have you been hearing these things?' Jessica asked.

'About a year.' Sophy put her hands palm upwards before her as if she were trying to read her own fortune. 'I was always rather nervy by nature, you see, and I do have a vivid imagination so in the beginning I didn't take much notice, but I kept thinking that if I only looked hard enough, turned my head quickly, I might see something – someone. Ridiculous really. Probably something to do with my age. I have been having rather a difficult menopause.'

'I'm not menopausal,' Jessica said bluntly, 'and I don't think I've ever been particularly nervy and I've heard things too. Does the name Polly Winter convey anything to you?'

'Polly Winter?' Sophy considered for a moment, then shook her head. 'No, I can't say it does. Rather a pretty name, isn't it? Why do you ask?'

'It's just a theory that I'm playing around with,' Jessica evaded. 'I was wondering if my predecessor heard anything either.'

'Miss Reynolds? No, she never spoke of anything. Of course she only stayed a week or two. She was a temporary secretary somewhere or other, and I suppose she found a better job elsewhere.'

'Didn't she say?'

Sophy shook her head. Her hands were still now. 'I went down to see my parents for the weekend and she left while I was away,' she said.

'But your husband was here?'

'Yes, John was here.' Sophy glanced at her and tittered slightly. 'Oh, I hope you're not fancying that John was flirting with her or anything like that. Quite apart from the fact that John is one of the most devoted husbands any wife could hope to have, Dorothy Reynolds had a face like the back of a bus, poor soul.'

Waves of icy cold ran up and down Jessica's back. She swallowed painfully.

'Do you – would you happen to have a forwarding address?' she asked.

'She came from Birmingham originally, I think. We probably have it somewhere. But she certainly never mentioned having seen or heard anything. She was in her mid-thirties, kept herself to herself all the time. I was very pleased when you turned out to be so bright and friendly, not to mention much younger and prettier.' Sophy paused for a moment, then said, 'You aren't thinking of leaving, are you? I mean nothing very frightening has happened, has it? I do hope that you'll stay to finish your research.'

'Yes, of course,' Jessica said automatically. 'I thought it might be interesting to contact her and find out if by chance she had heard anything, that's all. If we can get someone else who has heard these footsteps then we could get the matter investigated.'

'By whom?' Sophy looked at her.

'Isn't there a Society of Psychical Research or something like that?' Jessica enquired.

'Oh, I doubt if John would agree to that,' Sophy said, looking worried. 'He hates people prying into things, you know, and if it were to become known that some rather awkward events – footsteps and bells ringing – people might come along and stare and take photographs and things. We'd both hate that.'

'I'm sure they'd keep the matter confidential,' Jessica began.

'Oh, I think it's best to let matters lie,' Sophy said. 'Honestly, it's very little to make a big song and dance about. Actually it's a relief to find out that someone else has heard it. I can stop thinking I'm going dotty or something, and now perhaps we won't hear anything more. So let's leave it for the time being.'

'If that's what you want,' Jessica said.

The hands were moving again, aimlessly plucking at the edge of the table.

'Did you have a nice time last evening with your young man?' Sophy was asking. 'He did seem very nice. I said to John that I thought he seemed very nice. I hope he didn't think us rude going straight up to bed in the way that we did, but really our day was quite hectic. Would you like some coffee or a drop of sherry? I usually have a little drink about this time.'

'I ought to go up and get changed,' Jessica said. 'Adam is taking me over to the Wirral this afternoon.'

'Oh, parts of the Wirral are very pretty,' Sophy said with enthusiasm. 'I see you have a lovely day for it too. John and I will be in tonight. Are you planning on being late? I only ask because we can leave the bolt unlatched or the chain off, whichever you prefer.'

'I'm not planning to be late,' Jessica said. 'Oh, there might be a phone call for me – a Darren Parks. If it comes could you ask him to ring back after eight?'

'Yes, of course. How nice that you're getting to know people,' Sophy said as she watched Jessica go out into the little servants' room.

She climbed the stairs to the half landing, went into her bedroom and sat down limply on the bed.

So now there was another Dorothy who'd left suddenly while Sophy Clare was down in London visiting her parents. Plain, mid-thirties, a transient – had the extraordinary coincidence of names revived some old event or were certain people being drawn together to replay something that hadn't been ended but was doomed to be repeated over and over when certain conditions applied?

She went to the small table and sat down, drawing the typewriter towards her, her fingers tapping rapidly.

Dorothy Reynolds, thirties, secretary(?). Left abruptly. Dorothy Larue?

Mrs Tate, housekeeper, left abruptly and hasn't been seen since she caught the local bus but is obviously home since her coat and scarf are there. Why hasn't she phoned? Similarity of name and job to Mrs Tatum but Mrs Tatum didn't disappear.

Julian and Robina Clare, left home, trainee social workers. Julia and Robert?

John Clare and Sophy Clare. No name resemblance to Edward and Amelia Makin, but is there some parallel of character?

What did Polly Winter do after the Makins went abroad?

Jessica took her fingers from the keys and frowned at what she had typed before unrolling the paper and folding it into her bag.

She had renewed her make-up and changed into a simple shirtwaister that looked cool and fresh when the doorbell sounded. Snatching up bag and jacket she ran down the stairs in time to see Sophy letting Adam in, her voice fluting in welcome.

'Do come in. Jessica will be down in a – ah, here she is. How nice you look. I think pastel shades always suit blondes. Well, have a nice time. Have you got your keys?'

'In my bag. 'Bye.' Jessica preceded Adam through the front door.

'I was expecting her to enquire into my intentions,' Adam said with a grin as they got into the car. 'Rather motherly today, isn't she?'

'She probably misses her own two,' Jessica said. 'Adam, did you bring a picnic?'

'In the back. Why?'

'Could we go somewhere else first?'

'Sure. Where?'

'Wilson Street.'

'Where's that and why are we going there?'

'I'll direct you and it's where Mrs Tate and Linda live.'

Adam gave her a startled look. 'She's back then?'

'I don't know,' Jessica said slowly. 'I drove into town this morning, just to have a look round – curiosity, I suppose. Anyway

Linda was out. I went round to the back door and it was unlocked so I – well, I went in and called. There wasn't any reply so I went upstairs – I know I hadn't any business to do that but it seemed odd that the door had been left open and yet the house was empty.'

'I'd have done the same thing myself,' Adam said. 'Where was Linda?'

'Not in the house,' Jessica said. 'But Mrs Tate must have returned because as I trod on a loose floorboard in the bedroom the wardrobe door swung open and there were her coat and scarf hanging there. Unless she has two identical coats and scarves then she's back. Anyway I came out and – Adam, there was a boy by the car. He said he was keeping an eye on it because there'd been a little girl in a frilly pink dress hanging round.'

They were approaching a side road. Adam swung the car into it, stopped and turned towards her.

'So she doesn't just exist in your brain,' he said.

'There's more,' Jessica said breathlessly. 'When I drove back to The Cedars Sophy Clare was finishing the dishes in the kitchen and we started talking.'

'You told her you'd been to Wilson Street?'

'And that Linda wasn't in. I didn't mention the fact that I went into the house. Anyway she started telling me about feeling nervous when she was alone in the house. She's heard footsteps too, but she's never seen anything and of course I didn't tell her. About seeing Polly, I mean, though I did ask her if she had ever heard the name of Polly Winter but she hadn't. She mentioned the lodger they'd had before me. She was a temporary secretary from Birmingham and she only stayed a few weeks. Her name was Dorothy Reynolds.'

'Alias Dorothy Larue?' Adam looked at her.

'The name's very like. It can't be a coincidence. It can't!'

'She didn't happen to disappear, I suppose?'

'She left suddenly while Sophy Clare was down in London visiting her parents.'

'I hope she left a forwarding address.'

'Sophy said it was around somewhere. She didn't seem very keen on my contacting her but she's afraid of publicity if anyone gets wind of the fact that the house might be worth investigating psychically. It's natural.'

'True, but it'd be interesting to get her point of view. Look, leave that part of it with me,' Adam said thoughtfully. 'You don't happen to know where Dorothy Reynolds worked while she was in Liverpool, do you?'

Jessica shook her head.

'Leave it with me. I'll enjoy playing detective. So let's drive to Wilson Street and find out if Mrs Tate and Linda are there. You think she'd have rung the Clares.'

'Evidently she hasn't. That isn't like her either,' Jessica said. 'She's the devoted retainer type. Turn here. By the way, Wilson Street used to be called Victoria Street. I've been working it out that perhaps Polly Winter was born there and then went into the brothel. If she were a slum child or an orphan – and then Edward Makin took her in as housemaid. Or am I making connections where there aren't any?'

'I think we ought to concentrate on the here and now,' Adam said. 'Let's sort out the Tates before we start figuring out what happened more than a century ago. Agreed?'

'Agreed. Right and then left. It's number forty-seven.'

Obeying her instructions he drove into the long, narrow street with its mean houses and defiantly coloured doors.

'The curtains are partly open anyway,' he remarked, parking neatly.

'That was me,' Jessica confessed. 'I drew them and didn't close them properly, so that probably means the house is still empty.'

'Let's take a look then.' Adam sounded brisk and businesslike.

Following him down the alley to the back yard Jessica felt a decided sense of relief. It was pleasant to have a companion who clearly had his wits about him.

'The back door was unlocked.' She stepped ahead of him to open it.

'Someone's been getting breakfast ready?' He had noticed the frying pan at once and stepped over to look at the three strips of dried and hardened bacon.

'She didn't start cooking it though,' Jessica pointed out. 'When I came this morning it was already dried out.'

'Two used coffee cups in the sink.' Adam went over to look at them. 'Two people having a coffee together? Or one person having two cups with an interval between? This is the time when it would be very useful to have the talent for observation of Sherlock Holmes.'

'No thanks. I never fancied being Miss Watson,' Jessica said with a grin.

'Let's work out the scenario anyway.' He walked through to the front room and stood, frowning slightly as he went on talking. 'Linda Tate is about to fry herself some bacon for breakfast and her mother returns. She's naturally excited so she forgets all about the bacon and they have a cup of coffee together instead.'

'And Mrs Tate goes upstairs, hangs up her coat and scarf – puts on a Sunday coat? There wasn't an empty hanger in the wardrobe.'

'Which doesn't prove anything. She might hang two or three things on one hanger. Perhaps she went out without a coat. It is warm today.'

'Mrs Tate,' Jessica said firmly, 'is the kind of person who always wears a coat. And she wouldn't go out and leave the back door unlocked. Only she apparently did, just as she left the back door at The Cedars unbolted. It doesn't make any sense.'

'I suppose her coat is still here?' They looked at each other as he asked the question and turned with mutual accord towards the narrow stairs.

The coat and scarf hung still in the wardrobe.

'There's the used stub of the bus ticket she bought yesterday in the pocket,' Jessica said.

'I think,' said Adam, 'that it wouldn't do any harm to postpone the picnic and call in at the local police station.'

'And tell them we broke in?'

'The door was open and we haven't taken anything. You didn't touch anything much when you were here this morning, did you?'

'No, of course not,' Jessica said. 'But I don't see –'

'If Linda's gone missing too then the police are going to pay much closer attention to what's happening,' Adam pointed out. 'Your fingerprints and mine are going to be everywhere, and you said that the boy saw you coming out.'

'You're saying that something might have happened to them both? Why?'

'I'm not saying anything of the sort, but it might be prudent to make sure we're entirely in the clear. Is the local station over in Blundell Road direction handling the case?'

'I think so, and I wish you'd stop calling it a case. It makes me edgy.'

'There's probably a simple explanation.' Adam gave her a swift, consoling, unsexual kiss on the cheek. 'Let's go.'

They went downstairs and through to the kitchen again. Already the house was acquiring the peculiarly stale smell of an unused building.

'Sunday paper?' Adam pounced on it.

'I left it here. The newsagent who told me where the Tates lived said that Linda hadn't been in to collect the paper this morning, so I bought it and left it here.'

'No neighbours.'

'Outside in the yard he paused to look round.

'I think a lot of the houses are empty nowadays,' Jessica said. 'People move away from the run-down areas and the houses stay until some property developer comes along.'

'Depressing. She'd have been more sensible to move into The Cedars, since there are so many unused rooms.'

'She probably clung on to her independence,' Jessica said, walking into the alley. 'The late Mr Tate was an alcoholic apparently and after he died she probably appreciated being able to enjoy a decent night's sleep in her own bed – oh, I forgot to tell you. The double bed in the main bedroom had been slept in. I figured Linda slept there, maybe feeling a bit miserable because her mother wasn't around.'

'You'd think the Clares would have come round to see her.' Adam held open the passenger door for her.

'I daresay they didn't think of it. They both strike me as very nice but a bit self-absorbed. I mean if Linda were weeping on the doorstep they'd be very kind but out of sight out of mind –'

'Like Dorothy Reynolds?'

'Let's concentrate on the here and now,' Jessica reminded him. 'And let's not mention missing governesses or little girls in pink dresses or the police will think there's something wrong with my brain.'

'You went round to see if Linda Tate was all right and she wasn't there,' Adam said promptly. 'You found out the back door was open and you went in and ran upstairs and found Mrs Tate's coat and scarf in the wardrobe. When you found out that she hadn't rung the Clares you told me and we went back together.'

'Well, all that's true,' Jessica said. 'You don't have to make it sound as if we're concocting a story to avoid being arrested or something.'

'Arrested for what?' Adam asked mildly, ignoring her suddenly petulant tone.

'I don't know.' The little flare of tired irritability died as she turned to look at him. 'For trespass, I suppose.'

'Or murder,' Adam said.

'That's ridiculous! Who on earth would want to murder Mrs Tate?'

'I have no idea.' He swung the car into the main road again. 'All I have is a peculiar feeling that won't go away. And you have it too, don't you?'

'Yes,' said Jessica. 'I wish I didn't, but I do.'

Twelve

Sergeant Penton nodded his thanks to the constable who'd just put a tray of coffees on his desk and looked again at Jessica and Adam.

'Lucky you caught me,' he observed mildly. 'I generally spend Sunday with the wife and kids but she's gone off to see her mum, so I popped in. So you went over to Wilson Street? Strictly speaking they're the ones who should be dealing with all this, but since Linda Tate reported her mother missing to us and they've got their plates full down in town – well, anyway, it landed on us. There's been no word of Mrs Tate since she was seen getting off the bus at Friday lunchtime and going into the supermarket. I rang Linda around six last evening just to check with her that her mother hadn't returned. She had promised to let us know immediately but she strikes me as being a bit slow on the uptake, poor kid – speaking off the record, of course. Anyway she hadn't seen or heard from her.'

'So Linda was there at six last evening,' Jessica said.

'I made a note of the call. Regulations. I could have gone round to the house but Wilson Street isn't the kind of neighbourhood where it adds to your reputation to have a police car at the front door.'

'Then Mrs Tate went home after six,' Jessica said.

'We've no proof of that,' the sergeant said irritatingly.

'Her coat and scarf were hanging in the wardrobe. I told you.'

'You having – effected an entrance?'

'Me having trespassed,' Jessica said. 'I know it was terrible to barge in, but the back door was unlocked and there was no sign of Linda and I went in. The wardrobe door swung open when I trod on a loose board. I wasn't prying.'

'And the coat and scarf were there? Well, unless she had two identical coats and scarves then it certainly looks as if she came back.'

'And didn't report it to the police? Sergeant, I only knew Mrs Tate slightly but she was conscientious. She wouldn't do that.'

'And then the two of you went back later on this afternoon. Why?'

'I felt uneasy,' Jessica said, flushing slightly. 'I know that sounds silly.'

'A fair number of our cases hinge on a mixture of good luck and hunches,' Sergeant Penton said tolerantly. 'Sensible of you to check. The coat and scarf were still there?'

'And bacon in the pan ready for frying.'

'Sounds as if Linda was starting breakfast when her mother came back.'

'Mrs Tate would have put the bacon back in the 'fridge,' Jessica said. 'I'm positive she would. And Linda never popped in to the local newsagent to collect her Sunday paper. I made some enquiries there because I wasn't sure where the Tates lived exactly, and the man there mentioned it, so I bought it and left it at the house.'

'I'll get a car over there. Excuse me a minute.' Rising, he went out.

'At least he isn't threatening to arrest me for trespass,' Jessica whispered.

'Keep your fingers crossed.' Adam gave her a grin as the sergeant came in again.

'Lucky that it's Sunday and nobody got carved up last night,' he said. 'Look, would you mind if we took your fingerprints for elimination purposes?'

'No, of course not. Are you going to –?' Jessica hesitated.

'We've no reason to yet,' he told her. 'Linda Tate's a free agent. There's no law says she can't go out leaving bacon in the pan and the door unlocked. However, as you're here we might as well anticipate, so to speak. After that, I wonder if you'd be willing to follow us back to Wilson Street. Since you were there earlier you'd be able to tell if anything had been altered since you left.'

'Yes, of course. We do want to help,' Jessica told him.

'Very public spirited of you, Miss Cameron.'

Was there a faint dryness in his tone? Going after him towards the fingerprinting session Jessica felt an unwarranted sense of guilt. At least he hadn't made any remarks yet about bungling amateurs.

The fingerprinting over, they went out to Adam's car. Sergeant Penton got into a waiting police car; Adam obediently got into his own and, Jessica at his side, followed.

'At least he didn't laugh,' she said.

'No, he's taking it seriously.' Adam glanced at her as they rounded a corner. 'What's your view? Do you still have that uneasy feeling?'

Jessica nodded.

'I've my fingers crossed that the Tates will be enjoying a belated Sunday lunch,' she said.

'Speaking of food –' He sent a brief look towards the back seat where a picnic basket reposed.

'Adam, I'm so sorry.' Jessica felt a pang of guilt. 'We were going to have a pleasant afternoon over in the Wirral and instead I've dragged you into a police investigation.'

'I didn't need much dragging,' he assured her. 'Anyway the food won't spoil.'

The police car had already drawn up before the Tate house. Sergeant Penton and his constable got out and stood looking round. In a house at the other side of the street a curtain twitched aside and was as swiftly withdrawn.

'Right then, let's find out if anyone is home.' The Sergeant rapped the knocker briskly.

'The back door is down the alley,' Jessica said.

'Right then, then take a look. We'll go slowly and you can tell me if anything's changed since you were here last,' he said.

They went down the alley. Jessica felt a thrill of anticipatory nervousness. Odd, but when she had come here alone she hadn't felt anything but a curiosity tinged with anxiety. The presence of police seemed to crystallize all her nebulous fears.

The back door opened as before, the kitchen appearing as before with the cups in the sink, the bacon curled and dry in the frying pan.

'I pulled back the curtains here and there,' Jessica remembered. 'They were all closed when I arrived.'

'If you notice anything different point it out at once. Oh, and try not to touch things more than you can help. Right then, let's go.'

His 'right thens' made it like a military exercise, Jessica thought, going through into the narrow hall.

'Is this the paper you left?' He nodded towards it.

'Yes.'

'Well, doesn't look as if anybody has read it. Let's take a look upstairs.'

In the main bedroom Jessica trod on the faulty board and watched the wardrobe door swing ajar. The coat and scarf were revealed.

'There's a used bus ticket in the pocket,' Jessica said.

'Let's have a look then.' He had donned a pair of plastic gloves. On his large hands they looked clinical, sinister.

'Seems quite innocuous.' He used the word almost delicately as he lifted out the coat on its hanger. 'On the other hand one never knows. Harry, might be a good idea to have the lab boys take the once-over?'

'Can't hurt,' the constable agreed.

'Right then, let's get them in a bag and you two will have to sign a form, just to witness that I took the coat and scarf for inspection. We can't go nabbing people's belongings without a by-your-leave. Problem here is that there don't seem to be any relatives or friends to start worrying about them – except yourself, of course.'

'I'm not exactly a friend,' Jessica said uncomfortably. 'More nosy.'

'Heaven bless nosy young women then. Very helpful they can be. Anything else you noticed?'

'Someone slept in the bed here but not in the bed in Linda's room. The indentation is still faintly there.'

The sergeant walked over to the double bed and stood looking down at it.

'Anything there, Sergeant?' Constable Harry who had been busying himself with a large plastic bag looked alert.

'Would you know how tall Mrs Tate and Linda are?' he enquired.

'Not in exact measurements. Mrs Tate is of medium height, rather square in outlook. Linda's about an inch shorter than I am.

Maybe a little more than an inch, but her hair is frizzy at the crown.'

'Whoever slept here must have lain on top of the covers,' the sergeant said. 'The bed's too neat. If they made it after they'd got up the indentation would've been smoothed over. Mrs Tate and Linda aren't particularly heavy, are they?'

'Linda is quite slim,' Jessica said, trying to picture the girl without her outdoor garments. 'Mrs Tate isn't fat but I think she could be quite heavy. But why would she lie on top of the bedclothes? Unless she'd been travelling all night and lay down for ten minutes after she'd taken off her coat?'

'Then she wouldn't have left such a deep indentation,' he said. 'Harry, get on the car blower. I'd like a photographer here. And get Simpson. He can start a few house to house enquiries. He needs the exercise.'

'You do think that something has happened to them, don't you?' Jessica said.

'I think it's better to be too careful than miss out on salient facts in the beginning,' he returned without expression. 'Nothing else you can recall?'

Jessica shook her head. The neat, impersonal house had an emptiness about it that chilled her. She wanted to be out breathing fresh air. And eating. In sympathy with her thought her stomach growled.

'Right then, that seems to wrap things up,' Sergeant Penton said. 'Now, if you'll just witness to what we've removed for examination you can go. You've both been very helpful. It's appreciated.'

'What happens now?' Adam asked as they went downstairs again, and the other spread a form on the table.

'The lab boys will take a look at the coat and scarf,' he told him. 'It might give us an indication of where Mrs Tate went after she walked into the supermarket. Shoes.'

'Shoes?' Jessica looked at him.

'If she changed her coat and went out again you think she'd have changed her shoes as well. There was a pair of courts, a pair of fluffy mules and a pair of sandals in the bottom of the wardrobe.' He screwed his eyes up slightly as he recalled them to memory.

'I never even thought of looking,' Jessica said, chagrined, and almost leapt out of her skin as a loud rat-tat sounded at the front door.

'I'll get it.' The constable went out into the narrow hall and opened the door.

'Is Miss Cameron there? I've a message for her.' The voice was young and in the face of officialdom extremely respectful.

'It's Darren Parks,' Jessica said. 'I saw him earlier on when I was here. He came over to take a look at my car. He's a friend of Linda's. Just a casual friend, nothing serious.'

'Let's have him in then.' Sergeant Penton raised his voice slightly as the boy appeared in the doorway with the constable hovering behind.

'Hello, Darren. What's the message?' Jessica asked. She spoke quickly since the newcomer's face had fallen slightly at the sight of yet another policeman. She had the distinct impression that he would have liked to bolt.

'It's not exactly a message, Miss,' Darren said. 'Only you said to tell you if anything turned up. Anyway my mum saw Mrs Tate last evening.'

'She's sure?' Jessica spoke sharply.

'Yes, Miss. While we were eating just now – we eat later on Sundays on account of Dad's going to the pub for a couple of pints – and I said as how Linda wasn't home and Mum said, "Well, her mum's back because I saw her going down the road last night when I was letting out the cat". I asked her if she'd spoken to her but she said no. Mrs Tate was on the other side of the road but she passed under the street lamp, so she saw her clear.'

'What time does your mum put out the cat?' Sergeant Penton asked.

'Ten sharp. Like clockwork – sir.' He added the courtesy uneasily.

'I think we'd better come along and have a word with her,' Sergeant Penton began.

'I'm not lying,' Darren said. 'She did see her. Said she was walking funny.'

'How funny?' The sergeant looked alert.

'All hunched up,' said Darren, contorting his own lanky frame. 'She was walking fast otherwise Mum'd have called across to ask her if she was all right. But Mrs Tate always keeps herself to herself, so she didn't like – like.'

'Suppose you go along home and tell your mum we'll be along for a word,' the sergeant said.

'Did you phone me?' Jessica asked.

'I was going to but then I saw the police car and the other car so I came along here first,' Darren told her.

'Sensible lad.' The sergeant nodded approvingly. 'Right then, off you go. We'll be along in a few minutes.'

Darren went, less inclined to bolt after his friendly reception.

'We'll give her just enough time to get her apron off but not enough time to start imagining some tragic incident she just recalled,' Sergeant Penton said. 'Well, looks as if we're getting somewhere. Mrs Tate came home or towards her home at ten o'clock last night. If we can get a positive identification then we'll be a lot further forward. I'll be in touch with you, Miss Cameron.'

'We can call in later if you're still in the station,' Adam suggested.

'Oh, I daresay I will be. Nothing much on the telly this evening. See you both later then.' He was gathering up his things, taking a last, all encompassing look around.

Jessica went out on to the pavement and breathed deeply, letting out stale air.

'Let's go.' Adam was holding open the passenger door. 'This street is depressing.'

'All the same I'm glad that we went to the police,' Jessica said, getting in. 'The sergeant's going to carry on investigating so that means he thinks that something is wrong. It isn't just imagination.'

'And since you didn't mention Polly Winter –'

'She wasn't imagination either,' Jessica said sharply. 'I saw her, Adam, and so did the boy, Darren. I wonder if he'll mention it to the police – no, that's unlikely. When he mentioned to me having seen a little girl in a pink dress hanging round my car I didn't react to what he was saying. He has no idea that the child he saw lived more than a hundred years before. Adam, if Mrs Tate came home last night then where was she between then and Friday lunchtime? Why didn't she inform the police? And where are she and Linda now?'

'That's what the police will be trying to find out,' Adam said. 'Look, let's drive over to Formby and eat on the sandhills there. We'll go to the Wirral another day.'

'Are you staying that long then?' She felt a surge of pleasure.

'To the end of the month. I might stay longer. I never could resist a mystery or a pretty girl,' Adam said. 'The girl, let me add, is the greater attraction. When are you coming round to visit me?'

'Soon. Your landlord won't mind?'

'Not at all. I told you that I've taken over someone else's apartment. As soon as I can get another commission then I'll be striking camp.'

'A free spirit,' she teased.

'I'm hoping to get something down in London.' He shot her a smile. 'It would be rather nice if you and I could start seeing each other in a more normal setting, don't you think?'

'Yes. Yes, I do.' Jessica smiled back, sensing a promise for the future. It was unwise to allow herself to fall in love at a time when odd events were happening and she'd be more apt to see him as a rescuer rather than a man who might or might not become a romantic partner.

His words had removed a pressure she hadn't even been aware of experiencing. The sensation of release continued when they reached the grass grown sand dunes that held in their sunlit sweep no hint of the near proximity of any town. The food was unspoilt, the wine only slightly too warm. Adam had taken some trouble, she reflected, to provide the sort of finger foods that could be eaten without making too much mess. There were even paper napkins and tablecloth.

'If I'd known this was waiting,' she joked, 'I'd have postponed the visit to the police station.'

'We'll call in later and see if anything new's transpired. I've been thinking about Dorothy Reynolds.'

So decidedly had she banished any thoughts that didn't blend in with the present idyllic setting that, for a moment, she stared at him.

'Oh, the secretary who had my room before I came. Yes, what about her?'

'Well, leaving aside the coincidence that Dorothy Reynolds is pretty close in name to Dorothy Larue, it does seem that people connected with The Cedars seem to make a habit of leaving rather suddenly.'

'It's more than a hundred years since Dorothy Larue and Julia vanished,' she objected. 'I mean it's possible to make connections where there aren't any.'

'True. Probably I phrased it wrong.' Adam bit on a chicken leg, chewed meditatively for a minute or two, then resumed. 'In 1859 we have husband, wife and two small children. One of the children vanishes with a recently appointed governess. Today we have husband, wife, two grown-up children who've left home, a lodger who leaves while the wife is away for a weekend, and then a housekeeper who vanishes and her daughter who follows suit.'

'But Mrs Tatum didn't vanish. She stayed on after the Makins left,' Jessica said. 'And we don't know anything about Dorothy Reynolds. She's probably alive and well and living in Birmingham.'

'Then the pattern isn't repeating itself exactly,' Adam said. 'What we need to do is find the connecting link between two sets of circumstances that almost but don't exactly mirror each other.'

'Polly Winter,' Jessica said, and felt the breeze sharpen as it stirred the reeds.

'Perhaps. For someone who's been dead for – I wonder when she did die?'

'I've no idea. She isn't in the photograph of the Laurence family with Mrs Tatum.'

'That doesn't mean she'd died,' Adam said. 'The Laurences might have sacked her or she went back to her old profession or took another position.'

'If we could find Dorothy Reynolds she might be able to tell us something.'

'Or nothing.' He dropped the chicken bone into an empty paper cup. 'She might have simply got the chance of a better job and left. Anyway, I propose visiting the agent first thing in the morning.'

'I could ask John Clare for the forwarding address she left.'

'Didn't you say that Mrs Clare wasn't keen on investigating the odd noises she'd heard? She might not be too happy if you go on asking questions. On the other hand I can go and talk to the house agent and get the address that Dorothy Reynolds gave him when she came looking for lodgings. I've a Press card so I can lean on that a little.'

'Do you want me to come with you?'

'It'll probably be better if I go alone. You get on with your own research for this Victorian exhibition that's being planned, and I'll pick you up tomorrow afternoon. If I get a telephone number d'ye want me to give her a ring?'

'That would be marvellous,' Jessica said. 'I don't think I'd know how to approach the subject. She might think I was crazy or something.'

'I'll use my well-known charm.' Adam reached out to wind one of her short curls about his finger. His smile faded slightly as he said, 'Look, I don't want to spook you, but be careful, won't you? I won't feel happy until I meet Mrs Tate and Linda with a convincing explanation of where the devil they both went.'

'You don't seriously think that I might disappear like Mrs Tate and Linda?'

'And Dorothy Larue and Julia Clare and possibly Dorothy Reynolds too,' Adam said.

'Well, I've no intention of going anywhere,' Jessica said firmly. 'If anything odd happens then I'll either ring you up or come round. I promise.'

'Right then.' He imitated Sergeant Penton's flat, nasal tone so accurately that Jessica choked on a giggle. 'Tomorrow I will go and see the house agent and spin him some yarn that'll get me Dorothy Reynold's Birmingham address. I'll call round for you in the afternoon and we can go to my place and make toast and see where we're at. What do you plan to do?'

'Spend the rest of today and tomorrow morning getting my portfolio together for the committee to approve,' Jessica said with decision. 'I have to keep reminding myself that I came here to plan the theme of an exhibition and not get involved in someone else's mystery.'

She was afraid that he might question, tell her that the mystery seemed to be hers since she had seen Polly Winter. That was a possibility she didn't want to consider. It was more reassuring to believe that she'd landed in it by accident.

'Come on.' Adam was gathering up the remains of the food. 'We'll call in at the station and see if there's any news and then I'll drop you off at The Cedars.'

At the station Sergeant Penton, behind his desk, greeted them like old friends.

'Got yourself something to eat, did you? Coffee? No? Right then, you'll be wanting to know if we've got any further forward. In one sense yes. In another no. Oh, pull up a couple of chairs.'

'You spoke to Mrs Parks?' Jessica asked, obeying.

'Nice lady. Knows Mrs Tate to say good morning to, but she says the Tates aren't neighbourly. The father drank like a fish and she reckons his death was more of a relief than anything else. Anyway she's quite sure that it was ten last night when she let the cat out and she definitely saw Mrs Tate just passing under the street lamp on the other side of the road. Scuttling along very fast, she said. I

wouldn't have taken much notice of that – witnesses often pep up
what they've seen a bit for the benefit of the police, but she'd
already mentioned it to her son. She said she'd have called out but
Mrs Tate was going too fast, hunched over in a funny kind of way.
Anyway that was all. She went in, locked the door, and thought no
more about it. She said Mrs Tate was wearing her usual coat and
flowered headscarf.'

'So she did go home,' Adam said, frowningly.

'She was headed in that direction. We're still making house to
house enquiries, but that's a pretty run-down neighbourhood in
Wilson Street and half the places are boarded up. So far we haven't
struck gold. The question we're chewing over now is what
happened then. Assuming she reached home she presumably went
in, hung her coat and scarf in the wardrobe and then – what? Only
one person left an imprint on the double bed, indicating that Mrs
Tate may have slept on top of the covers. We can't say that Linda
slept in her own bed or not, because she might have got up this
morning and made her bed. And then what? Two soiled coffee
cups in the sink, bacon left uncooked in the frying pan, curtains
drawn – first thing that most people do in the morning is open the
curtains. And then mother and daughter go out again, leaving the
back door unlocked. Doesn't add up.'

'Haven't you got any theories?' Jessica asked hopefully.

'About a dozen but none of them quite fit. One thing does puzzle
me though. I'm wondering why you two are taking such a close
interest in all this. Now if it were the Clares who were fretting
that'd make more sense. After all Mrs Tate and Linda work at The
Cedars. But you've only just arrived in town.'

Jessica, meeting the probing eyes, was suddenly relieved she had
no crime to conceal.

'I'm here to arrange an exhibition on nineteenth-century family
life,' she said, choosing her words carefully. 'It occurred to me that
as I was actually lodging in a Victorian house it might be interesting
to base my work on an actual family. The last owner was a
bachelor, a Mr Laurence, but his father bought the property from a
clergyman, Edward Makin. He wrote a book of very dull memoirs
but he was married with a couple of small children, so the family
struck me as possibly fairly representative. Anyway I started doing
research and – it seems they employed a governess for their
daughter, Julia. A Miss Dorothy Larue. She was with them six

weeks and then one day she took Julia for a walk and they both disappeared and were never seen again.'

'Where did you get all this information from?' Sergeant Penton asked.

'A book from the local library,' Jessica told him. 'A hotch-potch of unsolved mysteries – Jack the Ripper, that kind of thing. There was a chapter about the Makins. Apparently they went abroad shortly afterwards and never returned to England.'

'When did all this happen?'

'1859.'

'A bit before my time.' He spoke solemnly. 'The entire force has been reorganized since then. However there'll be a file on the case somewhere in the archives, I daresay. I suppose you were reading up about that when Mrs Tate went missing?'

'I thought it was an interesting coincidence,' Jessica said cautiously.

'I agree, but it can't be more than that. Coincidences do happen.' He leaned both elbows on the desk, regarding her thoughtfully. 'Anyway it explains your own interest. Are you thinking of using that old mystery as part of your exhibition?'

'I hadn't thought of that,' she said truthfully.

'Might prove interesting. Show the sinister side of the nineteenth century underneath all the middle-class respectability. Tell you what, I'll have a bit of a snuffle around in the archives. If I come up with anything I'll let you have it. Right then! Nice talking to you. We'll be in touch.'

Leaving the station she mentally congratulated herself on having talked about the former mystery without having mentioned children in pink dresses who were only visible now and then to certain people.

Thirteen

The television was on when she let herself into The Cedars, calling, more for reassurance than anything else, that she was back. The sitting-room door was open and she could see Sophy Clare in what appeared to be her customary seat, eyes fixed on the hall. She answered cheerfully, however, rising to open the door wider.

'Did you have a pleasant afternoon?' she enquired. 'Would you like a cup of tea? I can bring another cup.'

'Thank you, no. I have to get on with some work,' Jessica said, pausing politely.

From his chair John Clare flicked her a quick abstracted smile and then turned his gaze back to the screen again. A war film, she noticed, with steel-jawed, steel-helmeted men scrambling up a hill. It wasn't surprising that his wife couldn't summon up much interest in the subject.

'Going well, is it?' Sophy said encouragingly.

'It seems to –' Jessica paused as the telephone shrilled.

'I'll take it.' John Clare was out of his seat and moving fast. Perhaps the film wasn't engaging his attention as much as it seemed to be.

He spoke briefly, identifying himself, replacing the receiver.

'Not anything of any importance,' he said.

'I thought it might be Mrs Tate,' Jessica said.

'Oh, I suppose we'll hear from her sooner or later,' he said.

'Yes, well I'll get on.' Jessica began to mount the stairs, wondering why she hadn't mentioned her visit to Wilson Street or her interview with the police.

On the gallery she turned briefly to glance back. The Clares had moved close together and Sophy was looking up into her husband's face with an earnest and questioning look while he nodded at her several times, smilingly drawing her into the curve of his arm.

She turned and went on into her room, dismissing the little piece of by-play, fixing her mind on the outline she intended presenting to her firm.

The exhibition must be easily moveable since it was taken round schools and halls. She would have to borrow some furniture of the period, hunt out some clothes for the papier-mâché models that would eventually be made. The public would see the silent shells of people who had lived more than a century before – clergyman, demure wife, small girl, baby, governess, housekeeper and servant girl. Man who went round brothels 'rescuing soiled doves', wife who took little doses of laudanum for her nerves, governess who went for a walk and never came back. Perhaps Sergeant Penton was right and she ought to plan for an exhibition that would show the truth behind the façade of crinoline and frockcoat.

She sketched out ideas for the styles of costume she would be seeking. Little lace cap for the proud mamma, black bombazine for the governess, black for the housekeeper too. Too much black. Still the little girl could be in – pale blue with a wide sash and a fringe of pantalette. Whatever she managed to borrow would have to be insured against loss or damage. What she couldn't obtain would have to be faked. Fakes impersonating fakes, she thought suddenly. Edward Makin with his obsessive affection for his stern mother could have been driven to do more than rescue girls from a life of social degradation. His wife might have hated his attentions and drugged herself regularly with laudanum so that her consciousness could float elsewhere while he performed his marital duty.

She took out the photograph of the Laurences and looked closely at the plump frame of the elderly Mrs Tatum. Well, nothing had happened to her at all events. She had stayed on to minister to the Laurences, then probably had used her savings to retire to a small cottage somewhere and died peacefully in extreme old age.

'Births, marriages and deaths,' Jessica said aloud.

There was St Catherine's in London where records were kept and local archives. With a little digging she could find out much more about the inhabitants of The Cedars, put neatly printed notices on the papier-mâché models.

'Edward Makin.' She typed rapidly. 'Born 1827. Entered Cambridge 1847, obtained Classics degree and was ordained as an Anglican clergyman in 1850. Succeeded to the living of his maternal grandfather in 1851. In 1853 married Amelia Benson (24). Julia born in 1854 and Robert in 1857 just after the death of Mrs Makin Senior. Two years later a governess was employed to care for Julia and six weeks later she and the child failed to return from a walk. In 1860 Edward Makin took his wife and son abroad and died of typhoid in Venice during that summer. Amelia Makin remained abroad, dying in 1875 and the son, Robert, was killed during a tiger shoot in India in 1881.'

Jessica lifted her hands from the keys and read over what she had written. She'd include the information in the portfolio she was getting ready for her boss to approve. Then it was up to the firm to decide if the subjects she'd chosen would make a good subject for the exhibition.

There was nothing definitely proved that she could put into a notice about either Dorothy Larue or Polly Winter. She would do some ferreting in the city archives the next morning. Having reached that conclusion she went briskly down the stairs and through to the kitchen to make herself a snack.

Odd how every time she walked into the main kitchen she expected to see Mrs Tate seated at the table. Odd because she hadn't known the cleaning woman for very long and she could count on the fingers of one hand the number of times she had actually seen her seated at the table. Usually she was at the sink or moving stolidly on her reliable looking feet about the kitchen. Why not expect to see her doing something active? It was as if Mrs Tate had left an impression of herself on a particular area of the atmosphere.

'A glass of champagne, Jessica?' Sophy Clare came in, heels tapping merrily, glass already filled and bubbling.

'Thank you.' Somewhat bemused, Jessica took it and sipped. 'What are we celebrating?'

'It would be a sad thing if we had to wait for a celebration before we enjoyed a glass of champagne,' Sophy said gaily. 'Are you going out again this evening?'

'No, as I said I'm going to work when I've had a snack,' Jessica said.

'So you did. Well, John and I are going to spend a quiet evening in and then have an early night. Oh, there wasn't any telephone call for you by the way.'

'Thank you,' Jessica said, putting the glass on the table and going to check on what she had left in the cupboard.

'Help yourself to anything you need,' Sophy said generously and went out again, humming.

Something had clearly cheered her up immensely, Jessica thought. She wondered if the telephone call had had anything to do with it. Certainly neither she nor her husband seemed in the least concerned about Mrs Tate's non-appearance. She quelled the impulse to go into the sitting-room and tell them that now Linda was missing too.

She ate her snack, choosing cheese as it was quick and easy, because even with the lights on and the back door locked and bolted there was an emptiness in the large kitchen with its shiny surfaces which contrasted so markedly with the old table and the row of disconnected bells.

It was no use. She pushed her plate aside, finished the champagne and went through to the sitting-room.

'I've changed my mind,' she said, putting her head round the half open door. 'I'm going for a drive round to clear my brain.'

'I'll leave the back door unbolted,' Sophy said. She was sitting near her husband and her face was tranquil. He, for his part, merely nodded, not taking his eyes from the screen. Was reality so unpleasant for him that he needed to absorb himself in unreality that could be switched over to something else if it proved uncomfortable to watch?

'See you later maybe,' she said, feeling awkward and went upstairs to fetch her jacket, wondering why the urge to get out for a while had suddenly become imperative. It was stupid when she still had work to do and had been out for most of the day already.

Not until she had backed the Mini neatly into the road did she realize that she was going back to Wilson Street. There was neither rhyme nor reason in it. She was aware of that even as she drove towards the traffic lights. No doubt the police had put a seal on the door. They might even have left a man outside, though she doubted that. On the other hand she might see lights on inside the house and when she rapped at the door Linda might answer it, or Mrs Tate.

'You'll never guess what happened. It was such a surprise but –' But what? What sequence of events could possibly explain what had happened?

She drove on steadily into town, wishing as she neared the long, narrow street with its boarded-up windows like blind eyes under the neon lights that she had called at Adam's lodging. Company would have been nice. Having reached that conclusion she scolded herself for being stupid and slowed as she came to the Tate house.

Not a light gleamed in the front windows. Mrs Tate then hadn't returned, unless she was sitting in the kitchen, having a cup of coffee with her daughter, the two of them marvelling over whatever had happened.

Parking the car she got out and went down the side alley. It wouldn't do any harm to take a look. Not that it was possible to see much in the gloom as she walked along and turned left into the yard.

The back of the house was in darkness too. Jessica stood for a moment, biting her lip in indecision. Whatever impulse had brought her here had been a mistaken one, wasting her time.

She turned towards the alley and stood, her eyes riveted on the small figure who barred her way.

The child wore the same trailing pink frills, the hem ragged, the heels of the shoes too high for a little girl to balance on without risk of falling. Under the tangle of curls the dead white face with its scarlet beestung mouth was too clearly seen in the darkness as if it carried some lurid light within the skull behind. Only the eyes were black pools rimmed with black with the fugitive glitter of silver on the lids as they were briefly closed and then opened again, staring at her with a feverish intensity. She stood about ten or fifteen feet away, holding out her skirt with thin little hands. It was not, of course, possible that she was there at all. Any real figure would have been no more than a blur in the darkness. As it was, Jessica could see the dirt that rimmed the long, scarlet nails on the child's hands.

Jessica felt the slow, cold horror creeping through her veins, a horror that was out of all proportion to what she was looking at. There was, after all, nothing frightening about a little girl dressed up in clothes an older girl might have graced, her face as crudely painted as if she'd been let loose among her mother's make-up boxes. Nothing frightening, but no power on earth could have induced her to pass it.

She backed away, holding down screaming. What had Adam said? Talk to it? It? Why did she think of the figure as an 'it' rather than a 'she' or a 'her'? It was a memory, she reminded herself, an echo on the ether of no more significance than the repeat of a television programme. What she was looking at was no longer there. If she walked steadily forward it would dissolve into the darkness again.

She took a tentative step, willing dissolution. The child made a tiny movement, no more than the slight lifting of her chin, but it stopped Jessica in her tracks. Then the little figure took a small, silent step towards her, the painted mouth opening in a smile of recognition. That was the final horror, that the child recognized her.

Jessica's nerve broke and she fled, stumbling wildly across the yard, scraping the back of her hand on a jutting stone at the end of the wall. She looked back once, heart thudding, and saw that the thing – oh, she couldn't think of it as a child – was taking short, teetering steps after her, the smile of recognition still opening the mouth where the scarlet paint looked black under the faint glow of an emergent moon.

There was a door ahead of her. Blindly, instinctively, Jessica pushed it open and stumbled through into darkness. The warehouse? Had she come into the warehouse? Her hand groped along the wall, pressed down a switch. Please God, don't let the electricity be disconnected.

Above her a bulb lit palely. The door had swung close behind her, impelled by its own momentum. Ahead of her empty cartons and boxes tumbled to the skylight. The floor was dusty. Small spirals rose up and made her cough as she stood there. She stifled the cough with her hand, shaking her head as she did so. What did she think she was achieving, for heaven's sake? This ghost, this – thing, would obey the laws of its own level, would appear and disappear at will with doors and walls no barrier.

Or would it? Staring at the closed door she tried to remember what Adam had told her. He had read somewhere that a ghost couldn't speak unless it were invited to do so. Perhaps it couldn't come in unless it was invited either.

At the other side of the door was a tiny, scratching sound. The sharply pointed, black-rimmed, scarlet nails of a child who had ceased to be a child more than a century before.

'It can't come in unless I ask it to come in.' The silent sentence was like a mantra of protection. It was not, after all invincible. Certain places it could not penetrate. Perhaps places where the child had never actually walked during its life.

The scratching came again, more sharply than before, rasping her nerves. She could open the door, see – what? A small girl in a pink dress, desperate to tell someone something? Or a thing in the likeness of a child, grave dirty, the scent of corruption in its breath?

Jessica backed away, slowly, her eyes on the door. Thank God it was a heavy door – too heavy for a small child to push open without help. She kept the fragile comfort in her mind as she moved into the gloom beyond the light bulb.

Her foot struck sharply against an overturned filing cabinet, its drawers gaping and empty. The whole place looked like a general dumping ground for abandoned office supplies and old packing cases. The far corners were thick with shadow.

If there was another door, she reasoned, forcing her mind to practicalities, she could unbolt it, push it open, find herself in the next street, go back to the car. The mental image of a small girl waiting expectantly in the back seat rose in her mind and was instantly suppressed.

She saw another switch and pressed it down, illuminating another dusty and naked bulb. Overhead was a cracked and filthy skylight, rafters that looked none too secure. The scratching had grown fainter, no more than a faint rasping on the edge of her consciousness. Her own feet, tapping the bare wooden floor, made more noise. She stumbled at the edge of a pile of black binliner bags and put out her hand to save herself.

Her hand sank into something solid yet not completely solid. It shuddered away of its own accord and she landed heavily on one knee, slippery black plastic heaped about her, the one filled bag tied with green twine.

A very large bag, Jessica thought, her eyes on it as if it were some rare archaeological find. Of course the police would surely have looked through this great echoing amphitheatre already – wouldn't they? Wouldn't they? Her hand moved again, tracing outline. Was this too fantasy? Some figment of the mind? The scratching had stopped. Her fingers, poised to pull at the twine, stiffened.

If she opened the bag would she see the smiling, heavily painted little face? She wanted to jump to her feet but something held her there. Her fingers moved again, tearing at twine and plastic.

The face was covered with clear plastic, pulled tight, twisted at the back of the frizzy hair. Apart from the hair she wouldn't have recognized Linda Tate.

She was scrambling to her feet, running back the way she had entered, all remembered horror swallowed up in the new terror that lent wings to her feet. She jerked open the heavy door, took a second to gulp in cold, moonlit air and ran again, across the clear space towards the yard, into the alley. Her hands shook violently as she fitted the key into the car door, her breath coming in sobbing gasps.

Then she was behind the wheel, slamming the door, automatically snapping on the safety belt, her mind going into automatic pilot.

She drove in the same automatic manner, stopping obediently at traffic lights, keeping down the speed, not thinking. Not thinking about anything.

There were lights at the police station, a strange officer behind the desk. Walking in she brushed dust off her hands, tried to control the jerking of a tiny muscle near the corner of her mouth.

'Yes, Miss?' The policeman behind the desk was looking at her.

'Is Sergeant Penton here, please?' How calm her voice sounded. As if she had mislaid a pet cat, an empty handbag –

'The sergeant went off duty hours ago. Is there anything I can do, Miss?'

'It's his case, you see,' Jessica said stupidly. 'He'll want to know about it.'

'You'd better sit down, Miss.' He had come round the desk, transforming himself into the father figure.

'Thank you, yes. I feel quite dizzy,' Jessica heard herself say.

'Put your head between your knees,' the policeman said. 'Pat, get us a good strong cup of tea – on the double. Now take it easy. No hurry.'

'I'm all right now.' Jessica forced the room into focus. 'I've found a body, you see, and it gave me a shock. In the warehouse in Wilson Street.'

'A body?' He had stepped back, father figure stiffening into investigator. A policewoman came in with a cup in her hand.

'I just brewed up.' Her voice sounded blessedly normal, a voice that sent away the shadows. 'You drink it down now, and you'll feel fine.'

Drinking the scalding, over sweet brew she felt normality shawl her round.

'Now if we can have your name, Miss.' He had notebook and pencil out.

'Jessica Cameron. I'm staying at The Cedars in Blundell Road.'

'And you say you've seen a body in Wilson Street?'

Over the rim of the teacup she nodded.

'And Sergeant Penton would want to know?' His voice was leading her slowly along.

'It's Linda Tate,' she said on a long breath. 'Her mother –'

'Has been reported missing,' the young policewoman said brightly. 'I reckon Sergeant Penton will want to hear.'

The other policeman went over to the desk again and picked up the phone.

'I didn't know that Linda Tate was missing too,' the policewoman said. 'She's the daughter, isn't she?'

'She's not officially missing but Sergeant Penton's taking a bit of an interest,' the other said, having spoken briefly into the receiver. 'He's on his way over. You don't mind waiting a few minutes, Miss?'

'I don't think,' said Jessica, trying to smile, 'that I could stand up if I tried. My legs feel like two sticks of jelly.'

'Must be a nasty business,' the policewoman said sympathetically.

'I'll get a car over there, just to keep an eye on the place,' the policeman said, going into an inner room. He sounded vaguely excited. Probably they didn't often get someone stumbling into this particular station to report a murder, Jessica thought. She had an almost uncontrollable urge to giggle but restrained herself, fearing it might be construed as hysteria.

'What exactly happened then?' the policeman asked, returning.

'I went into the warehouse and found Linda Tate's body in a binliner,' Jessica said. 'She had plastic over her face – clear plastic, I mean, twisted at the back of her head. She died like that, I think. Her face was –' She swallowed painfully, willing herself not to be sick.

'More tea, Pat,' the policeman said. 'Ah, here's Sergeant Penton now.'

He came in swiftly, coat tails flying, unlit pipe in hand. He looked large and solid and she felt some of the inner trembling steady.

'Well now,' were his first words. 'Still busy, are you?'

'I'm afraid so.' Jessica spoke meekly.

'And found Linda Tate? Right then, then we'll make a start.' He sounded pleased.

Fourteen

To her surprise her legs had developed bone and muscle, enabling her to walk into the office. Sergeant Penton had settled himself at the desk and was lighting his pipe. By the time it was glowing her nerves had settled down too.

'Right then.' He looked up at her from beneath greying brows. 'Let's hear what happened.'

'I felt restless and decided to go for a drive.'

'To Wilson Street.' He nodded.

'I know it sounds stupid but I kept thinking about Mrs Tate and Linda, so I drove down there. I went round to the back. I wasn't going to go in or anything but I thought they might have returned and be sitting in the kitchen. I know that sounds foolish too. Anyway –' Jessica took a long breath.

'We sealed the back door just to be on the safe side,' Sergeant Penton said.

'I didn't try the door. I – I ran into the warehouse.'

'And found the body of Linda Tate.'

'Yes. Ought not someone to –?'

'There's a car on its way,' he said. 'Go on.'

'I tripped over a pile of binliners. One of them – it felt as if there was someone inside it. I undid the twine and pulled it down and –' She shivered.

The telephone rang. He picked it up, listened intently, said, 'Right. Get the forensic boys on it,' and rang off, returning his attention to her.

'What caused you to run into the warehouse in the first place?' he asked.

Jessica, who had been considering and discarding various white lies, heard herself saying in a matter-of-fact tone, 'I saw a ghost and I ran.'

'I see.' He puffed slowly on his pipe.

'I know it sounds insane,' Jessica said desperately. 'It sounds that way to me too, but I did see one.'

'What exactly did you see?'

'A child of about eleven or twelve in a pink frilly dress with her face painted,' Jessica said. 'I have seen her before – in the street by the Blundell traffic lights when I first arrived. I didn't realize she wasn't real then. I saw her again at the Rainbow Club when I was there with Adam Darby, and then again tonight. I've seen her at an older stage too, thirteen or fourteen – hanging washing in the yard, looking through one of the ground-floor windows of The Cedars, dressed in blouse and a droopy skirt. I assumed it was Linda Tate until I met Linda and saw she was quite different. I think her name is Polly Winter.'

'And what makes you think that?' he enquired. It was impossible to tell from the mild interest of his tone whether he believed her or not.

Jessica took another long breath and launched into an account of the footsteps in the gallery, the slip of paper fluttering from the pages of the old cookery book. The words, halting at first, poured out.

'And you're the only one who sees this child?' He drew on his pipe.

'Yes – no, Darren Parks, the boy whose mother saw Mrs Tate on her way home – he told me there was a little girl in a pink party dress hanging round my car when I went the first time to Wilson Street. Of course he didn't realize it wasn't real.'

'You don't know it was the same child.'

'I can't believe there's more than one running round in high heels and a frilly pink dress.'

'True. Well, I think that's all for now.' He knocked the glowing ashes from his pipe into a large ashtray and rose. 'I'll get someone to drive you home. Don't worry. He can walk back. Our men don't get enough exercise since they stuck policemen in cars. And you're probably still a bit shocked.'

'What about –?' She hesitated.

'I have to get over to Wilson Street. No need for you to come now. Tomorrow morning you might not mind coming down with me. Someone will have to identify Linda too. No other known relatives.'

'Someone killed her,' Jessica said. 'She didn't put herself into that binliner.'

'Yes.' He looked at her thoughtfully. 'And you found her. Nasty business.'

'Don't they say that the person who finds a body is usually the prime suspect?'

'Sometimes, but I think you can rule yourself out. No motive as far as I can tell, not much opportunity if she was killed last night because you were in the Rainbow Club with Adam Darby. No, I can't see you as a prime suspect. Now I'll have someone drive you over to The Cedars.'

'If the Clares ask –?'

'No harm in telling them. The Tates worked for them after all. I wouldn't go into too much detail.'

'I won't.' She hoped the Clares would be in bed though it seemed unlikely.

'I'll call round about nine tomorrow morning. Too early for you?' He had the father figure persona again.

'I'll be ready,' Jessica said, and went out, handing the car keys to the pink-cheeked young constable who stood waiting.

A few minutes later she had bidden him goodnight, locked the garage and let herself into the kitchen where someone had thoughtfully left a light on. When she opened the hall door she could hear music coming from the television set in the sitting-room.

The first shock had subsided. She wanted suddenly to tell someone about the death, driven, she supposed, by the same compulsion that leads people to gather in groups and discuss disasters.

'Did you have a nice drive?' Sophy Clare looked up from the tapestry she was stitching as Jessica came in.

'Not very.' Jessica hesitated, then said, pitching her voice slightly higher than the television, 'I'm afraid something has happened. Linda Tate is – she's been found dead.'

Sophy's needle jerked and she uttered a small cry, a drop of blood spurting on to the canvas. Her husband had looked up, the expression of mild irritation on his face becoming something else – terror? Disbelief? The expression was gone too swiftly for her to analyse it. Then he leaned to switch off the television and looked at her.

'Dead?' he said.

'Yes. There's a warehouse at the back of where the Tates live. She was found there.'

'John?' Sophy looked across at him imploringly.

'Good Lord, what a dreadful thing,' John Clare said with no emphasis on the words at all. 'Saw the police, did you?'

He had apparently jumped to the conclusion that she had met them somehow. At least it saved long and complicated explanation.

'Yes.'

'But how? It was an accident? An accident surely?' Sophy said.

'She'd been suffocated by a large piece of plastic,' Jessica said.

'And no sign of Mrs Tate?' John asked. He had risen and was pouring drinks at a cocktail cabinet in the corner.

'Not yet.'

'You think that Mrs Tate –?' His wife looked at him. 'Oh, surely not. She was devoted to her daughter. She would never have –'

'We never know what goes on behind closed doors,' John said. 'Jessica, you look rather pale. A drop of brandy will do you good. Do you know when Linda was – when she died?'

'No. Late last night perhaps.'

'Oh, that's all right then,' Sophy said.

Jessica looked at her.

'She might have been asleep and felt nothing,' John supplied. 'Who is going to identify the poor girl? There are no relatives, are there?'

'Only her mother,' Jessica said.

'I'll call in at the station first thing in the morning,' he said. 'It is fortunate that I will be able to make an identification without your having to be troubled, my dear.'

'Poor Linda! She was never terribly bright but she was always very willing,' Sophy said. 'Shall I be expected to stay in tomorrow? I have my old ladies to see.'

'I shouldn't think so.' He moved to refill the glass she was holding out.

'And Jessica will be busy too, I daresay. You won't mind being in the house by yourself?'

'Not everybody is as nervous as you are,' John said.

'I'll probably be out for part of the day anyway.' Jessica debated whether or not to mention that Sergeant Penton was calling for her but decided against it.

'There we are then.' He sounded satisfied.

'I will say goodnight then,' Jessica said. 'Oh, I bolted the kitchen door.'

'Thank you, dear. Isn't it nice to have a considerate lodger?' Sophy appealed.

'Wasn't your last one?' Jessica ventured.

'Miss Reynolds? We scarcely ever saw her. She went off to Birmingham or some such place.' He sounded dismissive.

'Good night then.'

Climbing the stairs she felt her legs beginning to shake again. What had happened was crystallizing in her memory like some vivid waking nightmare. She had almost reached the stage of looking back and marvelling at her own behaviour. What had possessed her to drive back to Wilson Street, to go round to the back and stumble into the warehouse? The idea that she might not be entirely in control of her actions struck her with peculiar unpleasantness.

She stuck the chair under the door handle without allowing herself to think too deeply about why she chose to do that, pulled off her clothes, and slept without a single dream rising to disturb the long and peaceful night.

Morning brought a shower of rain, bending the branches in the garden.

From the gallery Sophy called, 'We're off now. See you later.'

Jessica hastily moved the chair and opened the door a crack to acknowledge the greeting.

'Old people's home,' Sophy said, pausing briefly. 'Terribly sweet old dears. Of course they call it sheltered accommodation these days, don't they?'

She waved a gloved hand and went on down the stairs.

It was almost half past eight. Jessica wondered if they'd run into Sergeant Penton when they called at the station. They might think it rather odd that she hadn't mentioned she was the one to find Linda's body. On the other hand she doubted if the sergeant ever revealed the slightest bit of information he wasn't obliged to reveal.

She was drinking a second cup of coffee when he tapped at the back door.

'Hope you don't mind the informality. I've brought Constable Harry along, and he'd thank you on his knees for a cup of coffee.' He stepped in, large and placid.

'He needn't go that far. Would you like one yourself?'

'Why not? I need an extra shot of caffeine. Oh, Mr and Mrs Clare called in at the station. He kindly offered to make the formal identification,' Sergeant Penton said.

'I didn't mention that I'd found her.' Jessica hesitated.

'No reason why you should,' he said. 'Mind you, you'll have to give evidence at the inquest. If I were you I'd say you were scared by a cat or something because the coroner may be a bit disinclined to take your evidence seriously if you start talking about little girls in party frocks.'

'Do you take it seriously?' she asked bluntly.

'I've an open mind. Harry here's a bit of a believer.'

'My auntie reads cups,' the younger man said.

'I don't,' Jessica said quickly. 'I've never had a psychic experience in my life until my poster –' She stopped.

'What about a poster?' The sergeant stirred his coffee.

'That was how it started,' Jessica said slowly. 'I forgot about that.'

'Go on then.' As she hesitated, Sergeant Penton added, 'We won't go putting you down as daft without a great deal more evidence.'

'When I came here I brought a poster of a girl dancing that I bought in Spain – just a touristy souvenir. The girl had a scarlet dress on, very vivid. I put it up on the wall when I arrived here and that same evening, when I went into the bedroom, the dress had turned pink. It's stayed pink ever since.'

'Could we see the poster?' he asked.

'Yes, of course. Would you like to come up?' She rose and led the way through to the hall and up the stairs, hearing the stolid, reassuring tread of the feet behind her.

'Nice room.' Sergeant Penton looked round approvingly. 'Is that it? The dress was scarlet?'

'The name of the firm that distributes them is at the back so you can check.'

'I wasn't doubting. Could you let us have it for a few hours?'

'For the forensic boys? Yes, of course.'

'I see you're picking up the jargon,' he said with a grin. 'Take it down, Harry. You have a bag?'

'Here.' The constable produced one.

Looking at it Jessica saw Linda's face, mouth and eyes open and fixed like some gargoyle trapped behind a film of ice. She turned abruptly and went out on to the gallery again.

'Right then.' The sergeant was behind her. 'We'll have this looked at and find out why it faded. Now, if you'd like to drive over to Wilson Street, we can take you through your movements of last night. No need to use your car.'

Going out through the back door, locking up, she reminded herself that Linda wouldn't be there. There would be chalk marks to denote the position where she had been found. Linda's body would be – elsewhere.

'We won't keep you too long,' Sergeant Penton was saying. 'You'll be wanting to get on with your work.'

'Believe it or not, but I have got it more or less under control,' she assured him.

'Must be interesting, digging up the past. You didn't notice anything in particular when you were driving down here last evening?'

'No, I was driving automatically, not even thinking about where I was going. It seemed such a foolish thing to do,' Jessica apologized.

'Like going back to make sure you turned the gas off?' Sergeant Penton suggested.

'Something like that,' she admitted. 'I kept hoping that Mrs Tate and Linda would be there.'

They were turning into Wilson Street. A small knot of people, women with scarves over their heads and pre-school age children were gathered at one end.

'News still spreads like wildfire even though the old neighbourhood solidarity is breaking down,' the sergeant said. 'You parked – where?'

'Outside the house.' She indicated where a solitary policeman now stood.

'You didn't knock at the front door?'

'No. I don't know why I didn't, but I didn't. I walked down the alley to the back. I had some idea there might be a light in the kitchen but the house was in darkness.'

'Let's do that then.' He alighted, held open the car door politely. Everything looked shoddy in the morning light, with patches of darkness where the earlier shower had soaked into gravel and stone.

'You didn't try the back door?' he asked when the stood in the yard.

Jessica shook her head.

'Stand where you were standing and then just walk us through everything else as near as you can remember,' he instructed.

'I stood looking at the house.' She suited words to action. 'Then I decided that I was being stupid so I turned towards the alley and the child was standing there.'

'You saw her?'

'Yes, I know – it was dark and there's no street light just here, but I saw her clearly – more clearly than if I stood in daylight. I don't know the exact time. I never thought of looking. Nine – nine-thirty? Around then anyway. The moon came out as I stood there and she was still there. I told myself she wasn't. I told myself that she was only in my imagination, that if I took a step towards her she'd dissolve or something. So I took the step and she – it took a step towards me and smiled. And then I ran.'

'Towards the warehouse?'

'Yes, but at the time I wasn't aware – I panicked and ran and banged into a door. It was open and I ran inside and it swung shut behind me.'

'Right then, let's walk the way you took,' he said placidly. At his heels Constable Harry held a notebook as eagerly as a terrier carried home a newspaper.

There was another policeman by the door of the warehouse. He stood aside as she pushed open the door, as the other two followed, the constable making a note as she reached for the light switch, then realized the lights were on.

'We've already got your prints so they can be eliminated,' Sergeant Penton said. 'What did you do then?'

'There was a scratching sound on the other side of the door. I stood for a minute and then I went further in. I turned on the other light over here, and then I skidded on one of the binliners and put out my hand to save myself.'

The chalk marks were there as she had envisaged.

'I grasped the bag,' she said, 'and felt something – yielding. I undid the twine. It was tied in a bow – I only just remembered that and then I pulled down the bag a bit and saw – and then I ran.'

'Back the same way?'

'I didn't even think about the child. I just ran. I got in the car and I drove straight back to the station. Do we have to stay here?'

'No, not at all.' He turned and led the way back into the open.

'Have you found out anything – anything you can tell me, that is?' she asked.

'We've built up a possible picture of what happened,' he said. 'Want a smoke?'

She hardly ever did but she took one anyway, drawing the smoke down into her lungs and coughing slightly.

'Difficult to tell the exact time of death, but around ten or eleven the night before last,' Sergeant Penton said, 'so that lets out you and your friend, Adam Darby, since you were in the Rainbow Club. Linda was killed from behind. A plastic bag twisted over her face and pulled tight. It'd have been over in seconds. We reckon she was about to make herself a bit of bacon for supper.'

'I didn't think of that.' Jessica shivered.

'We reckon she put the bacon in the pan and then sat down to finish her cup of coffee before she started frying it,' Constable Harry continued. 'She had her back to the kitchen door. Whoever came in killed her before she had a chance to turn round.'

'There were two used cups in the sink.'

'She had had a cup earlier and not bothered to wash it up. Anyway she was put feet first into one of the binliners. We figure the killer went into the warehouse first and had a bit of a nose round. Then Linda was carried over to the warehouse and dumped there.'

'Someone had slept on the bed upstairs,' Jessica said.

'He or she probably came back, had a bit of a snooze and then left. Of course the time of death is only approximate. Could have been a couple of hours each side.'

'Between eight and twelve,' Constable Harry said helpfully.

'Didn't Mrs Parks see Mrs Tate on her way home at ten o'clock?' Jessica asked, then shook her head violently at the thought that had occurred to her.

'And sticks to her story. Seems like a reliable witness. So Mrs Tate could have done it herself or it was done earlier and Linda had already been taken to the warehouse,' Sergeant Penton said.

'And Mrs Tate had a nap on the bed? With the back door open and her daughter missing? I can't see her doing that,' Jessica said.

'You're probably right,' Sergeant Penton said. He sounded gloomy.

'And I can't see someone who just killed someone coming back and having a lie-down,' Jessica said.

'One never knows with people who kill.' He had taken out his empty pipe and was biting the stem. 'Most of them do something irrational sooner or later.'

'Surely murder is irrational?' she said sharply.

'Sometimes murder is the rational solution to an otherwise insoluble problem,' the sergeant said. 'You're not yet a cynic, Miss Cameron.'

'It couldn't have been Mrs Tate.' She spoke with decision. 'She would never hurt her own daughter. She's a nice woman. I don't know her very closely, but I do know that. Sergeant, how does the child I saw fit in with all this? Or am I simply imagining things?'

'I don't know,' he said frankly. 'If you are imagining, then why are you imagining this particular figure? Why not a little boy? I've an open mind on the subject.'

'I don't feel as if I've any mind left at all,' Jessica said frankly. 'I feel as if I were in the middle of two different stories that get wider and wider apart. I feel stupid.'

'The murderer,' Sergeant Penton said, 'is probably feeling very clever. Most of them do. However we shall carry on plodding.'

There was a small twinkle in his eyes. Jessica looked at him and managed a contrived smile that trembled a little at the edges.

'It couldn't have been Mrs Tate, could it?' she said.

'There wasn't any struggle,' he said. 'Now, if you're sitting alone in a house, would you be prepared to do so while a complete stranger stepped up behind you and put a large piece of –?'

'No,' Jessica said. 'And if my mother had disappeared I wouldn't be sitting in a house with the door unlocked either.'

'We haven't found Mrs Tate's handbag yet,' he said.

'Her handbag?' Jessica threw away the unsmoked stub of her cigarette and blushed slightly as Constable Harry stamped it out and retrieved it.

'We'll need to do a lot more searching, Miss,' he said with a shade of reproof. 'Don't want to muddle them up, do we?'

'Sorry. What about Mrs Tate's handbag?'

'There's a small white leather one that is empty in the wardrobe,' Sergeant Penton said. 'Probably kept for best. No other handbag, which would contain her purse and her keys. Evidently she still has it with her. Did you ever notice Mrs Tate's handbag?'

'No, I'm sorry.' Jessica screwed up her eyes and tried to picture the kitchen with Mrs Tate seated at the table – 'No, I'm sorry. She may have kept it in the cupboard with her coat and scarf or in a corner of the kitchen. I simply don't recall ever having noticed it.'

'No reason why you should,' he said amiably. 'Of course when we find Mrs Tate then everything will become a lot clearer. Well, we'll be getting on with the investigation as we always do. Constable Harry will run you back to the station to make a statement about finding the body and then he'll give you a lift back to The Cedars.'

'And you don't want to have me mention the child in the pink dress?'

'Not unless it becomes absolutely necessary. Coroners are apt to get muddled,' Sergeant Penton said. 'I'll have a word with him myself perhaps. You've been very helpful, Miss Cameron.'

He gave her a smiling nod and wandered off to talk to a policeman who'd appeared around the corner of the warehouse.

'He's getting there,' Constable Harry said. He sounded like a proud child watching an elderly parent compete in an egg and spoon race. 'Very thorough, very sound is Sergeant Penton.'

'I'm sure.' Jessica walked with him back up the alley.

There were more policemen in the street, standing about as if they had nothing better to do than watch the increasing crowd of spectators.

In the car she looked at Constable Harry as they drove away.

'What do you think?' she asked.

'About Linda Tate's death, Miss? I think it'll turn out to be pretty much as the sergeant thinks it was. Mrs Tate might be a very nice lady but there are queer things happen in families. On the other hand why did she go missing before Linda was killed? I mean that's getting things the wrong way round.'

'And the child I keep seeing? I really don't go round seeing things that aren't there.'

'Neither does my auntie,' Constable Harry said, 'but she can tell you what's liable to happen in the next month or two, and she's right more often than not.'

'I don't suppose you'll have time to look up in the archives about the governess and the little girl who disappeared now this has happened?'

'Sergeant Penton and I had a bit of a chat about that. I reckon when he gets a spare half-hour he'll do a bit of digging,' the constable said. 'Now we'll get a brief statement from you typed up and then I'll run you back to The Cedars.'

'I'll be fine walking. It's only a ten minute stroll. And you'll want to get back to the warehouse, won't you?'

'It's a queer business,' he admitted. 'Nasty too. The sergeant's got daughters of his own. He gets irritable when young people are murdered. And if it's the mother who did it – it doesn't bear thinking about, does it, Miss?'

Polly's Tale

Well, this is a carry on and no mistake. Who would have thought it? – as the mistress says whenever she hears a bit of gossip.

There I was, minding my own business and getting on with my own life – such as it is these days – and along comes the new governess. New isn't the right word, because we ain't – haven't had a governess before. Master says it's important to speak nicely. I could've told him that it wasn't in Madam's place that my grammar upped and died on me. I was born speaking common. People living in Victoria Street are common. A lot of the girls in Madam's speak ever so nicely.

Anyway you could've knocked me down with a feather when I saw who the new governess was – is, since she's still here. Dot Larue, with her hair netted back and a dress on that covers up more of her than any dress did before. Well, I ask you. Oh, she recognized me straight off. She never let on and I never let on, but we both knew. We're not stupid.

It's funny but when I first saw her she looked different. She had short hair as if it'd been cut off for illness and the face was different, but when I saw her next it was Dot Larue, large as life, with her hair like it always was only more like a lady's and her face the same but without paint.

You know, sometimes I think that this house is haunted. No, don't laugh. I know we're past the middle of the nineteenth century and nobody believes in them things any longer, but there's times I catch glimpses of other people who don't live here. Like seeing Dot Larue with short hair. And then last evening when I had to go on an errand.

'Take the omnibus,' says Mistress. 'You know where to go?'

I know where to go better than she realizes. She tells me the stuff's for her nerves and she doesn't want Master to find out because it'd worry him. She doesn't know that I spent half my time in Madam's running out to buy those little packets. I mean, who wants squalling babies in a brothel? And Mistress doesn't want any more now that she's got her two either. Nerves is a laugh.

Anyway I put on my coat and off I go. On the omnibus. It's a bit of a treat for me to get into town. Master won't trust me farther than the local shop, but he's gone off to a clerical conference. That means he won't be back until tomorrow, so we'll all get a bit of a rest.

Well, I get off and I walk along, keeping my eyes firmly on the ground, looking like a good little servant girl. I get to the shop and go in and slide the note and the money over the counter. Funny, but he doesn't recognize me. I must've changed a lot since I was at Madam's.

I get the packet and stick it deep in my pocket and slide out again. The dusk is stealing down over the town and the lamps are being lit one by one. This was the hour when I put on my pretty dress and one of the girls painted my face up and I went down to hand drinks round and wait until a masher who licks his lips at the sight of a young girl comes along.

Well, it had its drawbacks did that life but I tell you plain that it had its moments too. It was a hell of a lot better than living in Victoria Street. And while I'm thinking about that then I find myself at the end of the old road.

'Well, stone the crows!' I say and look round in surprise. The old street looks really run down. Honestly, you'd never have known it. And there's a sign at the end says – WILSON? Wilson. So what happened to Victoria then? Makes me dizzy the way things are changing all the time. But it's the same road.

I know I ought to turn round and go back to catch the omnibus, but my feet are carrying me onward down the street. I can't remember exactly where I used to live before I went to Madam's. Somewhere round here for certain. There's an alley leading down one side. Now why do I find myself going down this alley? I don't like dark alleys any more, but I go along it anyway as if something's calling me. There's nothing at the back but a yard and the old warehouse. I have a bad feeling about that warehouse. And I feel as if I had the pink dress on. Maybe I'm getting sick, muddled in the head.

There is someone standing in the yard.

'It's Dot Larue,' I say aloud, but no sound comes out of my mouth. I'm opening it like a fish and nothing's coming out.

And then she starts running. And maybe it isn't Dot Larue after all, but I chase after her anyway and a door bangs in my face and I'm scratching, scratching, scratching ...

Fifteen

She had spent the morning at the university library, pushing out of her mind images of murder and concentrating doggedly on aspects of mid-Victorian family life – the meals eaten, the floors polished by generations of housemaids, the rigid moral codes when women

were either angels or soiled doves. She paused only for a coffee
break and then went on until aching shoulders and a twinge of cramp
in her arm told her that it was time to stop. What she had to do now
was go and see Adam. He would have read the headlines in the
newspaper, announcing that the body of Linda Tate had been
found. No details had been given and her name hadn't appeared.

Packing up the notes and sketches she had made, she headed for
the nearest telephone and rang the number Adam had given her.

An adenoidal voice at the other end informed her that Mr Darby
had gone to Birmingham and would be in touch.

Which meant, Jessica mused, replacing the receiver, that he must
have been given a useful lead by the house agent and, possibly
having failed to contact her at The Cedars had rushed off on a trail of
his own. Her best bet was to return and sit tight until he contacted
her from Birmingham.

She drove back to Blundell Road and turned in at the gate just as
the Clares appeared at the front door. They were clearly dressed for
travelling and Sophy carried a small overnight bag.

'Jessica, I'm so glad we didn't miss you.' Sophy spoke rapidly, her
voice high with worry. 'My parents are sick and we've decided to
drive down and see what we can do. I've left a note for you on the
table. Are you going to be all right here? Perhaps your friend can
come over and spend the night? He seemed such a pleasant young
man.'

'I'll be fine,' Jessica said. No point in worrying them further by
telling them that Adam was out of town. 'I'm sorry about your
parents. I hope you have good news when you get there.'

'Thank you. The extra keys are on the table and there's plenty of
stuff in the 'fridge if you don't feel like shopping. Do let's hurry,
darling.'

'Be sure to lock up. We'll ring later on this evening,' her husband
said, following her.

Jessica went slowly into the house. The day was sunny and
patterns of colour from the stained-glass windows dappled the hall.
She put the chain up at the front door and checked the back.
Everything was still and peaceful. Through the open window of her
bedroom she could hear the whine of a motor mower from one of the
nearby gardens. Placid suburbia had a lot to recommend it, she
decided, and went into the kitchen to make herself some lunch. She
had just finished washing-up after herself when a tap on the kitchen

window revealed the arrival of Sergeant Penton.

'I hope you don't mind the informality, Miss Cameron.' He stepped into the kitchen as she unlocked the door. 'All by yourself?'

'The Clares were called down to London. Apparently Mrs Clare's parents are both sick. Tea?'

'Nothing, thanks. You're not all alone here?'

'For the moment. I'm fine really.'

'Where's Mr Darby then?' he enquired.

'He went to Birmingham.'

'Birmingham?' The sergeant's eyebrows were elevated. 'Not very gallant of him to rush off at a time like this. Leaving you by yourself, I mean.'

'We're not a regular duet,' Jessica said with a twinge of amusement.

'Even so. Will you be here by yourself tonight?'

'I'll be fine.' Even as she spoke the confident words she wondered if they were true.

'Well, if you get worried about anything don't hesitate to ring,' he said cordially. 'I'm doing a bit of overtime this evening so you can reach me directly; I've scribbled down the number for you.'

'That's very kind of you, but I'm sure I won't need to ring. Sergeant, have you anything particular to tell me? I take it that this isn't a social call.'

'There's nothing further on Mrs Tate,' he said gloomily. 'That woman seems to have disappeared into thin air. No, I've been doing a bit of digging into police records. About the Makins and that governess who went missing.'

'I planned to search the city archives myself,' Jessica confessed, 'but then I decided to postpone it and get on with the work I'm paid to do. Did you find anything interesting?'

'Not very much. You know during the bombing in the last war a lot of records were destroyed. However the Makin case was kept on the books which explained how someone was able to write about it in that book of notorious mysteries you read.'

'And?'

'No arrests were ever made and no bodies were ever found,' Sergeant Penton said. 'In those days the police didn't have the scientific and forensic resources that we enjoy today, and they strike me as having been a whole lot more naive about the upper classes in those days too.'

'Meaning?' She looked at him sharply.

'In my opinion I think that I'd have questioned Edward Makin for a lot longer. He was a clergyman and so in the current climate of opinion beyond suspicion, but it strikes me as odd that he devoted so much of his time to hanging round brothels and rescuing "fallen women". I suspect the governess, Dorothy Larue, may have been his mistress. Either she threatened to make trouble and he killed her or she took off with the child out of spite because he'd rejected her or something of that nature. I fancy the police may have had the same idea with nothing to back it up, and they'd hesitate before embarrassing a clergyman of impeccable reputation. The family went abroad not long afterwards and the case was tacitly closed though it stayed on the books, but nobody was looking for the governess or the little girl any longer. Unsatisfactory ending.'

'The housekeeper, Mrs Tatum, stayed on to work for the Laurences when they bought the house. Did you find out anything about the servant girl?'

'Polly? Not a thing. She left and went into service elsewhere, I suppose. Who knows what happened to her? She probably married someone and moved away and lived a life of placid respectability and died peacefully at the end. Anyway there doesn't seem to be any point in carrying on down this particular dead end.'

'Well, it was kind of you to bother,' Jessica said, disappointed. 'I did see the child though – it wasn't imagination.'

'I'm prepared to accept there are more things in heaven and earth – did Mr Darby mention why he was going to Birmingham?'

'There was a woman lodging here before I came,' she reminded him.

'Dorothy Reynolds? We checked on that. She left, didn't she? You think she might be of some help. It seems doubtful to me.'

'Perhaps she left because she saw the little girl?' Jessica suggested.

'Perhaps.' He looked doubtful, then smiled. 'It would likely set your mind at rest if she had. Anyway, you'll not forget what I've said? At the first hint of anything not quite right give me a ring. And don't let anyone in unless you know who they are.'

'What if Mrs Tate turns up?'

'I've a gut feeling that she won't, but we'll see. You take care of yourself now.'

He gave her an avuncular pat on the shoulder and left. After he had gone she remembered that Darren Parks had seen Polly too – the child in a grubby party dress hanging round her car in Wilson Street. Perhaps she ought to have mentioned it. On the other hand what had happened here more than a century before had no material link with the murder of Linda Tate or the disappearance of her mother.

She locked the back door and went up to her room. Her notes and sketches were piled on the table – proof that despite everything she had managed to do a fair amount of work. She sat down and started typing up the notes she had taken that morning. The family that would serve as an example of Victorian family life was taking shape in readiness for the proposed exhibition. She would use the Makins, without mentioning the disappearance of Dorothy Larue and Julia. Such events were not typical of an average middle-class family.

She had left her door open so that she could hear the first ring of the telephone but it remained quiescent. The neighbour had finished mowing his lawn and the house was quiet. No childish footstep sounded along the landing; in the orchard the pears hung heavily from the trees with no thin figure reaching up to twist them free. The Cedars had no more atmosphere than any other place. Only Jessica's overstretched nerves twitched now and then as she raised her head from her work and listened to the emptiness.

Without warning, footsteps sounded in the yard beneath her window. She stood up and moved to look out, meeting the upturned gaze of a fair-haired young man who stood beneath. He was carrying a duffel bag and his expression was one of mild enquiry.

'I can't get in,' he complained.

'Why do you want to get in?' Her voice was sharp. 'Who are you?'

'Julian Clare. Who are you? Mother's generally home in the late afternoon.'

'I'm Jessica Cameron. I lodge here for the moment. Can you give me some proof of your identity?'

'Is Mrs Tate here? She'll vouch for me. I've no passport or anything on me.'

'I suppose it's all right. Wait a minute and I'll come down and unbolt the back door.'

She unbolted it and stepped aside as he came in, heaving his bag
on to the table. His expression as he turned to look at her was
wryly amused.

'You've caught Mrs Tate's security mania. I really am Julian
Clare. Where is everybody?'

'Your parents haven't told you? Mrs Tate went missing and your
parents went down to London. Your grandparents are both sick.'

'Meaning they feel neglected and want a visit. What d'ye mean,
Mrs Tate went missing?'

'Her daughter, Linda –'

'Kid with blonde hair. What about her? Is there anything to eat?
I'm starving.'

'In the 'fridge. I can make you a sandwich.'

'That would be charity indeed. I got a couple of days off without
any warning and decided to come home. My car's in dock so I had
to get the train. Go on about Linda Tate.'

'She's been – killed,' Jessica said, taking bread and ham and
butter out and beginning to make sandwiches.

'These drunk drivers –'

'Suffocated by a plastic bag,' she interrupted. 'Her body was
found in the old warehouse near her home in Wilson Street. Her
mother – Mrs Tate left here last Friday and never arrived at home.'

'My God.' He looked at her blankly. 'That's horrendous. Why
didn't someone ring up and let me know?'

'I suppose they didn't want to worry you or your sister. Tea or
coffee?'

'Coffee, please. What sister?'

'Your sister Robina –' Jessica stopped short, staring at him. He
had taken a seat at the table, unzipping his anorak, his glance on
the sandwiches she was making.

'Let me get this straight.' He moved his gaze to her face. 'You
say I have a sister called Robina?'

'Your parents said –' Automatically she put the plate of
sandwiches in front of him and switched on the kettle.

'Miss – Cameron? Miss Cameron, I had a sister called Robina.
She died.'

'Died?' Jessica stared at him blankly, her mind racing. 'What
d'ye mean – died?'

'Passed away – kicked the bucket – sorry, that sounds flippant
but it all happened a longish time ago. We were on holiday up in

the Broads – Father had hired a cabin cruiser; Robina was fooling around on deck and she slipped and fell. She was caught in the undertow. It was – unpleasant. She and I were closer than many brothers and sisters, you see. My parents were devastated, but I never dreamed – my mother started drinking a little too much from time to time – a crutch against the pain. I simply didn't realize that she'd carried her fantasy that far.'

'Mrs Tate didn't mention anything about it.'

'I daresay she figured it wasn't her business to go relating past family tragedy to a newcomer,' he said thoughtfully. 'She's fond of my mother, but someone ought to have said.'

'You are a trainee social worker?' Jessica asked, pouring two coffees.

'I am indeed. Ought to get my final qualifications before very long. Look, I think I ought to ring up my grandparents and find out if anything's seriously wrong. Excuse me.'

He went out into the hall, looking worried.

Jessica sat down, sipping her coffee while her thoughts rearranged themselves into a different pattern. Robina Clare was dead, a fact her parents had refused to admit. She must have been buried on the Norfolk Broads, and only Mrs Tate would have known the truth. And probably Linda too. Sophy Clare had no close friends; she could pretend to everybody else that both her children were still alive. It was the stuff of tragedy.

'The old people aren't too bad, as I suspected,' Julian said, returning. 'I am afraid my poor mother panders to them over much. Age isn't all sweetness and light. That's one thing my training is teaching me.'

'You're specializing in the care of the old?'

'It's a neglected field. Too much talk about euthanasia and not enough research done into the advantages of hospices and similar institutions. These are excellent sandwiches. You're not in the catering trade, by any chance?'

'I arrange exhibitions for a firm specializing in social history.'

'Sounds interesting. Why here?'

'I go where I'm sent and Liverpool and its suburbs are a rich field for Victoriana.'

'Like this house. Awful old pile, isn't it? My parents could never afford to furnish it properly. Look, this might be a bit awkward – I mean, I'd reckoned on staying here for a couple of nights. With you here –' He paused, looking embarrassed.

'I promise to lock my door,' she said, amused. 'Look, I'm not a cordon bleu cook like your mother but I can manage steak and salad for an evening meal, if you like?'

'Sounds good. I'll go up and have a bath and change. See you later.' He finished the last sandwich, shouldered his duffel bag and went out into the hall.

An attractive young man, Jessica decided, with his father's height and his mother's blue eyes and faint reddish tinge to the hair. His arrival was certainly opportune. Quite suddenly she knew that the prospect of spending the night here alone had been less than enticing.

Meanwhile she had a meal to prepare. Despite his having wolfed the sandwiches, she guessed that he'd probably eat a hearty dinner. Steak, baked potatoes and salad then, with fruit and cheese to follow – and it served Adam Darby right for rushing off to Birmingham without letting her know. She grinned happily to herself as she ran hot water into the sink, feeling the burden of apprehension lifting from her.

She had just finished grilling the steaks when Julian reappeared, freshly shaved and changed into polo-necked shirt and grey slacks. It was a pity he was so young, she thought – scarcely more than twenty-one or two – very young to be faced with the responsibility of old people.

'This smells marvellous.' He had poured out two glasses of wine and profferred one with a little bow. 'Shall we eat in the breakfast-room? I'll lay the table. Do you like Chopin?'

'Yes. Yes, I do.'

'I'll put on a record. After we've eaten I want to hear more about what's been going on here. My parents ought to have told me.'

As she had suspected he began talking about the recent events before they had finished the cheese and coffee, as the last strains of music died away.

'Tell me what happened. You met Mrs Tate, of course?'

'She was friendly.'

'She's a nice old girl – not so old, I suppose. Her husband drank like a fish. I think it was a relief when his liver finally gave out. Why would she disappear?'

'Nobody knows. She left here and went off on the bus as usual, got off at the supermarket before her stop; someone saw her walking home at about ten the night before Linda was found –'

'With a plastic bag over her head. That's – awful.' He crumbled a bit of cheese on his plate, his head bent. 'I don't like to think of someone so young dying.'

'It is dreadful. Coffee?'

'Just a splash – thanks. So how long d'ye think you are going to stay here? Is this research job a long drawn out affair?'

'Fairly long. Provided I don't turn the whole exercise into a holiday and get my lists and estimates in on time then I've a fairly free hand. Not that I feel in much of a holiday mood with – excuse me, there's the phone. It'll be a friend of mine. I'm expecting it.'

She sped across the hall, switching on the light as she went.

'Jessica?' It was Adam's voice. 'Thank goodness. I've been trying to get you for hours. I've met Dorothy Reynolds. She's still working in Birmingham, and she says that she left because she felt so uneasy at The Cedars.'

'Then she did see Polly?'

'She –' The voice stopped abruptly.

'Adam?' Jessica jiggled the receiver up and down and swore softly under her breath. 'Damn, damn, the line's gone dead.'

'Anything wrong?' Julian appeared at the door of the breakfast-room.

'The telephone went dead.'

'Try the operator and she'll reconnect you.'

'It's no use,' she said a moment later. 'It's completely dead.'

'Was it important?'

'I guess not.' She bit her lip, wondering what news Adam had been going to impart. The sound of his voice had been unexpectedly reassuring, like an arm laid over her shoulders in the darkness.

'Shall we listen to some more records?' Julian was carrying their coffees.

'Yes, yes, if you like.'

'The big sitting-room's more comfortable. You're not a television fan, I hope? I'm afraid my father spends so much of his time glued to the set that it's rather turned me against it.'

'I'm not a couch potato. Music would be fine.'

'I'll get something cheerful.' He carried the cups through to the large sitting-room and, after a scowl at the telephone, Jessica followed.

He had set the coffees down and was drawing the curtains across the windows. Two of the lamps were switched on and made bright pools of light over the armchairs at each side of the high fireplace.

'How about some Gilbert and Sullivan?' Julian enquired.

'Sounds fine.' Jessica sat down in one of the armchairs and sighed deeply. It was good to have company, to feel the night close round without the tingling of fear.

An instant later she was on her feet, her heart pounding. Someone had walked past the window. She had seen something – a shadow moved fleetingly close up in the tiny gap between the drawn curtains; a faint crunching sound came to her ears and wasn't repeated.

'Julian!' She uttered the name sharply.

'Just coming.' He walked briskly across the room. 'What's wrong?'

'Someone's prowling about outside.'

'Wait here, I'll go and see.' He put down the record he was carrying and started kitchenwards.

'He's at the front,' Jessica hissed.

'Then I'll approach him from the rear. Don't look so scared.'

'Do be careful,' she breathed, watching him push open the baize-covered door. The peace and security had vanished as if it had never been.

It was beyond her powers of self-discipline to wait quietly in the echoing silence of the hall. She moved to the front door, slid the chain off it, opened it a crack. Outside the front path was faintly illumined by the light from the hall. She stepped outside cautiously, and almost sprawled headlong as something snaked about her ankle. Gasping, she clutched the wall for support and pulled her foot free. A long length of telephone wire made a faint tinkling noise as the wind lifted it and blew it a few inches.

Telephone wire. She bent down and picked up the straying end. Someone had cut the cord outside while she was talking to Adam – someone who didn't want her to be able to contact the outside world.

She stepped back inside and closed the door with a snap. Silence came down again, but in the silence small sounds rustled – the ticking of a clock, the swish of something in the breakfast-room across the hall. She went across the hall, pushed wide the door, her eyes moving to the open window – it had been closed while they

were eating their meal. Now it was wide open and the curtains were
blowing against a vase of dried grasses on the sill. She leaned to
close it and pull the curtains to again.

'Julian?' She spoke the name again, her voice tentative.

There was no answer from outside. There was nothing but the
sound of the wind that still sounded in her ears.

This was stupid. Even if someone was prowling about outside
Julian Clare was here. He looked fit and athletic; he knew the
situation.

'Not a thing.' His voice made her start violently as he walked
through from the kitchen area. 'What are you doing?'

'This window was open. The telephone wire's been cut.'

'That must have been why the telephone went on the blink. I've
locked the back door but I think we ought to check the windows,
just in case.'

'I'll do the ones upstairs.'

It was a relief to have something practical to do. She went up the
stairs and along the railed landing, switching on lights as she went,
even humming a little tune under her breath like a child singing in
the dark.

Julian had put his duffel bag in the spare bedroom and the
window was open at the top. She hurried in to close it. Once shut
with the sneck locked it was impossible to open from the outside.

Impossible to open from the outside. The sentence repeated
itself like a litany. The window in the breakfast-room had been
locked. She had glanced at it as they sat down to eat and her feeling
of security had intensified. That meant that the window had been
opened from the inside – someone had leaned out to cut the wire.
Someone inside. What had Adam said? 'I've been trying to get you
for ages?' But he'd got through in the end and then been abruptly
cut off. Julian Clare had telephoned his parents in London to
enquire about his grandparents. Or had he? Had he telephoned at
all?

Her eyes fell onto the duffel bag. The duffel bag was large,
swollen at the sides. Her heart was beating in her throat as she
walked over to the bed and leaned to unfasten the bag. A couple of
T-shirts bulged out. She pulled out the first one and saw beneath
the shabby black handle of the shiny handbag that Mrs Tate had
carried on her arm like an extra limb.

She pushed back the T-shirt and did up the bag again. Her hands were slippery with perspiration. She had to think fast; she had to get out of the house.

'Everything all right up there?' He was calling up from the hall.

'Yes, everything seems fine.' She had sped out on to the wide landing, raising her voice to answer him.

'Shall I make some more coffee?'

'Yes. Yes, that would be fine.' She kept her voice loud and steady, her hands twisting together at her waist. 'I'll be down in a minute.'

The chain was still off the door. She could open the front door quietly and slip out, run for help, hide. Her mind considered and discarded possibilities.

She waited a moment, then swiftly crossed the balcony and descended the stairs. If she could get to the front door then she would be safe. She reached it safely, her hand reaching for the handle.

'Do you take sugar?' He stood near the baize door, looking at her. There was a faint enquiry in his expression.

'I was just – checking the front door,' she said, keeping her voice level with an effort. 'One sugar, please.'

'Fine.' He stood there still, looking at her.

'I think I'll try the phone again.' She walked towards it.

'If the line's been cut then it'll still be dead. You said the line was cut.'

'Yes, I merely hoped –' She hesitated, then said brightly, 'Why don't we have a liqueur with the coffee? I'll slip upstairs and put on something a bit more feminine. Won't be a tick.'

She was past him and up the stairs, turning into her own room, closing the door and standing with her back against it. If she climbed out of the window she might be able to cling to the drainpipe for long enough to let herself down lightly. The possibility of breaking her leg – or even her neck – occurred to her. Then she opened the window, slung one leg over the sill, felt for the drainpipe, telling herself not to look down, not to hurry. Women were expected to take a little time in which to change their clothes.

The drainpipe was rough between her palms; she tried to use elbows and knees but there was an ominous creaking in her ears that warned her the pipe might begin to buckle. Incredibly she felt hard stone under her feet. She had, by some miracle, reached the yard. She flattened herself against the wall, looking sideways towards the kitchen window. It would be safer to go into the garden, to avoid the patio that ran across the back of the house. Among the pear trees she would be invisible, hidden by branches and leaves. She edged her way along the yard wall, and stumbled down the two steps that led into the garden proper. Her feet were silent on the grass.

There was no moon, but her eyes were becoming accustomed to the darkness. The branches of the fruit trees made a rustling sound in the wind. She stopped to gauge her position and a hand suddenly clamped on her shoulder.

Reaction preceded thought. She hit out wildly, hearing a tearing sound as she broke free and ran back towards the house. Dear God, but he had guessed her intention. She ran instinctively, her fingers twisting the knob of the kitchen door while her mind prayed, 'Please, let it be unlocked. Let it be unlocked.'

It was unlocked and she almost fell into the kitchen. The kettle had switched itself off and a thin stream of white steam rose into the air. She ran past it, through the shabby room where the servants had once sat. The hall was too big. The doors leading off it were partly ajar, the rooms beyond in shadow save for the sitting-room from which lamplight gleamed. She paused for a split second, her eyes moving to the front door. If she risked going out again that way – the handle was softly turning. Raw panic ripped through the last shreds of her composure. She fled up the stairs, wanting only to get away from that slowly turning handle. She turned automatically to the right with some primitive instinct driving her towards the room she considered as her own space, but the way was barred as Julian stepped out from the tiny landing, putting an arm out to block her way to the stairs.

'I wish you hadn't found out,' he said, shaking his head gently. 'Oh, I do wish you hadn't found out. You were going to tell Mother and Father, weren't you, about the things I wanted to do to you? I had to push you, Robina. I had to push you. And they suspected anyway – they put me in that place – they called me a voluntary patient, but they did everything they possibly could to stop me leaving. That was very foolish, because I don't like people telling me what to do. I don't like females telling me what to do.'

'Females?' Her voice was a ragged whisper as she backed away along the gallery.

'Mrs Tate told on me.' His voice was resentful. 'She told about me coming home and jumping out at that stupid lodger – Dorothy someone or other – Reynolds, that was it. Plain, stupid Dorothy Reynolds. She left without saying anything except to Mrs Tate, and Mrs Tate told and then I wasn't allowed to come home for a long, long time. But I got out. I came here and saw Mrs Tate sitting at the kitchen table – she just sat there looking at me. I walked up and put my hands round her throat and strangled her – she died ever so quickly. Well, she'll not tell on me again in a hurry.'

'You wore her coat and scarf,' Jessica said numbly.

'I put her in the garden under some firewood just for the time being and then I walked down the road and took a bus to the supermarket. I rolled up the coat and scarf and then I walked out of the supermarket as myself. I took a bus back here and got rid of the body – it was very easy to dig a hole and put her in it. Nobody saw me at all. Then I walked for a long time and then I found myself near Wilson Street. It was getting dark and I was still carrying her coat and scarf. I don't know why. I put the clothes on again and then I walked along to her house. I was going to put the coat back in her wardrobe. The back door was open. Isn't that silly – to leave a door open in these days? I could see Linda sitting at the table, drinking some coffee. There were some plastic bags on the window sill; she turned her head and said, "Mum?", and then her face changed and she didn't say anything else. I put her in the old warehouse across the yard, in a bin bag and then I came back to the house and slept for a couple of hours on top of one of the beds. It was necessary to kill Linda else she'd have told that I was wearing her mother's clothes. She'd have told on me too. After that, when I woke up I walked to the station and caught a train back to the place where I'm kept. I told them I'd been with my parents.'

She remembered, as if it had been a hundred years before, that she had seen the relief in Sophy's face when she had answered the telephone. She recalled the comings and goings of the Clares – their pitiful attempts to keep their son's name out of everything; no doubt they had backed up his story that he had merely spent a short period with them.

'And now you're going to tell on me too,' Julian said. 'I'm sorry about that, because you're a nice person but –'

He stopped speaking, his blue eyes shifting beyond her to something – someone who stood behind her. She heard the tapping of feet or it might have been her own heart beating, and then he stumbled backwards, his hands clawing the air, and leapt, trim and athletic, his head striking the wood of the rail as he fell, spinning like a feather, with infinite slowness to the ground floor below.

And the door burst open bringing with it a blast of cold air and two solid, blessedly solid figures.

Sixteen

'Feeling better?' Sergeant Penton came into the sitting-room where Jessica, with her feet on a stool, was sipping brandy and water.

'Much. Constable Harry is spoiling me rotten,' she assured him.

'Very nice of me considering that the young lady nearly knocked me out when she met me in the orchard,' the young constable said with a grin.

'It was you who passed the window earlier on?'

'We decided to keep an eye open,' Constable Harry said.

'A discreet eye,' his superior said quellingly. 'You were careless there.'

'And since Julian Clare was actually drawing the curtains at that moment I knew it couldn't possibly be him,' Jessica said, sitting up straighter. 'I even mentioned there was someone prowling outside but he said he hadn't seen or heard anything.'

'He probably did and realized the house was under surveillance,' Sergeant Penton said.

'I nipped round to the back just before he opened the back door,' Constable Harry said. 'He didn't actually come out – I suppose he felt that with you in the place he had an advantage. He knew we weren't likely to rush him.'

'Have you found Mrs Tate?' She asked the question shrinkingly.

Outside the headlamps of police cars still raked the driveway.

'In the orchard. He came back after he killed her and dug a shallow hole. It was well covered though in the end she'd have been found, of course. We were already discussing search warrants and the like.'

'He took risks,' Jessica said and shivered.

'That was probably part of the fun,' Sergeant Penton said with an expression of distaste. 'He killed his sister by pushing her off the boat while the family was on holiday. The Clares have made a full statement.'

'You contacted them in London?'

'They weren't in London, Miss Cameron. They had driven up north to the private mental home where Julian had been persuaded to sign himself in as a voluntary patient. They always suspected that their daughter didn't die by accident, but they were reluctant to inform the authorities, so they paid through the nose for an expensive private home. That's where the money went. They couldn't afford to finish furnishing the house or to replenish the things that wore out. Mrs Clare's parents are both deceased, by the way, quite naturally, some years ago, but their continued existence was a convenient fiction when one or both of the Clares went to visit Julian.'

'But why did he kill Mrs Tate?' she asked in bewilderment. 'He told me she was going to tell – tell what?'

'Probably about his sister's death, though she'd have done that years before if she'd had any suspicion. Mrs Clare had told her that Julian worked away, training to be a social worker.'

'And refusing to acknowledge that her daughter was dead,' Constable Harry said. 'Typical denial mechanism coming into play.'

'Harry here fancies himself as a bit of a psychologist,' Sergeant Penton said with a sardonic look.

'She told me that they were both training as social workers – with children,' Jessica remembered. 'Julian talked about the problems of old people – I ought to have suspected something then. I suppose he never really telephoned anybody?'

'The telephone's been out of order most of the day,' Sergeant Penton said. 'It must have been reconnected just before Mr Darby rang you from Birmingham. While you were speaking Julian Clare opened the window and cut the wire. Then he closed it again and later on – after you'd seen Constable Harry's shadow outside he nipped across the hall and opened it again. Clever because you'd immediately assume that someone might have got into the house already. Yes, Julian Clare was very bright. Psychopaths often are, they tell me. Plain old-fashioned wickedness isn't reckoned too much in these enlightened times.'

'He told me that he strangled her because she was going to "tell",' Jessica said. 'He hid her in the orchard and then he put on her coat and scarf and caught the bus to the supermarket. And while he was doing that I was upstairs.'

'You were very lucky he didn't realize the fact,' Sergeant Penton said soberly. 'The Clares hadn't told him they had taken another lodger. The last time they tried and let him know he signed himself out of the home and came and harassed the life out of the poor girl. She liked the Clares and she didn't want to hurt their feelings so she upped and went back to Birmingham. Your friend, Adam Darby, contacted her but she was naturally unwilling to say anything over the telephone so he hared off. He contacted us after he'd tried to ring you and we checked but the phone genuinely was on the blink at that time – roadworks somewhere. When he did get through and was suddenly cut off again he rang us and caught the next train back. In fact I rather think that's him now. We sent a police car to meet him at the station. I told the driver to fill him in on the situation.'

Another arc of headlamps, the sound of a door banging, and then Adam was there, his face a mixture of relief and dismay. Jessica had the comforting feeling that were it not for the presence of the police officers he would have kissed her passionately. As it was he perched on the arm of the chair, put his arm firmly around her shoulders and said, 'I've had the full story. I never should have gone to Birmingham.'

'I seem to have been well protected all the way along,' Jessica said.

'Not that well.' Constable Harry looked uncomfortable. 'We couldn't risk trying to effect an entrance so when we glimpsed you climbing down the drainpipe –'

'What!' Adam stared.

'I was always rather good at gymnastics at school,' Jessica said modestly.

'Anyway it gave us an opportunity to draw Miss Cameron away from the house,' Constable Harry continued. 'The Sergeant went to the car to radio for back-up and I made myself known –'

'By putting your hand on her shoulder and frightening the poor girl nearly out of her wits,' Sergeant Penton reproached. 'You can run too, Miss Cameron.'

'Straight back into the house,' she said ruefully. 'It didn't occur to me that the danger was there and not outside at all. I thought Julian had followed me into the garden. Seeing him again was – all I could think of to do was dash down the stairs again but he was blocking the way. It was –'

'A merciful end,' Sergeant Penton said in a fatherly manner. 'I wonder what made him jump – probably realized the police were about to enter. There was no point in holding back at that stage.'

'The Clares – how much did they know?'

'They knew he'd left the home,' Constable Harry said, 'but then they were informed he'd returned. They backed up his story of having been with them, but they must have been worried when they started comparing the time he was absent with Mrs Tate's disappearance. Then they had word today that he'd gone missing again, so they decided to drive up to the home and try to arrange for greater security without letting the people there know exactly why. Happily the people there had seen the newspaper account of Mrs Tate's disappearance and Linda's murder by today and contacted us.'

'Shutting the stable door when the horse had bolted,' Sergeant Penton said with deep disapproval.

'But why?' Jessica asked the question with a furrowed brow. 'Why did Julian Clare kill his sister in the beginning? He spoke of doing things – oh, I see.'

'Sexual advances,' Sergeant Penton said. 'Probably she threatened to tell, so he killed her. Very nasty young man. Sex is responsible for a lot of mischief in the world. You won't want to stay here tonight, Miss?'

'She's coming back to my place,' Adam said with decision. 'We'll be spending a lot of time together in the future.'

'Ah, that's what I like to hear,' Sergeant Penton approved. 'The past is dead and in my opinion it's best left alone. What matters is the future.'

'Yes,' said Adam and tightened his grasp about Jessica's shoulders.

'Yes,' said Jessica and turned her head to smile at him.

Polly's Tale

No, it isn't dead. How can it be dead when bits and pieces of tattered memory keep blowing down the years? And me, Polly, a part of it all still.

They won't bother to find out about me now. They'll go away and the Clares will sell the house and live in another town. Nobody knows what happened to me. Nobody ever cared much.

I could manage until the governess came. Governess! Dottie Larue from Madam's, same as I had been. And I knew when I saw her that Master wouldn't be content just sinning with me in the shed on days the gardener wasn't around.

I was right too. Off they went together while Cook was having her nap and Mrs Makin was busy with the baby. And little Julia went with them. I supposed they wouldn't be doing anything very much with her there, but then I remembered there was a nice railed churchyard where she could bowl her hoop while they went into a vestry – him a clergyman and all.

Master'd gone down to the church that afternoon and later on I saw Dottie going out with little Julia. Oh, she looked such a pretty thing with her hoop, holding tight to Dottie's hand and skipping along. Cook's feet were killing her that day – east wind and a spot of rain coming in – so she put them up and dozed off early. I waited a bit and then I put on my cloak and went after them. I'm not sure what I was going to do – probably nothing at all. Anyway by the time I got to the church there wasn't anyone around and I thought as maybe I'd made an error.

And then I saw Julia, wandering up to the side door with her hoop in her hand. She'd got bored, I daresay, and was going inside to find her governess. And when she got inside she'd see – and after that she wouldn't be pretty little Julia who thought the world was kind. She'd be like the little girl the man had taken from Victoria

Street and sold to Madam. And I started running and caught up with her just inside the door. I don't remember what I said, but I gave her a fright and I didn't mean to do that. I wanted her to be safe – not knowing. And then she pulled free and skidded on the stone and fell down the two steps inside. Doesn't make sense, does it? Falling down two little steps and hitting her head and her neck all twisted and the hoop bowling down the aisle by itself.

Then Master ran out of the vestry with Dottie behind him, her hair all loose and her dress untidy, and she opened her mouth to scream and he turned on her with his hands reaching out and his face a fury, saying, 'Bitch, shut your mouth.'

And she only screamed once after that.

Master and I stood, looking the one at the other, and I was cold – so cold.

And then he said, his voice thick with loathing, 'All bitches. All women are bitches to tempt righteous men.'

We had a secret, the Master and me. We had a double secret. He could have told on me and I could have told on him. Better for them to disappear, he said. I was to go back home like nothing had happened and he'd make things tidy and follow on. And when I got home there was Cook wanting to know why I hadn't answered when she called me to pick the pears. And then the day went on, and he pretended to go out and look for them and said he'd found a hoop on the common. The police was suspicious about that because I'd gone out earlier to look and not seen it. I suppose he couldn't get the hoop under the altar.

It was a good place to put them, wasn't it? In that great hollow space under the altar where there are kept the bones of a few old martyrs. Nobody would think of opening up that space, now would they?

They went away later on, him and Madam and baby Robert, and some people called Laurence bought the house. Cook stayed on, but I didn't. I went back to Madam's where wickedness was honest and nobody quoted the Bible at me. I think I was sick a long time there, and then I went back to the house. I wanted to tell someone what had happened. I wanted to tell them that I did try now and then to be a good girl. I wanted to tell people who I am. My name is Polly Winter. I learned to write that when Dottie came. I used to practise it. My name is – but nobody ever bothered to remember. It wasn't important to anyone but me.

I don't know what I'll do now. Hang around here, I suppose, until another family finds out what went before. And all the time I can feel myself getting more shadowy. I take colour from the pictures on the walls and a voice from the echoes on the wind. And just now Master came back – younger than I'd ever seen him, and that new governess was there, and it was going to start all over again. I was going to be left out. And that wasn't fair. I called to him, soft and sweet, and he fell down into the hall below. I was going to say that I wouldn't tell on him – I never would have told. He didn't seem to understand.

There are policemen here again. If they looked at me they'd see; if they listened they'd hear.

'Please, sir. Please listen. My name is Polly Winter.'